5/30/14

Miss Dimple Picks a Peck of Trouble

Center Point
Large Print

Also by Mignon F. Ballard and available from
Center Point Large Print:

Miss Dimple Rallies to the Cause
Miss Dimple Suspects

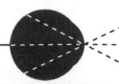

**This Large Print Book carries the
Seal of Approval of N.A.V.H.**

Miss Dimple
Picks a
Peck of Trouble

MIGNON F. BALLARD

CENTER POINT LARGE PRINT
THORNDIKE, MAINE

This Center Point Large Print edition is
published in the year 2014 by arrangement with
St. Martin's Press.

The text of this Large Print edition is unabridged.
In other aspects, this book may vary
from the original edition.
Printed in the United States of America
on permanent paper.
Set in 16-point Times New Roman type.

ISBN: 978-1-62899-086-7

Library of Congress Cataloging-in-Publication Data

Ballard, Mignon Franklin.
 Miss Dimple picks a peck of trouble / Mignon F. Ballard. — Center
Point Large Print edition.
 pages ; cm
 ISBN 978-1-62899-086-7 (library binding : alk. paper)
 1. Women teachers—Fiction. 2. Elementary school teachers—Fiction.
 3. Teenage girls—Crimes against—Fiction.
 4. World War, 1939–1945—Georgia—Fiction. 5. Large type books.
 I. Title.
PS3552.A466M58 2014b
813′.54—dc23
                                                    2014004013

For my friends through the years in the
Charlotte Wednesday Writers Workshop
with love and thanks
and in memory of my first editor,
Margaret Norton

ACKNOWLEDGMENTS

A peck (and more) of thanks to my friend and agent, Laura Langlie, who has been with me almost every step of the way!

CHAPTER ONE

"Did you hear that?" Dimple Kilpatrick added another couple of peaches to the basket on the ground and paused to listen.

"Hear what?" Charlie Carr, her fellow teacher and former pupil, stood on a ladder almost concealed by the leaves of the tree. Only her jean-clad legs were visible.

Dimple frowned. "It sounded like someone screaming." She paused to dab her forehead with a purple plaid bandanna. It was mid-July and the heat had been unrelenting. "Do you think someone could be in trouble?"

"I didn't hear a thing," Annie Gardner said. The younger teacher didn't want to say it, but in spite of her quiet demeanor, Miss Dimple Kilpatrick seemed to invite the opportunity to delve into a bit of detective work, usually at great risk of danger.

Phoebe Chadwick, who owned the rooming house where several of the teachers lived, planned to put up a few jars of spiced peaches with the help of her cook, Odessa Kirby, and the women had pooled their valuable ration stamps to help supply the necessary sugar. If they had enough left over, Odessa had promised to make peach ice cream.

"It's probably Delia and Prentice acting silly," Charlie said, speaking of her sister and her friend, who were working that summer at the Peach Shed down the road. "You know how those two are when they get together, and the Shed's not that far away."

Although Delia, at twenty, was married and the mother of a small boy, she seemed to act more like a teen around Prentice, two years younger. But Charlie knew her sister worried constantly over her young husband overseas with the army, and she was glad to see her have fun. The war had forced them all to take life more seriously, but most had learned to relish any fragment of happiness that came along, however slight.

"I don't know," Miss Dimple admitted. "Prentice hasn't seemed herself since Leola died so suddenly. One doesn't adjust to that kind of thing overnight." Leola Parker had helped to take care of Prentice since the child came to live with her aunt Elberta when she was three, and the two had always been close.

"I'll bet you heard one of that McKenzie brood," Annie said. "Don't they live around here somewhere? I had Wilbur in my class last year and his sister the year before. I'll swear you can hear 'em in the next county."

Dimple Kilpatrick moved quietly to the next tree. She hoped the others were right.

•   •   •

For a long time afterward, Delia Varnadore sickened at the rich, heady smell of peaches. But that morning, hurrying back to the Peach Shed, where she worked, all she could think about was standing in the shade of that big old gnarled oak, gulping her Coke and letting the cold liquid rush sweetly down her throat.

The two-lane asphalt road sizzled in the July sun, and Delia felt the heat clean through her sandals as she dashed across with a frosty bottle in each hand: a NuGrape soda for her friend Prentice and a Coke for herself. Steam rose from puddles left from a brief morning shower, and she avoided the worst of them as she made her way through wiry grass, trampled with foot traffic and red with clay, on the other side of the road. The Hershey bar in her skirt pocket bumped against her hip as she ran, and Delia hoped it wouldn't melt before she could eat it. She paused to wipe the inevitable mud from her thin-soled sandals. They had already been resoled twice since the war began, and, due to a shortage of leather and almost everything else, they would have to last the rest of the summer. Her family, like most others, had made do by cutting cardboard to line the insides of their winter shoes, but that wouldn't work with sandals. Delia didn't mind—not really—not while Ned Varnadore, her husband and the person she loved best in the world (well, except maybe for their adorable little Tommy, affectionately known as "Pooh"), was over there fighting along with her brother, Fain, and just about every boy she had graduated with from Elderberry High School. Had that been only three years ago? It seemed more like a thousand.

She looked around for Prentice. Something was bothering her friend, gnawing at her like a chigger bite in a place you couldn't scratch, and Delia couldn't worm it out of her no matter how hard she tried. Now Prentice had made it clear she was sick and tired of being asked. The NuGrape was a peace offering.

The Hershey bar was for Delia, and she felt a little guilty for not sharing—but not *too* guilty. After all, she'd earned it, hadn't she, sacrificing most of her summer sweating behind the counter and constantly itching with that blasted peach fuzz to sell peaches and produce when she'd rather have been at home with Pooh. And wouldn't Ned be pleased when he learned she'd been putting aside most of the money she'd earned along with a portion of the amount she received from his modest army pay? Delia could hardly wait to surprise him when this war was finally over and they could be a real family—just the three of them.

Not that she wasn't grateful to her mother and her sister, Charlie, for helping out with the baby this summer so she could put money aside. Her old baby bed had fit snugly in a corner of her upstairs room, its walls still a patchwork of high school snapshots and souvenirs. The corners of a program from her senior class play curled between a photo of Clark Gable cut from a film magazine and the dried and crumbling wrist corsage of once-pink roses from the prom. Her mother, Jo, worked faithfully three days a week at the munitions plant in nearby Milledgeville, and in September Charlie would begin her third year as a third-grade teacher at the grammar school they had attended as children, which was on the next block. When Ned was shipped overseas, the two of them had welcomed her home to the house on Katherine Street in the small Georgia town where she'd grown up and where Tommy was born a few months later. The same room in the same house in the same town. But everything was different.

Except for a brief shower that morning, it had been weeks since it had rained in Elderberry, and straggly weeds bent yellow with dust around the Shed's hand-painted sign with a picture of a lopsided peach the color of no peach Delia had ever seen. Knox Jarrett, who owned the orchard, had painted it so he wouldn't have to pay an artist. Trying to pinch a penny as always, Delia's aunt Lou claimed, which is why they had to use the bathroom at Grady Clinkscales's Gas 'n Eats across the road.

Yellow jackets hovered over mounded baskets of rosy Elberta peaches on the wooden counter. Delia had been stung twice already that summer and she despised wasps, yellow jackets, the whole hateful lot, but was grateful for the part-time job, and it was fun working with Prentice. Usually.

Although they were two years apart, Delia and Prentice Blair had been friends since grade school, and the money they earned now would be put to good use. Delia's for her future household; and, after working for a year at Lewellyn's Drug Store, Prentice planned to go away to college in the fall.

Just about everybody in town hung out at the Peach Shed at one time or another, so they always knew what was going on. If asked, Delia would begrudgingly admit she even liked the way the old place looked. The big, airy shoe box of a building squatted in the shade of a huge red oak. Its unpainted timbers had weathered the soft gray of a rain cloud, and the open sides allowed for a cross breeze if one were ever to come along. And several times a day, the NC and St. L, billowing smoke and cinders, would chug through on the tracks at the bottom of the hill, sometimes with fresh young recruits bound for Fort Benning, in Columbus, and the two always waved to them.

Delia took the two shallow steps in one stride and clanked the bottles onto the counter by the cash register. Since no one was about, she raised the hem of her cotton skirt to mop her wet face and looked about for Prentice. "Hey, I'm back! Brought you a surprise. . . . Where are you? Prentice?"

The room was a storehouse of heady smells and a palate of deep yellow, coral, and watermelon red. Bushels of green beans and sweet white corn lined the walls with green-striped watermelons and hills of pungent cantaloupe. Jars of Ida Ellerby's blackberry jelly marched along a table next to the register with Odessa Kirby's watermelon-rind pickles. But aside from the produce and Delia, the room was empty.

"Come on now, Prentice, I give up! Guess I'll just have to drink this nice cold NuGrape I brought you." Getting no answer, Delia opened the door to the small storage room in the back where baskets and cleaning supplies were kept, but only a beetle scurried away.

Prentice would never go off and leave the cash register untended. And where would she go? Prentice's aunt Bertie had dropped the two of them off earlier that morning, and they didn't have access to a car. The only place nearby was the Gas 'n Eats across the road. Delia's aunt Lou said they ought to call the station Eats 'n Gas instead of the other way around, and usually just the name of the place made Delia want to smile.

But she had a growing feeling this wasn't going to be a smiling kind of day.

Shoving damp hair from her forehead, Delia checked the cash drawer. Everything seemed okay. It had been a slow morning: Delia's neighbor Bessie Jenkins had stopped by for cantaloupe and tomatoes for supper, and Geneva Odom, who taught with Charlie, had purchased a watermelon for a family picnic. Their last customer, Dora Delaney, owner of the Total Perfection Beauty Salon on Court Street, had come for her weekly supply of peaches during her midmorning break.

"You oughta come by and let me do something with all that hair," she'd told Delia. "Must be hotter than the devil's kitchen in here, and look at all that mop on your neck! When's the last time you had a trim?" Dora swapped a couple of peaches in her basket for larger ones and examined Delia with her perfectly lashed green eyes. Dora Delaney would never see forty again, but she didn't look much older than thirty with her blond pompadour and cheerleader figure. Delia found herself envious of somebody who could look cool and trim while wearing a hot-pink smock.

"I've been thinking about a French twist," she said, handing Dora her change. "Only I never seem to have time to fool with it."

"Give me a holler," Dora said. "We'll make time."

Did she look that bad? When the local hair-dresser takes notice, it must be time to make a change. Delia shrugged. What did it matter when the only person she wanted to please was thousands of miles away?

Now frowning, Delia searched the road in front of her and watched as someone in a light blue Ford pulled into Grady's for gas. A truck rumbled past. Less than a mile away, her sister, Charlie, picked peaches with her friends and fellow teachers, Annie and Miss Dimple. But Delia couldn't imagine her friend deserting the Shed to join the pickers. She quietly set down her drink and stood waiting, listening. Her stomach had that same weak queasy feeling it did when she threw a stone into a deep ravine and watched it fall . . . fall . . . before it finally hit bottom. She wanted to be upset with Prentice for worrying her like this, wanted to find her friend and confront her, but her heart told her something wasn't right.

Prentice liked to tease, but since Leola's death two weeks before, her friend hadn't been in a teasing mood. Leola had been much more than a baby-sitter. She was a friend, somebody Prentice could talk with, turn to for advice. "I can tell Leola things I'd never dream of telling Aunt Bertie," she once admitted, and Delia knew Leola was the one who convinced Prentice to go away to college in the fall, a decision that had led to a breakup with her boyfriend.

Clay Jarrett, whose father owned the Peach Shed, had graduated in the class ahead of Prentice's, and the two had been dating for a couple of years. Prentice had recently confided to Delia that Clay had proposed. He wanted to marry right away and planned to enlist in the navy, but she wasn't ready for such a commitment. "I know it worked for you and Ned," she said, "but I've always planned to go to college, and Clay knows that. Aunt Bertie will help, and I've saved some from my drugstore earnings. Besides," she added, "Clay's content to stay right here in Elderberry after the war, and I'm not sure that's what I want."

Leola, of course, had agreed. An excellent seamstress, she'd been looking forward to making additional clothing for Prentice's college wardrobe, and the two had pored happily over pattern books, selected material, and shared excitement at the prospect of what was in store.

Prentice had been the one who found her body, and since then she hadn't acted like the same person: moody, jumpy, quick to cry. But there was something else, too. Delia had noticed a change in her friend even before Leola died.

Sighing, Delia lifted the heavy hair from her neck and fanned herself with a newspaper. *Prentice Blair!* Your drink's getting warm! Don't you want it?"

No answer.

"Prentice? Come on, now, answer me! Are you back there? This is *not* funny."

Still no answer.

She was probably crying. Out there behind the Shed crying—just like yesterday and the day before, but couldn't she at least answer? Or maybe she was emptying trash.

But not for this long. Bracing herself, Delia walked slowly through the cluttered storage room, out the back door, and down the steps. Two large garbage cans sat to the right of the door, the top of each anchored with a rock to discourage stray dogs and raccoons. Nothing but dust stirred in the narrow, grassy clearing. Beyond it, a stand of scruffy cedars and underbrush led into several acres of woodland that served as a buffer between the Peach Shed and Knox Jarrett's orchards and farm.

Why in the world would Prentice wander off into the woods unless somebody had called to her, needed her? Delia ventured to the edge of the knee-high weeds and called her friend's name, hollered it as loud as she could. Queen Anne's lace bobbed under the weight of bumblebees, and a small brown rabbit leapt from behind a clump of sumac and disappeared into the brambles. Nothing else moved.

Hattie McGee lived somewhere back there in a trashy old trailer. "Mad Hattie" everybody called her, and Delia was afraid of her. So was Prentice.

The old woman thought she was Scarlett O'Hara and wore a tattered green skirt that dragged the ground—stole rosebushes, too. Dug them up in the middle of the night and planted them around her trailer. Prentice's aunt Bertie was missing a Talisman, and Bessie Jenkins, her Mary Margaret McBride, a pretty pink hybrid she'd planted last spring, and neither would do anything about it. "Poor old Hattie's harmless," everybody said.

If it were up to Delia, she would make "poor old Hattie" dig them up and give them back—that is, if she weren't such a chicken. And she knew Prentice wouldn't have wandered anywhere close to Mad Hattie's—not intentionally.

Circling the Shed for a second time, Delia spied a peach partially hidden in rusty weeds beside the back steps. Testily, she tapped it with her toe, expecting to see a smushed, rotting underside, but the fruit was whole, firm. Delia picked it up and squeezed it. In a day or so, the peach would be ripe. It might have fallen from a basket as the fruit was being unloaded, except they always unloaded in front so they wouldn't have to carry it so far. She frowned. Customers usually parked in the gravel area out front, as well. It wouldn't make sense to go all the way around to the back.

So why? Delia thought she knew why, but hoped it wasn't true. Snatching open the screen door, she hurried inside.

Hardin Haynesworth Kirkland, crisp in beige

linen and smelling of some demure scent that probably cost more than Delia's entire wardrobe, stood at the cash register with her lips pursed. Delia hadn't heard her drive up. The woman held a cantaloupe in one hand and a jar of jelly in the other and sighed loud enough to stir up a storm. Delia ignored her.

Rushing past the pouty-faced matron, Delia squatted behind the counter, stretched her arm as far as she could, and felt, pushed far back on the lower shelf, the thing she had dreaded to find: Prentice Blair's purse.

The handbag was of tan imitation leather, but it looked almost like the real thing, Delia had assured her, and had been a gift from Clay when Prentice turned eighteen in May. *How could she simply disappear?* Delia crouched behind the counter until her heartbeat slowed. She had been across the street for hardly more than ten minutes. Only long enough to use the rest room, dash water on her face, and comb her hair. Then she'd had to wait to pay for the drinks while Grady went out to put gas in the tank for Emmaline Brumlow, who, of course, wanted her windshields cleaned front and back. She'd been held up by the train before crossing the tracks, she said, and her car had been showered with cinders.

"My dear, I am in rather a hurry. If you don't mind . . ." Delia's waiting customer drummed fingers on the counter and sighed again.

21

Delia stood slowly. She felt as if she had a stick jammed down her throat all the way into her chest. This couldn't be happening!

But it was. "Mrs. Kirkland, I'm afraid something's happened to Prentice." *Whose voice was this? It didn't sound like hers.* "I can't find her anywhere and I know she wouldn't just go off like this."

The woman tossed a dollar onto the counter to pay for her purchases and brushed an invisible hair from her cheek. "Now, Delia . . . it is Delia, isn't it?" She smiled like it pained her, and Delia wanted to vault over the counter and shake her. "She's probably in the back somewhere, or maybe she went across to the filling station. I'm afraid you've let yourself get overwrought."

"You don't understand! I just came from there and I've looked *everywhere*. Prentice is gone. GONE!" Her voice was only a notch below screaming. It was becoming obvious that Prentice had left with somebody, probably against her will, since she'd left her purse behind and the cash register untended.

"Exactly what is it you want me to do?" Hardin asked in a voice as stiff as her shoulders. Delia could tell she didn't believe her.

"I'm going over to Grady's to call the police, but my sister, Charlie, and some of her friends are picking peaches this morning in the orchard right up the road. Would you see if you can find them

22

and tell them to come? And hurry, please hurry!"

Whoever drove off with Prentice must have parked behind the Shed and enticed her into the car on the pretext of needing help to load the peaches, Delia thought, and since this had taken place while she was gone, *the abductor had to have been watching.*

"Who *is* this?" It was obvious that the woman who answered the phone at the local police station believed it was a prank. Delia gave her name and repeated the message. "My friend's been taken—probably kidnapped, and this is no joke! Please get somebody out to the Peach Shed as fast as you can. We've got to find her!" When the woman hesitated, Delia demanded to speak with Bobby Tinsley, Elderberry's chief of police. "Just tell him I'm Charlie Carr's sister and she's a friend of Miss Dimple Kilpatrick," she added, knowing that from past experience the chief was familiar with the two of them.

Minutes later, Delia stood among the knobby roots of the old oak, waiting for the police to respond. The tree had been there for over a hundred years, people said, withstanding drought, wind, and storms. Delia ran a finger along its dark, crusty bark. *If she could only draw strength from the massive trunk, calmness to ease the turmoil inside her.* Looking off in the distance, she saw a vehicle approaching and hoped it was

Charlie driving the old family car. Delia prayed under her breath that Mrs. Kirkland had been able to find them.

Seconds later, the familiar Studebaker skidded into the parking lot beside the Peach Shed and came to a jolting stop, scattering gravel in its wake. Running out to meet them, Delia Varnadore finally allowed the tears to come.

CHAPTER TWO

Delia, honey, what's wrong? Mrs. Kirkland said Prentice seems to be missing." Charlie Carr held her younger sister until the sobbing subsided. "Are you sure she didn't go across the street?"

Delia shook her head. "Oh, please don't make me have to go through this again!" But she rehashed what had happened earlier, adding that Prentice's handbag as well as the money in the cash drawer seemed to be untouched. "This isn't like Prentice, Charlie. You know it isn't."

"You're right. It isn't." Stepping from the car behind them, Miss Dimple Kilpatrick spoke up. "I believe we should get in touch with Bertie Stackhouse. Perhaps she can shed some light on this. After all, there may have been a reason Prentice needed to return home."

"What kind of reason?" Frowning, Delia glanced at the woman who had taught her, as well as her sister and generations of others, in her big high-ceilinged first-grade classroom at Elderberry Grammar School, and recognized the wordless communication understood by all women. In her modest way, Miss Dimple was reminding her that Prentice might have started her period and had found it necessary to go home.

"Oh," she said. "But how would she get there? She didn't even take her purse. And wouldn't she be back by now?"

"Did she seem sick?" Annie asked. "It's been so hot this summer, she might have come down with a bad cold . . . or something."

The four of them exchanged looks in silence. Everyone knew what "or something" meant. Swimming pools were practically empty in spite of the heat, and people tried to avoid crowded places because of the threat of polio. Their own president, Franklin Roosevelt, who had been stricken with infantile paralysis, often came to Georgia for treatments at Warm Springs, less than two hours away. Delia shuddered at the thought of having to spend the rest of her life in an iron lung with only her head sticking out, and although no one in Elderberry had come down with the dreaded disease, most of them knew of someone who *knew* someone who had it. The threat was as real as it was frightening.

"She's been upset since Leola died," Delia told them, "but she didn't act *sick*. Besides, she would've at least left a note if she meant to leave."

"Oh, Miss Dimple, you don't suppose . . ." Charlie turned to the older woman. "You thought you heard somebody scream. . . . Do you think it might've been Prentice?"

"When?" Delia demanded. "Do you know how long it's been?"

Annie frowned. "I'd say about thirty minutes." She clasped a hand to her mouth. "Oh, if only we'd—"

"Now, let's not jump to conclusions." Miss Dimple spoke calmly. "Quite possibly I could've heard children playing, as you suggested."

"Have you heard anything?" Mrs. Kirkland, who had parked behind Charlie, hurried to join them. "I'm sure there must be a rational explanation," she said when told the situation was unchanged.

Yet if Hardin Haynesworth Kirkland were a smoker, she would have worked through half a pack, Delia thought as they waited for the police to arrive. The woman paced from her car to the Shed and back again, pausing now and then to glance at her watch. She moved jerkily, like a mechanical toy. Thin, almost child-size, she seemed hardly large enough to bear her name.

Delia had never heard anyone refer to Mrs. Kirkland by two names. It was always *Hardin*

26

Haynesworth Kirkland, Haynesworth being her maiden name. Prentice's aunt Bertie had grown up with Hardin Haynesworth and their mothers had belonged to the same garden club. Hardin still belonged, but Bertie claimed she didn't care a fig about spending time with a bunch of women who wouldn't know a hoe from a spade, and besides, teaching English and literature at Elderberry High demanded most of her time.

Bertie had taken her niece to raise after the child's parents were killed when a train derailed during a picnic excursion. The little girl, then three, had been with them, but, except for a few minor scrapes and bruises, she had escaped unharmed. Bertie had never married, and Prentice was the only family she had.

"Perhaps we should wait until the police arrive to get in touch with Elberta," Miss Dimple suggested, and the others agreed. If Prentice had returned home because of illness or for whatever reason, they would find out soon enough, but if the young woman was indeed missing, as Delia feared, it would be best to inform her aunt in person.

Chief Tinsley, who had been on another call, arrived a few minutes later, and as soon as he saw Miss Dimple and her cohorts, he acted as though he intended to get back in his car and leave. "Well, Miss Dimple, I see you're here with your two accomplices. What kind of trouble have you three brought me this time?" he asked, shaking his head.

But he soon found out Prentice Blair's disappearance was no joking matter. After searching the area around the Shed, the chief sent another policeman, Fulton Padgett, to find out what he could learn from Grady Clinkscales at the Gas 'n Eats. Mrs. Kirkland gave her account to Chief Tinsley and left immediately afterward. Then, leaning on the counter inside the Shed, the chief spoke with Delia.

"You say Miss Bessie Jenkins and Dora Delaney were here earlier?" he said, taking a notebook from his pocket. "We'll follow up on that and find out if they saw anything, and of course I'll speak with Mrs. Brumlow, as well. It sounds likely she stopped over there for gas at about the same time your friend disappeared . . . *if* that's what happened," he added. "For all we know, she could be at home by now."

"Do you think Hattie McGee might've had something to do with this?" Delia asked. "She lives back there, you know, somewhere in all that jungle of underbrush and trees."

He smiled. "Old Hattie's harmless, but we'll check into it if your friend doesn't turn up soon. That property belongs to the Jarretts, and if they don't object to her being there, it shouldn't matter to the rest of us."

The chief paused to flip through his notebook, and Delia guessed he was probably marking time before expressing what was on his mind. "Do you think you might have heard her if your friend called out for help while you were across the road?" he asked.

But Delia shook her head. She was inside most of the time and a train had passed while she was there, so she didn't believe she would have heard anything. "But," she told him, "Miss Dimple thought she heard somebody scream while she was picking peaches in the orchard just down the road."

"How can you be so sure Prentice didn't decide to go off with her boyfriend somewhere?" he asked. "Hasn't she been seeing Clay Jarrett? I've noticed the two of them around town together, and the Jarrett place is just a ways behind us."

Delia nodded. "Yes, but she broke off with him a few weeks ago, and I really don't think Prentice wanted to be around Clay right now."

"Still, it wouldn't hurt to check. I'll have to speak with the Jarretts anyway. They'll want to send somebody over to take care of the Shed, but first we need to pay a visit to Miss Stackhouse, find out if she's heard anything from her niece."

Delia drew in her breath and glanced at her sister, who stood in the doorway with Miss Dimple and Annie. *This wasn't the time to cry again!*

"Chief Tinsley, I hope you won't object if we speak with Bertie Stackhouse first," Miss Dimple said, stepping forward. "I'm afraid she might become alarmed at seeing the police at her front door."

He nodded. "I see your point. We'll give you a few minutes, and if everything's all right there, you can wave us along."

Delia gave the cash box to Chief Tinsley to turn over to the Jarretts but kept Prentice's handbag to return to her friend. Charlie hadn't thought to park in the shade, and the car felt hot enough to bake a potato. Climbing into the backseat beside Annie, Delia remembered the Hershey bar she had left in her skirt pocket earlier and discovered it a brown syrupy mess. *Won't Prentice laugh when she hears about this!* she thought, forgetting for a minute the alarming circumstances.

If only she didn't have to think! If she could start the day over and begin anew. Delia looked at Miss Dimple, who sat in front, holding in her lap the straw hat with its trim of purple ribbon she had worn that morning. At least Miss Dimple was the same, always calm and reliable. She would know what to do. Delia was glad she was there.

During the drive to Prentice's, Delia prayed there had been some kind of emergency and that her friend's aunt Bertie had come and whisked her away, or that Prentice had experienced a sudden attack of appendicitis, flagged down a passing motorist, and was safely anesthetized and under the care of Doc Morrison.

But that wasn't to be.

Why couldn't he get her out of his mind? It had been over two weeks now, and he'd never thought it would come to this. *And the things she'd told him!* Prentice. *His* Prentice. He'd always thought she looked like the yellow-haired angel in that big book of Bible stories his grandmamma gave him one Christmas. Some angel she turned out to be!

Clay Jarrett skimmed down the ladder and carefully rolled his last basket of peaches into the waiting truck. The Georgia Belles bruised easily and his dad would have his hide if he brought in a damaged load. He had been picking since sunup and didn't have a dry thread on him. Even with the long-sleeved cotton shirt, his arms stung with the hateful peach fuzz.

He fanned his wet face with a dirty visored cap that said *Purina Feed* on the front and drew a sleeve across his forehead. Trickles of sweat mixed with tears drizzled salty into his mouth. Damn it! This was the last time he was going to cry over Prentice Blair, but she had been on his mind all morning and there was nobody around to see him cry. Nobody but those blasted yellow jackets and the mean sun that followed him wherever he went. Clay felt like somebody had poured acid into his heart, and when he thought of the flawless face of Prentice Blair, the awful bitterness rose in his chest.

It was all that old woman's fault. Leola. Prentice listened to whatever Leola Parker told her. "Go away to school, see something of the world," she'd told her. And Prentice had listened, hadn't she? Listened to Leola instead of to him. Well, she wouldn't be listening to her anymore. Clay felt kind of bad about that, about what had happened. And Prentice—Lord, he'd never seen her so crazy upset. And then there'd been all that talk about dating other people and she'd given him back his ring. Thrown it at him in the end.

That was when she'd told him. Knowing the way he loved her the way he did, she told him *that*.

It was almost noon by the time Clay got his peaches to the sorting shed, and he started to peel away his clothing even before he reached the house. In the shower, needles of hot water pounded him, renewed him, but it couldn't wash away the wound that festered inside.

In less than an hour, he would begin his shift at Mr. Cooper's grocery. Harris Cooper didn't pay as much as his dad did, but the grocer didn't mind if he stopped for a sandwich if the schedule wasn't too tight, and this week his clerk, Jesse Dean Greeson, was taking care of the store so the Coopers could spend some time with their new grandbaby in Columbus. Their son-in-law was serving there with the army at Fort Benning, where Clay would probably go if he was drafted into the army, although he preferred to enlist in the navy—and the sooner, the better, he thought. He would've signed up already if his mother hadn't carried on so.

Clay tried to slick down his wet straw-colored hair, but he knew it wouldn't do any good. It would be sticking up in all the wrong places as soon as he got out the door. He glowered at himself in the mirror. What did it matter now anyway?

Easing out the front door, which the family rarely used, Clay tried to slip away unnoticed. It didn't work.

"Clay? Clay, honey, don't you want some dinner? There's ham from last night and I saved some of that tomato pie you like. Won't take a minute to heat."

"No thanks, Mom. Gotta go—running late. I'll grab something in town." He gave her a blink of a kiss and hurried to climb into the old Chevrolet truck, its once-black sides now stained rust red with Georgia dust. He really wasn't late, but he didn't want to stay around the kitchen with her constantly hanging over him. Clay loved his mother and would fight anybody who said he didn't, but she was just about to drive him nuts since his breakup with Prentice. Lately he couldn't stand to be around anybody who expected him to carry on a conversation longer than two sentences.

Driving past the Peach Shed, he raised a hand to Miss Dimple, who was standing outside with a couple of others. If it had been anybody else, he wouldn't have even acknowledged them, the way he was feeling, but there was something about his first-grade teacher that made him want to "do the right thing." He didn't see Prentice and didn't want to, but he knew she was working there today.

Jesse Dean had an order ready when Clay pulled up in back of the store. A lot of Harris Cooper's customers were older people who either couldn't shop for themselves or didn't want to, and they were accustomed to special treatment. Whoever was delivering that day not only took the groceries to the door but carried them inside, and, on occasion, put them away. That was fine with Clay as long as he didn't have to talk.

Today his first delivery went to Miss Iona Satterlee, a retired teacher a few miles north of town on Russells' Mill Road. To get there, Clay had to pass the "special place"—his and Prentice's—an old logging road that meandered into nothing behind the vine-draped ruins of an old mill. When they had first parked there, they thought the spot entirely their own, but later, evidence led them to believe otherwise, and according to some unwritten code, they didn't take advantage of their secluded spot, but chose their nights selectively, infrequently, rationing the heady rapture of their visits. Or Prentice did. Clay would've parked there every night if she'd allowed it.

Her kisses sent him soaring into some sweet, wild place he'd never been before and didn't ever want to leave. And when he felt Prentice's firm young breast against his own, everything in him surged. Once, carried away by the thrill of his scoring the winning touchdown in a game with their archrivals in the next town and the dizzying essence of the autumn air, she had let him touch her breast. It was as smooth as a peach; soft yet firm, it fit into the palm of his hand as if God had made it that way. Her nipple felt like warm rubber and she moaned when he explored it.

Clay moaned, too. His hands moved urgently to the tentlike area beneath her corduroy skirt. Her stomach was flat, hot, shuddered when he touched it. Outside the car, an owl called, and through the windshield a honey-dipped moon hung from the top of a bare oak. Clay closed his eyes. At that moment, he could speak love in foreign tongues, hear music that had never been written.

"Stop!" She covered herself with her hands, curled away from him, and cried, struggling to button her blouse. "I can't. I'm sorry, it's wrong."

"Oh God, Prentice, don't do this to me! Sweetheart, *please*. It's me, honey, Clay, and I love you. You know I love you. It's all right, really."

"No, it's not all right. I love you, too, Clay, but it's too soon. I'm not ready. And what if something happened? What if I got pregnant?"

"You won't. Listen, I've got protection. I'll take care of you. Nothing like that will happen, I promise." Silently, Clay thanked his dad for the advice given more like a warning during one of their rare father-son moments.

She sat as if snapped by a rubber band and plopped her tempting bottom as far away as she could. "You mean you've been carrying around *rubbers* all this time? Clay Jarrett! I can't believe the nerve of you—the conceit! What would people think if they knew you had those things?"

He hoped the darkness hid his smile. "I don't wear 'em on a chain around my neck, but if they did happen to see them, I guess they'd think I was planning ahead."

"Well, you can just plan ahead with somebody else! Take me home." Prentice scrambled in her purse for lipstick and a comb. Her fair hair billowed to rival the moon.

"Prentice, look, sugar, I'm sorry. It's just that . . . well, other people do it. I don't see why we—"

"I'm not *other people*." She dabbed on lipstick in the dark, and when she twisted her mouth in that funny little way, his heart turned to pudding.

"Besides," she said. "I made a promise."

"What kind of promise? Who did you promise?" But he already knew.

"Leola. I promised Leola I'd wait until I'm old enough to know what I'm doing."

"But Prentice, sugar, I know what I'm doing. Isn't that enough?"

He made her laugh and she forgave him, and that was the end of that. But in all the time they went together, they never made love. Not once. Oh, they petted some, but after that night, Prentice always knew when to call a halt before they "went too far," as she called it. And because Clay loved her, he would wait just as long as it took.

And then she had to go *and tell him that.*

$\mathcal{C}$HAPTER $\mathcal{T}$HREE

When Elberta Stackhouse looked at Clay Jarrett with that hay-colored thatch so like his dad's, her yearning cut deep and cruel. Not that he could have been her son, but that hers could've been much like him.

In a little while, she would have to collect Prentice and Delia from the Shed, and God forbid that she should run into Knox Jarrett. Bertie wasn't comfortable with Prentice working for Knox; in fact, she didn't like it worth a damn. Of course she couldn't voice her objections without explaining why, and Bertie didn't plan to explain why. Ever.

The romance between Bertie Stackhouse and Knox Jarrett had gone to dust long before Prentice was born, but the bitter aftermath of that affair cursed her every day of her life. It was hard to live in the same town all those years and pretend nothing had happened.

If the child had lived, he (or she—Bertie had miscarried at three months) would either be in the armed services or possibly married, with a child of his own, and Bertie would write to him faithfully or brag about her grandchildren. Instead, each year Elberta Stackhouse counted the would-have-beens. Her child would be twenty-six if she had carried it full term.

Her periods had never been regular and she had been over two months along when she told Knox about her suspected pregnancy. In his sophomore year at Georgia Tech, he was less than pleased at the news. "We'll marry, of course, but first let's be absolutely sure. I'll need some time to decide how to tell my folks," he told her with a face as bleak as a January morning. "I'm afraid this is going to kill them."

"And what about *mine?*" Bertie had been carrying this all alone. Now, reaching for him, she needed the comfort of his arms. He held her stiffly and told her not to worry. They would do what they had to do.

They never told their parents about the pregnancy, and when she lost the baby a few weeks later, it was obvious Knox was relieved. For a short time, he consoled her as best he could, but when he came home for the summer, it was as though they had never been together. When Bertie saw him with Chloe Albright at a square dance on the Fourth of July, it was as if somebody had plunged a pitchfork right into her heart. Even after all this time, she would almost rather have a tooth pulled without anesthetic that be around Knox Jarrett, so when her niece Prentice broke off with his son, she was secretly relieved.

Yet in spite of that, Bertie smiled whenever she thought of Clay Jarrett. Everybody did. There was a Norman Rockwell innocence about him, a basic goodness. Lanky and good-natured, the boy reminded her of his father at that age, and he valued the same things: family, farming, and football—although not necessarily in that order. The Jarretts were a close-knit clan, content to live on the land that nurtured them and fill up three pews at the Methodist church on Sundays. Bertie had taught both their children and liked them in spite of herself. The older one, Loretta, went to work for a local florist after high school and married at nineteen. Her brother, two years younger, had always grinned and saluted her when they passed in the halls, calling her "Miss Peach," after the fruit that shared her name.

Yet there was an undercurrent of passion in this almost-man, a hint of something better left unstirred, and Bertie would be glad when Prentice left for college in September, putting some distance between them.

Now she stood in the doorway of the girl's room and shook her head, hoping the college experience would change her niece's living habits. Clothing tumbled from dresser drawers; more cluttered the bed. A trail of shoes led to the closet, where summer apparel fought for space with the winter things Prentice had promised to put away in April. Bertie sighed, but it was only a token sigh. She would never admit it to her niece or to anyone else, but it really didn't matter to her if Prentice Blair carpeted the entire house with her underwear and painted the walls with iridescent glitter.

When her niece first came to live with her, Bertie's heart had ached for the grieving and bewildered little girl as night after night she held the child and soothed her until Prentice finally slept. Then Bertie would go to her own bed and cry for the sister she had lost. Months would pass before Prentice stopped asking for her parents and came to accept her aunt's home as her own. Now, at forty-three, Bertie couldn't imagine what her life would have been like without her.

Bertie tightened the lids, wiped off the ten jars of peach preserves she'd put up earlier that morning, and treated herself to a second cup of coffee. This week's *Eagle* had come in the morning's mail, and she opened it to find Leola Parker's face frowning at her from the obituary page. Leola had disliked having her picture made and would carry on something awful if anyone even aimed a camera in her direction. She'd have a fit, Bertie thought, if she knew her likeness was right there in the public eye for every "Tom, Dick, and Harry" to see. A soft-spoken, retiring woman, she'd had to be cajoled into letting Josephine Carr write her up for the *Eagle* when her apple pie took first prize at the county fair a few years back.

The photograph was not a recent one. Leola's daughter, Mary Joy, must have dug it up from somewhere. Still, the younger dark-haired woman in the picture looked much like the Leola she knew: the same small brown face with eyes bright as buckeyes that never missed a thing behind those deceptive bifocals. The only thing missing was the familiar black felt hat with a jaunty green feather in the front that Leola had worn no matter the season. The first thing she'd done upon arriving was to place it carefully on its accustomed shelf in the hall closet until it was time to leave for the day. Bertie couldn't remember when she hadn't worn it.

Good heavens! The *Eagle* had published Leola's age. She would be mortified if she were aware that everyone knew she was seventy-eight.

Bertie had thought her much younger. Leola Parker's death had cast a pall over the town. There was hardly a family she hadn't cooked, cleaned, or baby-sat for, and a good many of Elderberry's inhabitants, including Prentice, could thank Leola Parker for their raising.

At her funeral the week before, the small brick African Methodist Zion Church on Blossom Street, which Leola had tended and attended since her mama brought her to the altar, overflowed with the local population, black and white. Prentice and Bertie sat in folding chairs in the aisle and latecomers lined the walls. The old woman's death had been sudden, and Bertie felt cheated, even resentful, at not being able to tell her good-bye.

Prentice had refused to go with her when she took a pound cake to pay her respects to Leola's family. It was Leola's recipe and her favorite dessert. She'd been baking it for over sixty years, and as far as Bertie knew, not a one of them had fallen or "gone sad." She hoped she had done it justice. Why, she wondered, did people take a favorite food of the deceased to their family? Leola wasn't there to eat it, to brag on what a *fine grain* it had—why, even better than she herself could bake! Which wasn't true and never would be. Still, Bertie felt somehow her old friend would know she'd let the ingredients come to room temperature, added the precious sugar a

42

little at a time, as she had been taught, and she hoped the hordes of Leola's friends and relatives who swarmed in and out of the small frame house would find some small comfort in eating it. She only wished she could find a way to comfort her niece.

Bertie set her empty cup in the sink and wandered outside through her small garden patch, hoping to find a ripe tomato for lunch. The tomatoes needed staking again and the gangling bushes drooped with the weight of green fruit the size of tennis balls, but not a one was ripe enough to eat. And she could just taste that good tomato sandwich—the kind you eat over the sink with the juice dripping down your chin. Be better with bacon if she had any, which she didn't, of course.

But she *could* get tomatoes. Hadn't Prentice mentioned selling homegrown produce at the Shed? She would ask her niece to select a few for her when she went to pick up the girls.

Bertie was searching for her car key when she heard someone at the door.

Delia made her way across the porch, feeling much like Dorothy in *The Wizard of Oz*. Suddenly, her world had turned upside down and nothing was as it should be. She touched the delicate fronds of an asparagus fern that cascaded from a stand by the front door. It was the same plant that had been there all summer, but today it looked different somehow. "Miss Bertie, is Prentice here with you?" she asked. *Please, oh please, say yes!*

"Delia? What are you doing here? Of course Prentice isn't here. Isn't she with you?" It was then that Bertie saw Dimple Kilpatrick standing in the background, and it took her only a minute to assess the situation. "Miss Dimple, what is it? Is something wrong with Prentice?"

"She's *gone,* Miss Stackhouse! It's been over an hour now and we've looked everywhere!" Delia was crying now. "She just disappeared. . . . *Nobody* can find her." She turned to Miss Dimple, who attempted to explain the situation in as calm a voice as possible. "There's probably a reasonable explanation, but to be sure, the police are looking into it," she began. "Chief Tinsley has already—"

Bertie stepped out onto the porch, letting the screen door slam behind her. "It's that damned Clay Jarrett," she said. "I just knew he was going to cause trouble." Fumbling in her pocket for a handkerchief, she sank into a rocking chair with a sigh so dark and so heavy, Delia felt the weight of it envelop her.

There had been tears when Prentice gave Clay back his class ring a few weeks before. And anger. Shouting. Prentice had refused to talk with him since, but Delia couldn't believe he would hurt her. How could he? How could anyone?

Prentice Blair was eighteen and so lovely, people often turned to stare. Sometimes Delia wished her friend would get a pimple right at the end of her nose or have to wear really thick glasses. It wasn't fair for somebody to look like that, but it was hard to be jealous of Prentice, because she didn't know how to be mean. Prentice liked everybody and everybody liked her. Who would want to hurt somebody like that?

Now the woman who had been a mother to Prentice, her face flushed from canning, stood as Bobby Tinsley pulled into her driveway and, hat in hand, started up the walk. She had taught Bobby Tinsley, as she had so many others, and knew he probably wouldn't be able to remember *Beowulf* from *Macbeth*, but he had been well liked by his classmates and greased lightning on the basketball court. Bobby knew the people in his town: knew their parents, where they lived, what kind of car they drove (if any), and where they went to church. He also knew of grudges, old and new; of jealousies and resentments. And he cared in spite of them.

Dimple Kilpatrick stood with her hand steady on Delia's shoulder and watched as Bertie waited on the steps to greet Bobby. On the woman's face she saw the same pain she felt inside, and for a moment she closed her eyes. She didn't like what she was thinking.

• • •

Chloe Jarrett wiped off her kitchen table for the third time that day and tossed the dishrag into a sink full of soapy water. No wonder Clay didn't want to hang around more than he did. The whole house smelled of tomatoes from yesterday's canning. The day before, it had been tomato sauce, then green tomato pickles. Chloe hated tomatoes. She saw them in her sleep. A never-ending procession of squashy red fruit spattered her dreams; the juice ran like blood, stained her hands, dripped onto her feet. And still they came, would keep on coming until late September or an act of God. Chloe prayed for an act of God. She sat at the table and sipped coffee—lukewarm now, but she didn't even notice. They didn't own the farm; the farm owned them.

She heard water running in the sink behind her but didn't turn around. Knox. Her husband made that irritating little sputter as he dashed water onto his face, then fumbled for a towel. Why did he insist on washing his face in the kitchen sink when they had a perfectly good washbasin in the bathroom?

Now he opened the door of the Frigidaire, clanked things about. From where Chloe sat, she could only see his fanny sticking out. How tempting it would be to give him one quick shove and send him headfirst into the custardy tomato pie, or, better still, that green Jell-O salad with gooey topping. Chloe giggled to herself.

"What's so funny? Phone's ringing. Aren't you gonna answer it?" Her husband backed out of the refrigerator, juggling platters of ham and sliced tomatoes. "Chloe—the phone! Didn't you hear it, honey?" Knox added dill slices to his collection, jars of mustard and mayonnaise.

Chloe didn't object to endearments—relished them, actually—but when her husband called her "honey" in that tone, it made her think of Miss Crenshaw, her piano teacher back in the fifth grade. *No, no, honey, we don't do it that way. I don't believe you've been practicing. . . . Maybe we'd better stick to the easier pieces for a while, honey. . . .*

Taking her time, Chloe picked up the receiver in the hall.

"Mama, there's something going on over at the Shed!" Her daughter spoke so fast, she had trouble understanding her.

"Loretta, what's wrong?"

"I just saw a police car down at the Peach Shed and there were people swarming all over the place!"

Chloe frowned. Sometimes her daughter exaggerated. "When was this?"

"Just now. I was coming back from the hospital—Alma Owens fell and broke her arm, you know, and her Sunday-school class sent her the prettiest gladiolas! Anyway, you'd better tell Daddy to get down there. Sure looks like something's wrong to me."

"Did you see Delia? And what about Prentice?" Chloe sighed. "Was *she* there?"

"Could've been, but I didn't see either of them." Her daughter paused. "Look, Mama, you've gotta get over this thing about Prentice. These things happen all the time. Believe me, Clay will live. Besides, whatever happened between those two is none of our business."

Anything that happened to one of her children was her business, Chloe thought. She hadn't been enthusiastic when Clay first started dating Prentice Blair. After all, she was *that* woman's niece, and now here she was working at the Peach Shed. Knox didn't think she knew about him and Bertie Stackhouse, but of course she did, and Chloe was tired of pretending. How could he think she didn't know? Didn't everybody? And she'd heard rumors there'd been more involved than a hot romance, too. If there had, she didn't want to know it.

In spite of that, it was hard not to like Prentice Blair. Such a pretty girl—nice manners, too—but she had hurt her son, hurt him bad. Of course Clay had never told her, but she could read it in his voice, his eyes, his every move. Chloe Jarrett felt his misery as though it were her own. And it was. She couldn't forgive Prentice for that.

"Probably somebody stopped for speeding," Chloe said. "You know how they come around that curve there, but I'll tell your daddy."

"Tell me what?" Ice cubes rattled as Knox refilled his glass with sweet tea.

Before she could answer, they saw a police car pull up behind the house.

CHAPTER FOUR

Nobody knew about the cave but her. Nobody knew what was in it. If they did, they'd be all over the place: police, soldiers, Yankees, Nazi spies. They'd want it. They'd want her.

Whenever Hattie McGee felt threatened, she hid in the bramble cave she'd hollowed out for herself in the thicket beside the creek. She hid there now. Something was wrong. The girl was in trouble and the enemy had taken her away, would probably torture her for her secrets. They did things like that, Hattie knew. But they wouldn't do that to her! The Nazis would never find her here, and even if they did, she wouldn't tell. Her secrets would die with her.

Now the police had come. Hattie heard them talking in their loud, coarse voices, listened to them poking about where they had no business—probably trampling her precious rosebushes, breaking off fragile blooms. If she stayed out of sight for a while, maybe they'd go away. They usually did, but this time things were different. Hattie didn't know why; she just knew they were and that she'd be better off to stay where she was.

Hattie smoothed her stained taffeta skirt beneath her and made herself comfortable on a bed of grass. Ashley had always liked that dress. She remembered how he'd looked at her when she wore it to the ball at that big plantation house with all the stairs. She couldn't think of the name of the place. Seems she couldn't remember a lot of things lately. What would Ashley think of her if he could see her now? Old and gray and thick around the middle—her with a waist so small, Mammy'd had to take in all her dresses. Dear Ashley! He would love her anyway. Of course he would.

But Ashley was gone now; Mammy, too. Everybody she knew and loved. Only she, Scarlett, was left to defend and protect what remained of their heritage. Hattie's eyes burned and she wiped her nose with a tattered handkerchief that once had been lace and tucked it inside the frayed neck of her dress. Sometimes she felt so lonely. So afraid. It was awful being *the last one*. Now it was all up to her.

With her long skirt spread around her, Hattie hunched in her den of twigs and vines and took a pack of cheese crackers from a string bag. The bag was attached to her wrist by a length of Christmas ribbon that at one time might have been red. Jesse Dean, who worked at the grocery store, had given her the crackers, so she knew they were all right. She had known Jesse Dean Greeson since he was a tiny little boy with skin so pale you could almost see through it and hair that wanted to be yellow but couldn't quite make it. Hattie reckoned God must've run low on paint when He made Jesse Dean, but he turned out fine just the same. Once in a while he would treat her to a cup of ice cream they kept in a freezer at the store, the kind with a movie star on the lid. She wished she had some now.

At least it was cooler here than it was inside that stuffy trailer. The enemy was watching the trailer; she heard them stomping bull-like through the tall grass, banging on her dented metal door. Hattie smiled to herself. Well, let them try to find her here! She had covered her tracks well. They would never know anybody had passed this way.

A blue jay scolded her from a tree stump beside her crawl-through doorway. Hattie threw the raucous bird a crumb to shut him up, then yawned and went to sleep.

"Dimple, you've hardly eaten a bite," Phoebe Chadwick said, frowning. "Doc Morrison brought us that cantaloupe this morning fresh from his victory garden."

51

Dimple Kilpatrick shook her head and pushed aside her plate. "I'm sorry, Phoebe. I just don't believe I can get anything down right now."

"I don't suppose they've heard anything?" Phoebe turned to Annie, who was silently toying with her tuna salad. Tonight the three women ate alone in the Chadwick kitchen, where blue checkered curtains hung limply in the open windows. A third boarder, Lily Moss, was visiting relatives in Atlanta, and Velma Anderson, who taught with Bertie at the high school, had gone to lend what support she could to her longtime friend.

"I'm sure Charlie would've telephoned if they had any news," Annie said. "Delia's so worried, she's threatened to go out and look for Prentice herself, and I can imagine how helpless she feels. I only wish I could do something—*anything*—to help. If only we'd listened to you, Miss Dimple, when you heard that scream! Maybe we could've helped her."

But Miss Dimple shook her head. "Think how long it would've taken us to get back to the car, Annie, and then drive out to the main road and around that long curve to the Shed. I doubt if we would've been there in time to make a difference."

"But we could've *tried!*" Annie rejected the comfort of her words.

Annie Gardner and Charlie Carr, who had

been roommates all during college, would soon begin their third year of teaching at Elderberry Grammar School, and she would be the first to admit that Phoebe Chadwick's rooming house was beginning to be almost as much like home to her as the place where she grew up. Charlie lived only a block away with her mother, Jo, her sister, and Tommy, the small son Delia called "Pooh."

"Delia's mother finally convinced her she'd be more help if she made phone calls from home to some of Prentice's friends," Annie continued. "Maybe *somebody* has seen her or at least might have an idea where she is.

"Charlie took little Tommy to her aunt Lou's for a while just to get him out of the house. Poor little thing doesn't understand why his mother's so upset."

Dimple took her plate to the sink and filled a dishpan with hot water. She had to do something to get her mind off the memory of the dainty little girl who had sat in her classroom twelve years before and delighted in entertaining her classmates with a wide selection of spirituals in her sweet soprano voice. Dimple knew without asking that Prentice hadn't learned them from Elberta Stackhouse, who was somewhat of a freethinker in spite of her longtime membership in the Presbyterian church.

"Has anyone thought to check the cemetery behind Leola's church?" Phoebe asked. "The child has grieved so over Leola's death, she might've gone there to try to find some kind of comfort. It's bad enough to lose someone suddenly like that, but poor little Prentice was the one who found her." She poured herself another glass of tea. "Odessa says Leola was in good health as far as she knew," she added, speaking of her longtime cook, Odessa Kirby. "They were cousins once removed, you know. She thinks she must've slipped on something and hit her head."

"Prentice's aunt Bertie seems to believe Clay Jarrett has something to do with Prentice's disappearance," Annie said as she added her plate to the pan of soapy water and began drying dishes. "What do you think, Miss Dimple?"

Miss Dimple rinsed out the dishpan and dried her hands on a flour-sack towel somebody had embroidered with a basket of daisies. "Clay's far from perfect, but I can't imagine him doing anything like this," she said. "I imagine his family is as worried as we are."

"Maybe the two of them eloped," Phoebe suggested, but Annie shook her head. "Not the way Prentice was feeling. Even if she changed her mind, she'd never worry her aunt like this, and from what Charlie tells me, this is not like her at all."

"There's still plenty of daylight left," Phoebe reminded them. "Maybe we'll hear some good news soon."

For a while, Delia thought everything was going to turn out all right, or at least some part of her did. She had been raised on fairy tales. The prince would kiss Sleeping Beauty and rouse her from her one-hundred-year nap; the woodcutter would hear Red Riding Hood's cries and save her from the wolf.

But nobody had come to rescue Prentice.

"It's sweltering out here, honey. Don't you want to go back inside? They'll call you if anything turns up." Delia's mother sat beside her on the porch swing, fanning them both with an old seed catalog.

"You go on, Mama, I'll be okay." Delia wanted to be there if anybody arrived with news, good or bad. Her eyes scanned the street—left, right, then left again. Prentice didn't own a car, but she sometimes drove her aunt's old blue Ford. Whenever Delia rode with her, Prentice beeped the horn twice as she pulled into the driveway, then turned around in back of the house and beeped twice more as she drew level with the porch. Delia closed her eyes and replayed the sound of tires on gravel, the playful toot of the horn, willing the ritual to happen.

She felt the warm touch of her mother's hand on her arm and the swing jostled as Jo stood. "I'll get us some lemonade," her mother said, shutting the screen door quietly behind her.

People acted like Prentice was already dead, Delia thought. Even her mother whispered around her, and Josephine Carr wasn't the whispering type.

Was the sun going to shine forever? It seemed like the day would never end. Late-afternoon shadows wrapped around the dogwood tree in the front yard and teased thirsty zinnias in the flower bed by the porch. It should be midnight by now, yet the sun was still blasting yellow heat over the town.

After leaving Bertie's, Delia had spent over an hour at the police station, going over details with first one person and then another. Had Prentice said or done anything to lead her to believe she might be planning to go away? How many times had they asked her that question? How many times had she asked it of herself? And the answer was always the same: *No! No! No!*

And her friend's aunt Bertie! She had tried to console her, to give her a wispy fiber of hope to hang on to, even if it eluded her own grasp. If only she hadn't taken so much time across the road at Grady's! If only the train hadn't made so much noise. If only she'd been more observant.

Delia had spent most of the afternoon on the phone, trying to track down *anybody* who might have seen or heard from Prentice, but it was as if she had disappeared down the rabbit hole like Alice did in Wonderland.

After she gave her information at the police station, Delia was asked to wait in a small, narrow room lined with mismatched chairs and smelling of stale cigarette butts and dirty ashtrays. It was sweltering in there and she was grateful when someone offered Cokes from the cooler. Thank goodness Charlie was with her. Delia had never felt so lonely or so desolate since her Ned left to be shipped overseas.

She heard Clay Jarrett's voice outside in the corridor. "What's happened to Prentice? Won't anybody tell me? What's wrong? Is she all right?"

A door closed down the hall and Delia couldn't hear him anymore, but she did hear his father's loud, angry words as he was apparently being ushered into another office. "Look, can't you see how upset my son is over this? He loves that girl! My God, how do you think I feel? She was working for me. If anything's happened to Prentice, I'll find the bastard who did it. You have my word for that, but it sure as hell wasn't Clay!"

Earlier, Chief Tinsley had talked with Delia privately about Prentice's relationship with Clay and asked if it was true they had quarreled and weren't seeing each other anymore. Delia had told him the truth. She liked Clay, considered him a friend, as did her husband, Ned. Why, he had been in their wedding! But if he had hurt Prentice, she would turn on him in a flash.

"About how long did the two of them date?" the chief asked.

"Over two years, I guess. Almost three."

"And who was responsible for bringing this relationship to an end?"

He meant, of course, who had dumped who. Prentice would've smiled at his description.

"She was," Delia told him.

"So Prentice broke off with Clay. Do you know why?"

Delia nodded. "She's going away to school. Believes they should date others."

"And her boyfriend didn't agree with this?"

"No, I don't think he did."

Chief Tinsley stood and walked to the window, and Delia noticed a dark oval of sweat on the back of his shirt. "I want you to tell me the truth about this next question," he said, turning to face her. "Think about it before you answer. As far as you know, has Clay ever become violent with your friend? Struck her? Threatened her in any way?"

"No," Delia told him. She didn't have to think about it. It was hard to believe Clay would ever hurt Prentice.

But it was beginning to look as if somebody had.

It was too hot to stay inside and Miss Dimple didn't think she'd be able to sleep a wink anyway, nor did any of the others, so the three of them were sitting on Phoebe's front porch later that night when Velma Anderson pulled into the driveway in her cherished Ford V-8.

"Still no word," she announced without waiting for the inevitable question. "Doc Morrison gave Bertie something to help calm her, but I doubt if it will. Adam's with her now and Evan just left. He's been with her all afternoon."

Dimple nodded. She liked the Presbyterian minister and thought if anyone would be able to bring comfort to Elberta Stackhouse, it would be Evan Mitchell.

"I'm glad Adam's there," Dimple added. "She needs a steadying influence right now, and he's always seemed level-headed to me."

Phoebe spoke up. "Well, he's certainly been persistent! My goodness, Adam Treadway's been after Bertie to marry him for years now, and it's obvious he adores her. I don't know what's been holding her back."

"I'm not sure Bertie has room for anyone but Prentice in her life right now," Velma told them, then drew in her breath when she realized what she'd said.

"And doesn't Adam live in Clifford?" Dimple asked, coming to her friend's rescue. "That must be—what?—at least forty miles from here."

"Yes, but they're looking to replace the head of the English Department at the high school there,"

Velma said, "and Bertie tells me they've been trying to talk her into coming for an interview. Adam owns a little bookstore in Clifford, you know."

Dimple knew. The Novel Pastime. She had shopped there with her brother, Henry, earlier that summer and found the small store doing a thriving business. Widowed, and the father of two grown sons, Adam Treadway seemed content with his life as it was, but it was obvious he'd prefer to have Elberta in it.

Velma sighed as she sat in the wicker porch swing, and no one spoke for a while as they listened to the creaking of the swing, the sawing of July flies in a nearby oak. Soothing summer sounds. The grass had been cut that day and everything smelled green and new. Now and then a car stopped for the light at the intersection on Katherine Street, and except for a pale square of yellow from the living room window, the porch was steeped in a soft summer darkness. But there was nothing soft about this night.

"I wonder," Phoebe said finally, "how Chloe Jarrett is going to take all this. The police are bound to believe Clay had something to do with this girl's disappearance, and you know how she dotes on that boy."

Dimple had rolled countless bandages with Chloe for the American Red Cross; the two had volunteered to head up the scrap drive, and served together on several PTA committees. Chloe Jarrett had more gumption than people gave her credit for, Dimple thought, and was on the point of saying so when Annie spoke up from her seat on the front steps.

"Why do you keep talking about things like that?" she asked, getting to her feet. "Prentice is missing, probably dead, and all you can talk about are things that don't matter! *Where is she? What's happened to her?*" And suddenly, she began to cry. She hadn't meant to cry. It just happened, and she couldn't do a thing to stop it. "People are dying every day—young people just like Prentice—and they aren't ever coming back!"

Phoebe made a move to go to her, but Dimple stayed her with a hand and quietly led the younger woman inside. Annie's pilot brother, Joel, who had barely escaped being shot down during the D-day invasion in June, continued to risk his life on subsequent missions, and the last she'd heard from her fiancé, Frazier Duncan, he was fighting somewhere in France.

Years ago, Dimple had found herself in a similar situation when her sweetheart fought the Spaniards and yellow fever with Teddy Roosevelt during the Spanish American War. Unfortunately, yellow fever won. His face was only a memory now, but her heart never forgot, and it ached for Annie and all the others who lived in fear of that dreaded telegram from the War Department.

But first they must get through this never-ending night. It was never too hot or too late, Dimple believed, for her favorite remedy of ginger mint tea, and later in the darkened kitchen, the two women sipped quietly and waited for a brighter tomorrow.

CHAPTER FIVE

Clay knew his mother was hurting. She'd barely picked at her supper. It was too hot to eat, she'd said. They left her there in the dusk on the screened porch with her glass of tea and her radio. She liked to listen to soap operas—*Young Widow Brown* and *One Man's Family*, soppy as lukewarm oatmeal, and old-time music so slow, he wanted to build a fire under it.

"Chloe? We'll be back in a little while," his dad said when they left. And she didn't ask where they were going. Clay had a pretty strong hunch she knew.

His mama didn't like Elberta Stackhouse, and Clay couldn't understand why. He'd gotten along fine in her class in high school, never made less than a B, but every time that woman's name came up, his mother acted real funny. It had something to do with his dad, he thought. His sister told him once she'd heard the two of them had dated when they were younger, but then sometimes Loretta got carried away with romantic notions. And even if it were true, if there *had* been something between them, his mom had won out in the end. So what was her problem?

They drove in silence with the window down while air that must have been close to a hundred degrees blasted in their faces. "I don't know why you want to go there," Clay said. "She isn't going to want to see us, Dad—especially me. We'll only be wasting our time."

His father glanced at him but didn't speak as they turned onto Court Street. The stores had closed for the day and the streets were deserted. Most of Elderberry's men had gone to war—at least those who weren't too young or too old to fight. Everyone but him, Clay thought. *Why hadn't he enlisted sooner?* He had been too young when the war started; then his dad needed help on the farm, for at least a few months longer, he'd said, and of course his mother had backed him up. Well, the few months had turned into more than a year, and still his number hadn't been called. He should be over there like the sailor with the duffel bag on the poster in Lewellyn's Drug Store window, who warned, *If You Tell Where He's Going . . . He May Never Get There!* When this mess was finally cleared up, Clay Jarrett would be going, too.

On the courthouse lawn, a recruiting sign for the U.S. Army Air Force featured an airman holding a large bomb against a backdrop of clouds and planes. *O'er the Ramparts We Watch*, it reminded everyone. Being in the service would give him a chance to travel, Clay thought, to get as far from the farm as possible. Why, he'd never even seen the ocean! Then, when the war was over, he'd come back home to Elderberry. Maybe.

Except for the fountain splashing in the park by the town library and a mutt lifting its leg on a geranium-filled planter in front of the Total Perfection Beauty Salon, Elderberry seemed asleep. Clay wondered if he'd ever sleep again.

"Maybe you'd better tell us what you know," Clay's father said at last.

"What do you mean?"

"Son, if Prentice doesn't turn up, you could be in big trouble, and don't pretend you don't know it. Seems you've done gone and stepped in a pile of shit. You think I can't tell you're holding something back?"

Was his own dad accusing him of doing something to Prentice? Clay felt like he'd swallowed fire; he struggled to find his breath. "You don't think I had anything to do with Prentice disappearing, do you? Dad, I thought you knew me better than that!"

"*I know* you didn't have anything to do with it,

but the police don't. I heard how Bobby Tinsley was questioning you this afternoon. Seems everybody knows the two of you broke up after some kind of quarrel, and now you're the likely suspect. Son, if you've got the sense of a gnat—and I kinda believe you have—you'll use anything you know to help yourself."

"I don't know what you mean," Clay muttered.

"I *mean* what if something . . . well . . . *bad* has happened to Prentice? She's been missing since this morning and I'm afraid it doesn't look good. The longer they concentrate on you, the longer it'll take to find out who's really responsible. Is that what you want? Do you think she would?"

Clay felt those treacherous tears welling up in him again. Damned if he knew what Prentice would want.

"Well, do you?" his father demanded.

Silently, Clay shook his head. But then everybody in town would know Prentice had been screwing around with somebody else.

"Elberta, we came to offer our help." Knox Jarrett spoke softly through the screen door. Bertie, on the other side, showed no signs of opening it.

"I think you've done enough," she said. Her eyes were red and swollen and her face splotched from crying. She didn't even look like the same woman who had stood in front of Clay's high school English class and lectured them on the evils of attempting to compare the word *unique* to any other word; the woman who'd served them cookies and hot chocolate when he brought Prentice home from a movie.

It hurt him that she'd feel that way, but he knew she was hurting, too. Clay thought he might choke on the tears in his throat. "Miss Bertie, I wish I knew where Prentice was. If I did, I'd tell you, but I didn't have anything to do with this. Please believe me! I love Prentice! You must know that by now." *And, oh damn! Those blasted tears again!*

How long were the three of them going to stand there staring silently at one another? Clay felt his father's hand on his shoulder and knew it was a signal to leave. He hadn't wanted to come here, but now he didn't want to go, not with all this hurt and pain straining through the screen door from both sides.

His father spoke again. "Elberta, I'll do everything I can to help find Prentice. I promise you that."

The two of them had turned to go, when Clay heard the hook dangle free on the door and Bertie stood aside to let them in. She walked, Clay thought, as though her shoes pinched as she led them into the familiar living room with the radio on the small side table by the squat lumpy club chair and a sofa slipcovered in a rose-flowered print that Prentice always said reminded her of

66

squashed peaches. Clay headed for the armchair, leaving the sofa to the other two, who sat as far apart as they could. A plate of cookies, probably brought by a friend, sat on the coffee table in front of them, but nobody took one, nor were they offered. Why was it that people brought food whenever something bad happened? When his grandma Gladys had died, he hadn't been able to eat a thing.

"Clay?" Bertie leaned forward. "I know you cared for Prentice. I don't want to believe you would do anything to hurt her, but it's been hours now, and we've heard nothing. I'm about to go crazy thinking about all the things that could be happening to her. I'm so afraid . . . I'm afraid I'll never see her again."

Twisting a handkerchief into a rope, she looked at him with eyes that mirrored his own hurt. "If you can think of any reason for this to happen, or *anyone* who might have had something to do with this, *please* tell me now."

He knew his dad was waiting for him to tell what he knew, but he couldn't bring himself to tell Prentice's aunt what she'd told him—not all of it anyway. "She said she was seeing somebody else," he admitted. "That's why we broke up. Prentice was—is—going away to college and she wants to see other people."

"But who?" Bertie stood and towered over him. "Who, Clay? Didn't she tell you who?"

He shook his head. "I wish she had. I wish I'd asked, but to tell you the truth, right then I didn't want to know." If he did know, Clay thought, he would probably have killed him.

Rose petals. He'd heard them talking about rose petals, although they hadn't meant for him to hear. In the hallway outside the room where he sat, people talked in low, mumbling voices, their words muffled, like they were standing in a coat-jammed closet where consonants burrowed into pockets, vowels disappeared through a crack in the door.

When they came for him that morning, he'd been eating breakfast with his parents: eggs and grits and some of his mama's buttermilk biscuits with sourwood honey. Now it seemed Clay Jarrett had been inside this room since he was born. Ages ago, a gruff man had talked to him, then Chief Tinsley again, not so gruff, but his anger was barely concealed. Both had asked questions about Prentice. Some of them, he couldn't answer; some, he just flat out wouldn't. For a long time, he'd been sitting alone, sagging forward in the cane-bottomed chair, or pacing the length of the room—seven steps if he didn't take very large ones. The one window looked down on a mulberry tree that dropped dark, squishy berries onto the rusting tin roof of Red Campbell's Shoe Repair next door.

Something had happened to Prentice and nobody would tell him what it was. Whatever it was, it was obvious they thought he had something to do with it. *And, oh, God, he didn't want to know!* But how could they think he could do anything to hurt Prentice? Okay, so he'd been madder than hell when she'd told him what she'd done, but even then he had no desire to hurt her. Not physically. But a cold, dark feeling had come over him and for the longest time he simply couldn't function. Clay stood at the dirt-streaked window and watched a squirrel leap from one branch to another. Sometimes he couldn't even remember how he'd made it through the last couple of weeks.

He jumped at a touch on his shoulder and a tall graying man in a navy blue suit smiled slightly and stuck out his hand. He looked like he'd stepped right out of an advertisement for Parks Chambers, that store in Atlanta that sold menswear.

"Clay? Sorry. Didn't mean to startle you. Curtis Tisdale. Your parents have asked me to represent you."

"Represent me for what?" Clay slung the man's hand away from him. This guy wasn't from around here. He'd never seen him before. "Look, will you please tell me what's going on?"

With one sweeping motion, the man drew two of the chairs at right angles to each other. "Sit

69

down please, Clay. There are some things we need to talk about." His voice seemed gentle, almost fatherly. "Can I get you anything? Something to drink?"

Numbly, Clay shook his head. Still standing, he grasped the back of the chair. "It's Prentice. She's dead, isn't she?"

"Son, I'm so sorry. . . ."

Clay turned away, but there was nowhere to go. His plastic face was melting all the way down to his stomach and it hurt. He didn't know this man, but when Curtis Tisdale offered an arm, Clay took it, and for the next few minutes he cried himself empty against the stranger's chest.

"We should've let him enlist, or go away to college—*something,*" Chloe Jarrett said.

"He didn't want to go away." Knox looked at her across the small, shaky table in the back of Lewellyn's Drug Store, a block from the police station where Clay was being questioned. Coffee sloshed on the tabletop as he lifted the mug to his lips. "Clay belongs here. When his number comes up in the draft, he'll go, of course, but he knows where his future lies."

"But we didn't give him a choice."

"Didn't want a choice. Seemed satisfied to me. Spoiled is all. Never had to do without."

The words were meant for her, like it was all her fault. "What's that supposed to mean? Clay works hard, always has. And if I remember correctly, you went to college, Knox. And just when did you have to do without?"

A bell jingled as the front door opened, and Chloe glanced up in time to see Dimple Kilpatrick walking purposefully toward them. If it had been anyone else, she would have wanted to hide behind the lotion display, but Miss Dimple had a calmness about her that seemed to affect everyone around her. "I'm so glad I found you here," she told them. "I know this is a most difficult time for all of you, and I want you to know I'll do anything I can to help."

Knox jumped to his feet and offered a chair. He'd always admired Miss Dimple and was truly fond of her, even though a few years back she'd made him clean the blackboards after school for throwing spitballs at Thelma Sue Honeycutt. But she waved the chair aside. "Thank you, no. I can see you have things to discuss, but I'm afraid we're facing some dreadful times ahead, and if you will, I'd like you to tell Clay I have great confidence in him." Miss Dimple reached across the table and took Chloe's hand. "We'll all get through this together," she said.

The troubled couple watched as Miss Dimple selected several greeting cards, paid for them, and left. They didn't know she was thinking of the time seven-year-old Clay confessed on his own to breaking one of the small windows in the back door of the school while playing softball too close to the building.

"Please don't tell my daddy!" he'd begged. "I'll be in such big trouble! My aunt Maud gave me a whole dollar on my birthday, Miss Dimple. Will that be enough to pay for it?" It was, and Dimple Kilpatrick never said a word. She also didn't tell the child if it had been more than a dollar, she would have taken care of it herself.

Chloe took a deep breath. She felt as if at least part of the load had been lifted from her shoulders. She knew from working with Dimple Kilpatrick that she had a sharp mind and a shrewd intellect and also had been instrumental in helping the police with several cases in the past. What a relief to have her on their side!

But what was keeping that lawyer? Chloe took a paper straw from the holder and wrapped it around her finger until it fell apart.

"Don't." Knox covered her freckled hands with his calloused brown ones. "Chloe, surely you don't believe for one minute that Clay had anything to do with this girl's death."

"Prentice. Say her name, Knox. *Prentice.* She was a person, a part of our lives . . . only now she's dead." Chloe had seen Elberta Stackhouse sitting like a wax figure at the police station, and for the first time she hadn't thought of her as competition for her husband's affections, but as a woman with a grief so deep there was no balm to reach it. She had wanted to go to her, but Knox had steered her away, and Bertie's hurt pulled at her until she thought she would drown in the awfulness of the thing.

Did Bertie believe, as the police must, that their son had something to do with Prentice's death? If so, she must hate him, just as Chloe would hate anyone who harmed one of her children. But surely the woman knew Clay better than that.

It was getting late now and people who worked downtown hurried past on their way home. It was too hot to linger. Had they heard about Prentice? How many of them had already made up their minds that Clay was guilty?

"Curtis Tisdale's the best," Knox was saying. "We're lucky to get him." He squeezed her hand. "They can't hold him, Chloe. We'll have Clay home tonight."

"I want to see him. Why won't they let us see him?"

"Right now, he needs Tisdale more than he needs us, I reckon. But it won't be long now." Her husband lowered his voice. "Sounds to me like that nut in Atlanta might've had something to do with this."

She looked up. "What nut?"

"The one who's been killing all those women. Surely you've read about it. Scatters rose petals over their bodies. They call him 'the Rose Petal Killer.'"

Chloe winced. She'd read about those murders in the newspaper but hadn't paid much attention. With the war and all, there was so much violence, so much killing, why read about more? "I thought maybe they'd caught him by now," she said. Chloe studied her husband's face, the sun lines around his solemn brown eyes, his lips working to maintain composure.

"They didn't find—were there rose petals on *Prentice?*" Her words were slow, shattered, like the flowers themselves. She grew roses—a few of them—in that plot behind the old smokehouse. Clay had never paid much attention to them, probably didn't even know they were there.

Again, Knox gripped her fingers. "Overheard two of the men talking at the station. One of them sounded like that detective who questioned Clay. 'Covered in petals,' he said. Didn't know I was listening."

Her husband leaned closer, beckoned her forward until she could feel his breath on her cheek, see the small scar where he'd nicked himself shaving. "Chloe, they found her—Prentice—out by the old mill. Said it was their necking place."

"Whose necking place?"

"Theirs. Clay and Prentice's. Hell, just about everybody in town has been there."

Chloe hadn't. In her day, proper young ladies didn't do things like that. "How do they know it was theirs?" The lemonade she'd drunk earlier pitched and spewed inside her. This baby boy she'd suckled, sung to, and, with great difficulty, potty-trained—she didn't know him at all.

"Guess he told them about it." Knox almost smiled. "Chloe, where did you think they went after those games?"

"Why, to get something to eat, I guess. I don't know." And I don't want to know, she admitted to herself. All Chloe Jarrett knew was that she wanted her son back home again. She wanted things to be the way they'd been before. The thought of Prentice—pretty young Prentice— lying dead somewhere was like coming upon a washed-out bridge. You couldn't get around it; you couldn't get over it; you simply had to deal with it. Chloe made herself ask the next question. "Knox, do they know how she was killed?"

He shook his head. "Maybe *they* do, but I sure don't." He stood and looked toward the doorway as Curtis Tisdale approached them, his face grim.

CHAPTER SIX

It wasn't real. Delia looked at the wrinkles in her green linen lap, her hands twisting the Lilliputian hankie her mother had pressed upon her. And what good would that little thing do?

Delia had stuffed one of her father's large handkerchiefs into her purse in case she needed to cry. Charles Carr had died when Delia was eleven, but her mother still held on to small reminders, and until recently she had kept a tin of his pipe tobacco on top of her chest of drawers.

But Delia hadn't cried, and it didn't look like she was going to. What was the matter with her? Her best friend was dead. Murdered. Kind, beautiful Prentice, who had never hurt a living soul, was gone forever from her life, from all their lives. And she had yet to shed a tear.

Next to her, her mother stared straight ahead, her face all drawn and tight, her hand barely touching Delia's arm, but touching it just the same. Delia was glad it was there. On her right, her sister, Charlie, sat with closed eyes, one hand shading her face. The sharp edges of her small white purse dug into Delia's thigh, and now and then she got a whiff of Charlie's Chantilly cologne, a gift from her fiancé, Will Sinclair, before he left to fly missions overseas. Like Annie's brother, Joel, Will was involved in helping to run the Nazis out of France, and Charlie wrote him faithfully every night.

It looked as if the entire community of Elderberry was wedged inside the small Presbyterian church, built to accommodate less than half that number. Delia felt a trickle of sweat ooze down her face and used her fancy handkerchief to blot her brow.

Miss Ella Clyburn, whose small cottage she had passed every day on her way to high school, sat in the pew across from her, a drooping white rose pinned to her navy blue dotted swiss dress, and Delia wanted to smile when she saw it.

Clusters of tea roses grew on either side of the gate to Miss Ella's house, and every day during blooming season, she wore a pastel blossom pinned to her sagging bosom. Delia and Prentice had once brazenly picked a couple of the roses and Miss Ella not only lectured them sternly but telephoned their homes to report the misdeed. If Prentice were here, they would giggle and nudge each other, share a secret little smirk.

But Prentice wasn't here. She was down front in that glossy brown box covered in a blanket of primroses, daisies, and Queen Anne's lace as dainty and sunny as she was.

Was. Not is. *Was,* as in gone, dead, the final exit, and there was no reason for it, no explanation.

The pianist began to play familiar hymns, Prentice's favorites. "Abide with Me," "All Things Bright and Beautiful," songs she used to sing in her clear, sweet soprano. Charlie wiped her eyes and their mother snuffled softly; others wept openly.

Delia wanted to swallow, but she couldn't because there was a rock in her throat. No, not a rock, a boulder, and her mouth was as dry as road dust.

Awareness settled upon her, as loud in its

stillness as a clap of thunder. Around her, people drew in their breath, exchanged stiff-necked glances. Fans fluttered into laps, hymnals slipped silently aside, and Delia sensed, more than heard, muted footsteps on the carpeted aisle behind them.

An usher leaned over and whispered to Miss Ella across from them, and she shifted to permit Chloe Jarrett to slide in beside her. Knox was seated in a folding chair in the aisle next to his wife, leaving Clay standing all sallow and hollow-eyed at the end of the pew while hundreds of pairs of eyes tried to look somewhere else.

Before the usher could return with another chair, Delia's aunt, Lou Willingham, who sat on the end on the other side of Charlie, gave her niece a firm poke in the arm and whispered for her to move down.

Delia sucked in and inched over as best she could, and with a minimum of shuffling and grunting, they made room for Clay at the end of their pew, but their resentment was like a spear ramming home, and the cutting coldness made her shiver in spite of the warm flesh on either side. Prentice was dead—strangled, they said— and the one who had killed her could be sitting close enough to touch.

It was almost over. The prayers that consoled and strengthened or fell on hearts that solace couldn't

78

heal; the words of the service spoken with tenderness and grace by the minister who had watched Prentice grow up, and whose eyes mirrored the hurt they all felt. Prentice had been raised in this church, and only last Sunday, she had sung in the choir.

Now Pauline Hobgood, the soloist, sang "Amazing Grace." Sang it without accompaniment in a deep, rich contralto that seemed to Delia to reach inside her spirit and lift it up. Listening, she kept her eyes on the window behind the pulpit. It was a large, round window of clear glass, and beyond it shreds of clouds hovered in a summer blue sky. She felt her mother's hand close firmly over hers as they stood for the benediction, and shut her eyes as Prentice's aunt Elberta and her friend Adam Treadway followed the casket up the aisle. She couldn't bear to look at them, to have their grief burrow into her heart on top of her own.

And then something happened that made some smile and others cry. As people began to slowly make their way outside, the pianist began to play "Angels from the Realms of Glory." She played it joyfully and she played it loud, as if she meant for it to reach Prentice herself.

"Isn't that a Christmas hymn?" someone behind them muttered, but Delia knew exactly why that particular carol had been requested. To Elberta Stackhouse, Prentice *was* an angel.

• • •

First Leola and now Prentice. Two funerals in a little over two weeks. Dimple Kilpatrick, sitting in a back pew with her friend Virginia Balliew, watched the crowd of mourners shuffle past. When an older person died, it wasn't unusual for people to smile and speak to one another or even to converse in respectful voices, but no one spoke here. What could one say? Their faces were grim; some were tear-stained. All seemed intent on reaching the doorway and stepping back into the living world. *Was one of them a murderer?*

Leola's daughter, Mary Joy, nodded solemnly to Dimple from the other side of the church. Someone patted her shoulder as he passed; another squeezed her arm, recognizing the sadness she felt at losing "one of her own" in this senseless way, for anyone acquainted with Dimple Kilpatrick knew she thought of those she had taught in that manner. It didn't matter if they had children or even grandchildren; she would always claim a part of them. And it had become increasingly difficult to lose the brave young men who had died in the service of their country.

The Jarretts, she noticed, had somehow managed to slip away through a side door. Everyone knew the police had questioned Clay but hadn't been able to hold him due to lack of evidence. He remained, however, at the top of their list of suspects. Chloe, already frail, seemed to be fading into gray, and Dimple was worried about her. Having made a promise to help, she would try to see Chloe tomorrow. Dimple didn't know who was responsible for Prentice Blair's death, but she was certain it wasn't Clay Jarrett.

Mary Edna Sizemore, the home economics teacher at the high school, passed by on the arm of the school chorus director, Sebastian Weaver, both openly crying. The drama coach, Seth Reardon, his eyes bleak, followed solemnly behind them. Prentice had been bitten by the acting bug her senior year in high school, when she landed a major role in her class play, and had even been considering taking courses in theater at the university.

Head down, Elias Jackson, the high school principal, paused to blow his nose before attempting to regain his composure.

Rather than subject themselves to the close confinement of the exiting crowd, Dimple and Virginia had agreed to wait until the sanctuary was empty before leaving, and now Dimple rose as the last person made her way out the door.

"You might as well sit back down, unless you want to stand outside and wait on me," Virginia whispered, tugging at her skirt.

"Whatever for?" Frowning, Dimple complied.

"Because I have to go to the rest room! I thought this church would never empty!"

"Well, my goodness, Virginia, why didn't you say so? We would've left earlier."

Virginia sighed. "Dimple, you should know by now my bladder doesn't like for me to stand and wait. When I have to go, it just doesn't do for anybody to get between me and the bathroom."

Dimple agreed her friend was right and decided she might as well stay where she was instead of trying to weave her way through those gathered around the front of the church. She had been sitting there only a few minutes when she overheard an exchange behind her in the narthex that immediately seized her attention.

Where in the world did her family get off to? You'd think they could at least wait! Delia wandered into the narthex after leaving the rest room, where she'd splashed cool water on her face. It hadn't helped. Her eyes still burned and her skin felt hot and sticky. She looked about before starting for the door. They were probably waiting for her out front to ride to the cemetery together.

Delia almost cried out when someone suddenly tugged at her sleeve, and she turned to find herself facing a black-veiled apparition in a huge rose-crowned hat. The woman's dress, the color and texture of long-dead leaves, looked and smelled as if it had been stored in somebody's basement for the better part of a century. The long skirt lumped and bunched over what looked to be about six or seven crinolines. *Hattie McGee.*

She tried not to flinch when the woman grabbed her arm.

"You watch out, girl! They'll be after you next." Hattie's voice was hoarse, unaccustomed as she was to talking.

"They? They who?" Delia found herself being herded into the hallway that led to the Sunday-school rooms. The air was close and stuffy, and Hattie hadn't bothered to bathe lately. Delia held her breath.

"Scarlett knows. Scarlett knows who. Don't you go back, you hear? Don't go back there again!" The words were almost singsong; the black-veiled face loomed closer. Delia ducked her head and inhaled quickly, noticing Hattie's gloved hand on her arm. The tattered lace mitt was edged in tiny seed pearls and felt scratchy on her skin.

"What do you know? Tell me. Where am I not supposed to go?" She wanted to pull away and run, but suppose Hattie really did know something?

"The Shed. I know what I saw there. I know what I found . . . but they don't. They don't even know I have it." The veil hid the woman's eyes, but there was triumph in her voice.

"Delia? Are you in here?" Delia heard her sister's voice and was relieved to see Charlie and Miss Dimple appear behind them in the narthex.

"She says she knows something," Delia told them. She was surprised at how shaky her voice sounded, and she wasn't sure her knees were going to support her. "Says she saw what happened to Prentice."

"Hattie, if you know something, you must tell the police. It could be something that would help." Miss Dimple spoke with a voice of reason, but reason was lost on Hattie McGee.

"No! That's just what they want. Don't you know that? It's in my secret place. They'll never find it there. They'll never find me."

There was fear in her voice and it went to the bone. Dimple felt it like an electric shock and it was obvious that the others reacted to it, too. Charlie hurried to her sister and pulled her out of Hattie's reach.

"What did you find?" Miss Dimple continued, speaking in a soft voice. "Tell me. What are you afraid of?"

Hattie shook her head, showering a flurry of wilted petals. A pink one caught on her veil; a red one seesawed into the water fountain and stuck there, looking like a big drop of blood.

"Why, the Nazis, of course, and you'd better be afraid, too. They took her, you know, and that's when they dropped it—right back there behind that shed."

"Dropped *what?*" Delia ignored her sister's calming hand on her arm. Mad Hattie couldn't help being as crazy as a bedbug, but Delia had lost her best friend. Her head ached, her dress stuck to her back, and she resented being cornered by this smelly creature who spoke in riddles. *"What did they drop?"* she asked again.

Hattie McGee lunged closer, her flowery hat tilting at an angle. "Why, it was gold!" she whispered with breath that could be used to subdue the enemy. "It was gold—*real gold!*"

"Look, we have to go," Charlie said, stepping between them. "Our family's waiting for us to go to the cemetery, but if you really know something, anything—" But before she could finish her sentence, Hattie turned and fled down the hallway, shedding rose petals like some macabre flower girl.

By the time they made their way outside, most of the people had dispersed except for a few groups murmuring sad good-byes in the shade of the old stone building, and the funeral procession was already winding its slow, antlike way to the cemetery.

Miss Dimple hurried to join Virginia, who had waited for her in the narthex and had overheard only part of the commotion in the hallway. "What was that all about?" she asked.

"I wish I knew," Dimple admitted.

Delia and Charlie made their way across the steaming asphalt parking lot to find their mother and aunt Lou, who were already in the car with the motor running. Charlie slid quickly into the backseat and Delia hurried to join her. It would be awful to be late for Prentice's graveside service because of Hattie's ridiculous ramblings.

What now? she thought when she heard running footsteps behind her and turned, to find Clay racing in her direction.

For a horrible minute, she thought he was going to take her hand. Clay's tie was crooked, his coat rumpled, and his face damp and flushed. He looked like an overgrown Boy Scout. But, damn him, he wasn't!

"I've got to talk to you, please!" Clay stumbled to a stop and put out a hand to brace himself against the car. Delia stepped back instinctively.

"Don't worry, I'm not going to touch you. Look, you know I wouldn't have done anything to hurt Prentice. You've got to believe me!" Clay glanced at Charlie, who was watching him with interest, and lowered his voice. "Delia, listen, I really need your help. Can you meet me some- where later?"

CHAPTER SEVEN

Jo Carr inched her vehicle into the somber line behind Dora Delaney's faded Plymouth, which was jammed with everybody who had ever filed a nail or shampooed hair at Total Perfection. Bertie always had her hair cut there, and Dora had closed the salon for the funeral.

"What does Clay want to see you about?" Charlie asked, having tried and failed to overhear the conversation.

Delia sank back against the seat and closed her eyes. "Says we need to talk."

"Whatever for?" her mother asked. Perspiration fogged her glasses and she snatched them off and wiped them on her sleeve.

"Wants to talk about Prentice. About what happened—or didn't happen, I guess. Clay swears he wouldn't have hurt her."

"Do you believe him?" Charlie asked.

Delia didn't answer. She could hardly bear to look as they drove past the grammar school, where playground swings hung limp and empty in the sun. How many times had she and Prentice played there to see who could swing the highest, made tiny houses in the roots of the giant oak?

Her mother turned left at the corner and

followed the chain of cars past Lewellyn's Drug Store where Phil Lewellyn, the pharmacist, stood respectfully in the shade of his green-striped canopy with the local dentist, Lou's husband and the girls' uncle Ed. There was hardly any traffic in town because almost everybody in Elderberry was in the funeral procession.

"Well, do you?" Charlie persisted.

Their aunt spoke up from the front seat. "I think we should at least hear what he has to say," she announced.

"*We?*" Delia glanced at her sister, who rolled her eyes. Their aunt was incredibly nosy.

"Well . . . *someone* should be with you, Delia. There's safety in numbers, you know."

Delia was grateful when her mother stepped in. "Your aunt Lou has a point," she said, "but I doubt if Clay would speak freely with one of us hanging about. He might be less intimidated if Charlie went with you instead."

"I don't even want to be in the same room with him," Delia said. "Why should I listen to Clay Jarrett if he had anything to do with what happened to Prentice?"

"But what if he didn't?" her mother said.

Jo spied her at the end of the block when a blob of dark skirt bobbed into view. She resembled a dusty balloon after most of the air had escaped. Hattie McGee. It was a wonder the woman hadn't dropped from heat exhaustion in all those under-skirts. Jo lifted her foot from the accelerator; they were practically crawling along as it was. "I can't believe she's out in all this heat," she said. "Do you suppose she wants a ride to the cemetery?"

Before anyone could answer, the old woman glanced behind her and darted into a side street.

"Seems to be going the other way—thank goodness!" Delia said. "Looks like she's planning to sit on Doc Morrison's wall."

Jo glanced down the narrow, tree-shaded street and saw Hattie McGee perched there, knees up, her back propped against the low column of the Morrisons' brick wall. She hoped Amanda Morrison didn't have any roses she'd mind sharing. "Guess she's only cooling off a little. I suppose she's all right." She hated to leave her there like that, but there was no time to stop. Jo gained speed to catch up with Dora's car before winding up the hill to the cemetery.

"That woman's never going to be all right," Delia said. "I like to have never gotten away from her back there at the church! Thought I'd die of asphyxiation."

"Honey, she can't help the way she is," her aunt Lou reminded her.

"Well, I'm sorry, but she nearly scared me to death . . . all the time carrying on about Nazis and gold and people chasing after her. Claims she saw what happened to Prentice."

"Poor Hattie." Jo slowed to a stop as the cars ahead began to turn into the cemetery gate. "She has this thing about gold—especially the Confederate gold. Says she knows where it's hidden, and to hear her tell it, the Yankees have been on her trail for years, but she's harmless, I reckon. Must've overdosed on *Gone with the Wind*."

"And now she thinks Nazis are after her, too," Charlie said. She ran her fingers through her blond shoulder-length hair and lifted it off her neck as her mother parked on the side of the road. "Has she always been this way?"

"Long as I can remember," her aunt said. "I think she had a high fever from some kind of illness when she was a young girl and it left her this way. Family's long gone, of course. Sister married and died somewhere in Texas, I believe. But Hattie was quite gifted, they say—played the piano and had a beautiful voice. Young girl like that. Her whole life wasted. What a pity."

Grass crunched underfoot as they followed the others up the dusty hillside to where Prentice's flower-decked casket waited under the bright blue canopy.

Pity is not a strong enough word, Delia thought.

The hat was hot and heavy and the veil tickled Hattie's chin. If only she could take it off for a minute, but Mammy would have a fit. It wouldn't do to get too much sun, bad for the skin. And what if she got *freckles?*

She'd never had freckles before. Had she? But somebody had. Somebody nice. A girl. Hattie couldn't remember her name, but she saw her face, saw it plain as day: blue eyes and freckles, and a mouth that laughed. They'd played together, made mud pies and baked them in the sun. The girl didn't care about freckles. Neither did she. Where was Mammy then?

Gone, of course, and the mud pie girl was gone, too. She was alone. Hattie closed her eyes and rested her back against the column. This was such a nice wall, and shady. They wouldn't think to look for her here. Surely these people wouldn't mind if she rested a spell, and there were roses, too—such a pretty color! She'd sure like to have one like that, almost an apricot it was. Maybe she'd come back when it was darker, cooler, and help herself to a cutting. She didn't think they'd care.

The music woke her. Somebody was playing the piano. Hattie had heard that piece before; her fingers stretched and arched, plucked at her skirt. "The Minute Waltz" it was called, and whoever had played it before did it much better than the person who lived in this house with the apricot rosebushes. The clumsy musician kept breaking off in mid-measure, starting all over again. Hattie wanted to burst inside that house and rap the pianist's knuckles, show her how to play it right. But she couldn't remember how.

Her hat slid over her face. Most of the roses had fallen from it, and, sighing, Hattie took it off and laid it aside. The sharp edges of the wall cut into her legs and she slipped off it and sat on the sidewalk just long enough to stretch. She hadn't had anything to drink since she left home for the funeral and her throat was so dry, it hurt to swallow. A little water from the hydrant by the porch would taste mighty good if only she had something to drink from.

Hattie McGee stiffened when a car pulled up alongside her and somebody blew the horn. It was a shiny black car, and at first she thought it was the hearse that had taken that poor girl's body to the cemetery. Now it was back for her.

Never show fear. Pretend . . . pretend . . . pretend. But Hattie's hands trembled as she quickly jammed her hat back on her head and snatched up her string bag. Her legs felt weak when she tried to walk. After a futile attempt to smooth her skirt, she began moving away from the car. If she wished hard enough, maybe the car would go away.

But it didn't.

"Are you all right?"

Hattie glanced over her shoulder and saw the big car backing alongside her. The driver leaned over the seat to speak through the window on the passenger side. "It's all right; I won't hurt you. I just wanted to see if you were okay. You looked . . . well, you were down there on the sidewalk, and I thought you might've fallen."

Hattie slowed but didn't answer. She knew that voice, knew the woman it belonged to. Hardin. That was her name. Hardin . . . Haynesworth . . . something. Couldn't let go of her maiden name so she dragged it along behind her like so much baggage. Why, Hattie didn't know. Granddaddy was poor as a church mouse, but at least she wasn't a Yankee. And it *was* awfully hot. She wasn't sure she'd be able to walk all the way home.

Hattie opened the door and, bundling her skirts about her, slid in beside the driver, oblivious to the woman's expression of distaste. "A ride would be mighty nice," she told her.

The woman had been drinking. You could smell it all over her—not that Hattie cared. She wasn't above taking a toddy herself if anybody were to offer, but nobody ever did. From beneath her veil, Hattie slyly eyed the driver and saw her slip a mint into her mouth. All the mints in the candy store wouldn't cover up that boozy breath, she thought, and a crooked little laugh angled out and strained through the limp black net.

"Did you say something?" The woman stopped suddenly at an intersection and Hattie steadied herself against the dashboard.

"Throat's dry," she croaked. She hadn't meant to laugh, but it did her good to know the Haynesworth woman had problems just like everybody else. She'd seen her earlier at the funeral, all cool and fresh in her pale blue dress and pearls, and she was still as spotless as a freshly ironed sheet, but something was surely gnawing at her. Hattie couldn't remember who she'd married, only that he had money.

The woman steered with her left hand and held a handkerchief to her nose with her right, like she had a cold or something. Or maybe she was upset over the funeral. She wore an emerald dinner ring on her right hand and a diamond as big as a peach pit on the other. You'd think she'd at least have manners enough to offer a mint, Hattie thought, but it wouldn't be polite to ask. What would Mammy say?

"Saw you at the funeral," Hattie said.

"That's right. I started to go to the cemetery, but there was such a crowd." The small woman behind the wheel glanced at her. "I suppose you've had a lot of commotion around your place. You must be glad it's all over."

"Who says it's over?"

Hardin frowned. "I beg your pardon?"

"They'll come back when they know," Hattie said.

"When they know what?" Hardin Haynesworth . . . whoever fluttered her hand kind of queenlike at somebody in a passing car as they turned into the road that led to the peach orchard and Hattie's rusting metal home.

"When they know what I found." Hattie closed her eyes. She sure was tired and the seat was as comfortable as any rocking chair. She could stand to ride a little longer if asked.

But the driver wasn't asking. She turned into the expanse of red clay and weeds that served as an access to the trailer Hattie called home. At one time, there might've been a road leading into the scruffy underbrush and pines, but now tall grass brushed the underside of the car as its driver circled and stopped. "And what *have* you found?" she asked.

"Never you mind." Struggling with the door handle, Hattie stepped out onto coppery dust. The woman didn't sound like a Yankee, or a Nazi, either, but Hattie wasn't sure she could be trusted to share her secret. Especially after she'd had too much to drink. She touched the brim of her hat with lace-mitted hands and made a coy little curtsy before plodding through the knee-high weeds for home. "Much obliged for the ride," she called over her shoulder.

The brief ride had relaxed her and Hattie knew a fruit jar of cold tea waited in her little box of an ice chest, but she had a strange prickly feeling something was wrong. *Like somebody was watching.*

Late-afternoon shadows melted into the thicket, but the sun still blew its scorching breath with a smothering kind of heat. Hattie turned and looked behind her, but the fancy black car was gone, leaving only a lingering halo of reddish dust. If only she weren't so thirsty, she would turn back. Grady Clinkscales at the Gas 'n Eats would give her something cold to drink. Hadn't he done it before? But now the trailer was in sight, and rusty and run-down as it was, it was home to Hattie. She pulled off her hat and veil and began working at the buttons on her skirt. How good it would feel to peel away all these clothes! And oh, lordy! She was about to wet her pants!

But as soon as she pushed open the door, Hattie knew someone had been there before her.

CHAPTER EIGHT

What a strange old bird, and about as batty as they come! *Batty Hattie*. And mercy, what an awful smell! Hardin Haynesworth Kirkland twisted her face into a grimace and rolled down the window on the driver's side. Hot air blasted her face and played havoc with her hair, but she couldn't stand the odor any longer. The whole car reeked of sour sweat.

At least her husband wouldn't notice she'd been

drinking. Somehow he always knew, even when she sprayed and gargled, sprinkled cologne on the upholstery. That was about all Griffin Kirkland noticed about her, unless she said or wore the wrong thing. He didn't curse, or even yell. Griffin never said anything worse than "darn," and she'd never heard him raise his voice. No, his strategy was aloofness, and his weapon, silence.

Hardin was accustomed to her husband's coldness, his criticism, but his terrible silences banished her into a state of isolation, made her feel less than human. Sometimes she wished he'd just haul off and hit her, which, of course, he never would. Griffin Kirkland knew she'd never stand for that. At the least little bruise or telltale handprint, she would take him for everything he was worth: his money, his estate, and, worst of all, his reputation.

Her husband had an image to uphold as a respected member of the law firm of Kirkland, Kirkland & Smith. The Smith partner had been dead for years, as had the founding Kirkland, but Griffin fully expected his son, Griffin Chenault Kirkland III, to join him after the war. Like his daddy and his daddy before him, Griffin Kirkland served as a steward at the Elderberry Methodist church. His own great-granddaddy had been minister there when the small brick church was built back in 1888, and the old man's unsmiling portrait hung in the vestibule, where he seemed to be looking over everyone's shoulder. Griffin was going to look just like him someday, and the thought of it made Hardin want to become one of those brave people who fled to some exotic place and never came back.

But Hardin wasn't brave. And she knew she wasn't even very bright. Her Haynesworth granddaddy had lost his money during the Depression and nobody had ever figured out how to get it back. Hardin's father had died when she was fifteen, but her mother managed to send her to business school for a couple of years, where she learned to take dictation and type other people's letters. She wasn't even a very good secretary, but Hardin Haynesworth was beautiful; she had looks and she knew how to use them. She had used them to get Griffin Kirkland.

And then there was Chenault, the one thing she'd done right. Her son, her saving grace. If it hadn't been for Chenault, Hardin would have left her husband years ago, but if she had, Griffin Kirkland would have found some way to take him away from her. He knew how to do things like that. *Well, he wouldn't be able to do that now!* Hardin smiled. Now that Chenault was stationed on the southwest edge of Atlanta with the U.S. Army Installation Management Command at nearby Fort McPherson, he could come and go as often as he liked. And wouldn't her husband be surprised if he knew she had been setting aside a portion of her household allowance for years so that one day she and Chenault wouldn't have to depend on him? She could stand anything now.

It was almost six when Hardin turned into the boxwood-lined drive to Silverwood, the Kirkland family home on the outskirts of town. The dark, dignified Tudor always greeted her with reserve, and even after all these years, she felt like an intruder there. Thank goodness Griffin had a meeting tonight and wouldn't be home for dinner. If Chenault dropped by, maybe they could have supper together, just the two of them. And a glass—or more—of wine. Hardin slipped another breath mint into her mouth before heading for the shower.

"I need your help," Clay Jarrett said. He stood on the Carrs' front porch in the darkening twilight of a summer evening, as he had on earlier occasions: double dates with Ned and Prentice, Monopoly games that went on forever, watermelon cuttings and high school dances. Happy times. This wasn't one of them.

Reluctantly, Delia stepped out to join him, leaving Charlie inside but within hearing distance. "What do you expect me to do?" she said. "My best friend is dead. You've come to the wrong place if you want sympathy from me."

Clay spoke softly. "She was my best friend, too."

His face was like a raw wound, and Delia looked quickly away. She hadn't expected to see such suffering there. "I don't think Hell could be any worse than this," Clay said.

He was nineteen, a year younger than she was. Too young to hurt like this, Delia thought. And so was she. Something in his voice wrapped around her heart, warmed it like a blanket. "I miss her so much," Delia said. And finally the tears came. She'd never thought what a relief it would be to cry.

She heard her sister say her name. The screen door opened and then closed softly, and someone took her hand and squeezed it. Clay. She could tell he'd been crying, too. "It's time to talk," he said.

Delia found the dainty hankie still tucked in her pocket and used it to blow her nose. "I don't know anything you don't know," she said.

"You might. She was seeing somebody, you know."

"Who?"

"I don't know, but I got the impression it was somebody from around here, somebody older, and they were doing more than holding hands."

Delia backed away. "I can't believe you'd say that when Prentice isn't here to defend herself! Who told you that?"

"Prentice. Prentice told me." Clay plucked a frond from the wisteria vine that shaded one end of the porch and leaned against the railing.

"When? When did Prentice tell you this?"

"When we broke up. You think I *like* telling you this?" Clay sighed. "I thought she might've said something. I got the idea Prentice told you just about everything."

"Not lately," Delia said. "But I've been busy with the baby—and I've been trying to help more around the house, too, with Charlie teaching and Mama working at the munitions plant three days a week." Suddenly, she needed to sit down. She had been to her best friend's funeral, and now this. Delia sank into the nearest rocker. "And then since Leola died," she continued, "Prentice had been crying a lot."

"About Leola?"

"Yes, but it was more than that. She acted like she was worried about something . . . kind of nervous and on edge, but she wouldn't talk about it." Delia hugged the chair's cushion to her chest. "I wish I'd made more of an issue of it. Maybe she would've told me what was wrong, but she always got upset when I asked. Do you think it might have something to do with this . . . person she was seeing?"

"I honestly don't know what to think," Clay admitted. "I guess she had a right to get upset with me. I didn't want her to go away to school next fall—acted like a jackass—but I would've been willing to see her on weekends or whenever I could. Prentice didn't want any part of it, wanted a clean break. The way she acted, you would've thought I was a kid. And then she told me they'd been . . . well, you know . . . what they'd been doing."

Delia frowned. "What makes you think he was older?"

He shrugged. "Just from the way she was acting, like all of a sudden I didn't have sense enough to get in out of the rain. She wasn't ready for a commitment, she said. There were things she wanted to do." Clay looked out at the quiet street, where moths whirled around the streetlight. "Seemed to me she'd already done enough. Anyway, that's when she gave me back my class ring. *Damn!* I've never been so mad at anybody in my life." He turned and looked at Delia, looked at her for a long time. "But not mad enough to kill her, if that's what you're thinking."

"And you don't have *any* idea who she was seeing?"

Clay shook his head. "I was sort of counting on you for that."

"What about her aunt Bertie? Maybe Prentice told her."

He shook his head. "She says not. And how would you ask her that anyway? 'Miss Bertie, do you have any idea who your niece was making out with?' Besides, I don't think the two of them talked about things like that."

"Leola might know," Delia said. *But Leola was dead.*

"She never mentioned *anybody?* Somebody she admired, maybe wanted to date?" Clay grabbed the arms of her chair, leaned so close that Delia could see the sunburn peeling on his nose. "It might even have been in a joking way. . . . Try to *think*."

"I'll talk to Miss Bertie," Delia said. "Oh, don't worry, I won't be explicit. Maybe she'll remember something."

"Does that mean you believe me?" he asked. "You'll help?"

Delia nodded. "I believe you, but if I ever find out you're lying, you'll wish you were the one they buried up on that hill today."

He closed his eyes, plopped back in his chair. "Good enough. I've told the police she was seeing somebody, but I can tell they don't believe me. If only I had a name—or even an idea—it would help. Look, be careful who you talk to about this, Delia—especially the part about . . . well, you know . . . the sex."

After a day that seemed as if it would never end, night had finally crept upon them, gently veiling the porch in darkness, but it wasn't dark enough to hide the flush on Clay's face.

"I will. I promise," Delia said.

"And you'll let me know if you think of anything, *anybody* Prentice might've been seeing?"

"I'll let you know." Delia could think of only one name, but it was too far-fetched to be true. She didn't want it to be true.

• • •

"Clay says Prentice was seeing somebody else, somebody older," Delia told her sister.

Charlie already knew it because she'd been listening, but she pretended otherwise. "Does he have any idea who it might've been?"

"Says he doesn't know. But why would she do that, Charlie? It doesn't make any sense. She and Clay have been a couple for ages."

Maybe that *was* why, Charlie thought, but this wasn't the time to say so, especially since Delia had married her Ned soon after high school. "Do you think she wanted to make him jealous?" she suggested.

"Why would she do that? Clay Jarrett hasn't looked at anybody else since tenth grade." Delia followed her sister into the kitchen and poured a glass of ice water from the green glass bottle. "I'll ask around, see what I can find out. Surely somebody has an idea what was going on."

"Are you out of your mind? If Prentice was seeing somebody else, he could be the one who killed her!" Charlie didn't realize she was shouting until Delia hushed her with a finger to her lips. "Keep it down. . . . You don't want to wake Pooh, do you? And how else are we going to learn anything? Any other ideas?"

"Just promise me you won't do such a foolish thing, Delia. If this person killed once, he wouldn't think twice about doing it again."

"But it might even be that Rose Petal Killer they've been writing about in the papers." For the first time that day, Delia Varnadore smiled. "And aren't you the one to talk, Charlie Carr? Seems to me you and Miss Dimple and Annie Garner attract murder like a magnet."

And we're pretty darn good at solving it, too! Of course there had been a few close calls, but Charlie knew if anybody could get to the bottom of this, it would be Miss Dimple Kilpatrick. "Remember you have little Tommy to think of and a husband coming home to you when this war's finally over," she said. "We'll look into this, I promise."

It didn't surprise her that she could hardly wait.

Upstairs, Delia smiled at her small son, who was sleeping froglike on his stomach, one hand clutching a woolly toy dog his father had bought for him before he was born. A quick bath had refreshed her and her bed waited, but as tired as she was, Delia knew she wouldn't be able to sleep right away. The room held too many reminders of Prentice. A lopsided friendship plaque of plaster of Paris, made when Prentice was ten, hung on the wall over her desk; a pillow cross-stitched with what was supposed to look like an angel was propped in the window seat. Letters Prentice had written when Delia and Ned first married and were living on an army base in Texas were still somewhere in her desk drawer, where she'd put them when she came home a few months before Tommy was born. Prentice wrote weekly at first; then her correspondence dwindled as the demands of her senior year increased.

Could Prentice have mentioned someone in her letters? The drawer stuck; it always stuck, but Delia gave a hard jerk and it squawked open. Thank goodness it hadn't wakened the baby! The letters, addressed neatly in Prentice's rounded handwriting, were written on blue paper. There were twelve of them.

Delia tiptoed into the lighted hallway and, sitting in the armchair where on rainy days she'd always liked to read, she spread them on her lap, arranging them in order of the dates they were mailed, but the postmarks blurred. *Prentice was really gone! She couldn't help her now, but maybe Prentice herself had left behind a clue.*

She didn't find a name until the sixth letter, dated October tenth.

It was the name she had dreaded finding.

CHAPTER NINE

I wouldn't jump to conclusions," Miss Dimple said. "After all, who hasn't experienced a schoolgirl crush?"

Charlie never imagined Miss Dimple had, but

then, she was constantly being surprised at her fellow teacher's daring and ingenuity and was learning not to be astonished at anything Dimple Kilpatrick pulled out of her hat.

An early-morning shower had refreshed the air and Miss Dimple and Annie were shucking corn for dinner on Phoebe's latticed back porch when Charlie joined them with the information Delia had found in her letters.

"It sounds like something you or I might have written," Annie reminded her. "Remember what a crush we had our freshman year on that—"

"Oh, never mind him!" Charlie told her, recalling the good-looking history professor with a fascinating English accent they fantasized about until they learned he was old enough to be their grandfather. "Clay says Prentice was seeing *somebody,* and his is the only name we've found that might be of interest. Delia said she hadn't thought anything about it when she first read the letter because it had become an ongoing joke between the two of them."

Charlie smiled when she thought of what Prentice had written in the letter her sister had shown her: *Guess who came to the game tonight??? Chenault Kirkland, and he was in his uniform, too! Oh, gosh! I thought I was going to melt! Anyway, he spoke to me—and I think he smiled—or maybe it was just gas.*

"When they were in high school, Delia and

Prentice used to concoct fantasies about Chenault Kirkland," Charlie told the others. "You know . . . like you might about Clark Gable or Cary Grant." She paused, thinking again of the letter. *Chenault is taking me to dinner in Atlanta tonight. . . . I told him I had to study, but the poor thing was so disappointed. . . .* "He sent flowers, invited them on dates to exotic places. But of course he was out of their reach. . . . It was a joke."

Miss Dimple stripped the shucks off the last ear of corn and added it to the growing pile. "Did she mention anyone else?"

Charlie shook her head. "Well . . . except for Clay, of course. It was Prentice's last year in high school and activities kept her constantly busy. As you know, the school chorus presented two concerts a year, and most Sundays she sang in the choir. Then cheerleading took a lot of time until football season was over, and in April, Prentice had a leading role in the class play."

I can't believe this is actually happening to me, she'd written Delia. *I never imagined how much I would love doing it!*

"What did she have to say about Clay?" Annie asked.

Charlie shrugged. "The usual, for the most part— where they went for hamburgers, a movie they'd seen together—and sometimes they double-dated." She paused. "It wasn't until the last letter that she mentioned Clay's objections to her going away to college, even though he knew she planned to stay in Elderberry and work for a year before leaving." *It's true, isn't it, that girls mature faster than boys? Clay Jarrett is a classic example!* Prentice had written.

"I guess he thought she might forget about it after a year," Annie said.

"If he could've read Prentice's letter, he wouldn't have been so surprised," Charlie told them. "'I can't help but be excited when I think of all that lies ahead of me,' she wrote. 'Remember that poem Aunt Bertie taught us? *I am the master of my fate. I am the captain of my soul.* . . . I never thought much about it before, but now I think I know what it means.'"

A robin in a nearby apple tree scolded a squirrel on the ground beneath. The blades of a push mower click-clacked in the backyard next door as eleven-year-old Willie Elrod reluctantly cut the grass, but for a few minutes none of the three women could bring themselves to speak.

"I can't help thinking of that scream you heard, Miss Dimple," Charlie said finally. "If only we had—"

"*If only's* will drag you down and bury you," Miss Dimple reminded her, "so put that in a box and lock it away. As it was, I honestly don't believe we could have reached her in time," she added softly.

"I wonder why Mrs. Brumlow didn't hear anything," Annie said. "The train had already passed at the time she was buying gas and having her windshield cleaned, but she said she didn't notice a thing out of the ordinary."

"Probably because she wasn't looking for it, and the sound came from another direction," Dimple explained. "I heard it because we were on that hill *on the other side* and behind the Shed. . . ." She paused. "And it might also be because I have *a few* years experience in being receptive to cries of distress."

Miss Dimple, realizing that all the grieving in the world would never bring back that wasted young life, gathered up her apron (purple, of course) and shook clinging corn silks onto a newspaper. "As you pointed out," she reminded Charlie, "Delia was away for over a year after she married Ned, and when she came home after he was shipped out, she had little time for anyone but the baby. Prentice must have had other close friends during that time."

Charlie nodded. "Delia said she was probably closest to Karen James. They were on the cheer-leading squad together. And Iris Ellerby was her best friend in the chorus. As far as I know, they stayed close after high school." She brightened. "You're right, of course, Miss Dimple. If Prentice was seeing somebody other than Clay, she might have mentioned it to one of them.

"I think Iris just finished her freshman year at Wesleyan," she continued, speaking of the girls college in nearby Macon, "and Karen took a secretarial course and went to work as a receptionist for my uncle Ed after Miss Mildred finally retired."

Everyone breathed a sigh of relief when Mildred Stovall "hung up her hat" at age eighty-one after years of faithful service to Ed Willingham, one of the town's two dentists. In the last few years, she had become so deaf that she mixed up names and dates for appointments, so patients only hoped they were showing up on the correct day and time, but genial Ed couldn't bring himself to let her go.

It was agreed that Delia should be the one to speak to Prentice's friends, as it would seem more natural, since she was nearer their age.

"I'll suggest it to her today," Charlie promised. "After all, I know she's as eager to clear this up as we are."

"And then what?" Annie frowned as she shoved the discarded corn shucks into a garbage can. Lately, it seemed, she became irritated and impatient at the least little thing. She knew her fiancé, Frazier Duncan, was somewhere in the thick of the fighting going on after the Normandy invasion in June, and it had been some time since she'd heard from him.

"I can't help thinking this all started when

Leola Parker died," Miss Dimple said. "Perhaps we should begin there."

"If you all want that corn for dinner, you'd better get it in here," a voice announced behind them. "Water's about come to a boil."

Phoebe Chadwick's longtime cook, Odessa Kirby, waved a wooden spoon at them from the kitchen doorway, from which came the aroma of green beans fresh from the victory garden, simmered long and slow with a chunk of streak o' lean. "Corn bread's hot, and Miss Velma's done got the table set in the dining room," she added.

Charlie's stomach rumbled. Although she didn't usually eat at Phoebe's during the summer months, today she had been invited to take Lily Moss's place, and had accepted gladly, hoping that lady would extend her visit in Atlanta. "Odessa," she began as they filed through the kitchen, "I know you and Leola were cousins, but did you know her very well?"

Odessa, busily scrubbing corn at the sink, answered over her shoulder. "Course I knowed her, but she lived way out at the end of nowhere and went to that Zion church over on Blossom Street, so we didn't see each other a whole lot." Odessa shook her head, and from the expression on her face, you could tell she didn't think much of her cousin's choice of churches.

Charlie smiled to herself. Odessa's idea of the "end of nowhere" was only a couple of miles from town and in easy biking distance from Bertie's neat brick bungalow, and through seventh grade, Prentice had been dropped off there afternoons after school until her aunt got home from work.

"Why, I was ten years old before I found out Leola wasn't my grandmama," Prentice had once confided to Delia. The afternoon Leola died, Prentice had bicycled the familiar route across fields and woods and through neighboring land the mile or so to Leola's to pick blackberries. Leola had promised to make them into a pie, and it was close to dusk when Prentice finally filled her pail from the bushes bordering the back pasture. Rounding the corner of the house, where she'd left her bike, Prentice found the old woman's body at the foot of the two cement steps leading to her small front porch.

"What a horrible thing for that poor girl to have to deal with!" Phoebe said when Charlie reminded them about it at dinner. Although they ate their main meal in the middle of the day, most people referred to it as "dinner."

Velma Anderson agreed. "It's tragic enough to come upon a stranger like that, but to find someone you love . . ." She shook her head. "I just can't imagine."

Miss Dimple helped herself to the homegrown tomatoes. "You taught Prentice, didn't you, Velma? Did you ever hear her speak of seeing someone other than Clay Jarrett?"

"I only had her for typing her junior year," Velma said, "and as far as I know, Clay was her one and only." Slowly, she stirred saccharin into her iced tea. Sugar had been rationed since the beginning of the war, and although most objected to the aftertaste of the substitute, they rarely complained. After all, what good would it do? "Prentice was a good student," she continued. "Well behaved, and so lovely. She had a leading role in her senior play, you know, and I believe she had some talent. Seth Reardon seemed to think so, too. I know he encouraged her."

"Ah," Miss Dimple said, and made a mental note to return to that subject later. However, first things first, she thought, and as soon as dinner was over and everyone was seated in Phoebe's comfortable parlor, where an electric fan whirred without much effect, she returned to the subject of Leola Parker's death.

"Do they know exactly how Leola died?" she asked Charlie.

"The coroner said her heart gave out when she apparently slipped and hit her head on the bottom step," Charlie said. "There was a gash on the back of her head."

She stood and went to the window, as if the sight of the pink climbing rose on the trellis by the porch would somehow lessen the grim reality of Leola Parker's death.

"Delia said Prentice told her Leola's hands

were still warm, but she couldn't find a pulse, and her frantic attempts to revive her failed. That was when she saw the smoke."

"What smoke?" Annie asked.

"It came from the underbrush on the other side of that little stream that crosses Leola's property," Charlie said, "and Prentice said it began as a wispy little curl and quickly spread into a billowing curtain of gray. She didn't want to leave Leola, but what else could she do? Prentice ran inside and called an ambulance and the fire department, but she said it seemed to take them forever to come. Meanwhile, she sat out there and held Leola's head in her lap while the fire spread along the dry grass until a section of the bank next to the road was smoking black."

Phoebe shook her head. "Poor child. She must've felt so alone. You know how far Leola's house is from the road, and her driveway is almost lost in all those trees. Imagine having to wait there like that without a soul to call on for help."

Restless, Charlie leaned on the back of the sofa. She simply couldn't sit and do nothing. It was too late to help Prentice, but it galled her to think the person responsible for her death was running around free. "Actually, the ambulance got there in less than ten minutes, but it must've seemed like hours to Prentice," she said.

"Leola probably saw or smelled the smoke and

went outside to see what was going on," Miss Dimple suggested.

"That's what Sheriff Holland thinks," Charlie said.

Velma nodded. "Some careless motorist must've thrown a cigarette into that dry grass, and that's all it took, but I doubt if Leola's place would've been in danger with that creek between her house and the road."

It was true, Charlie told them, that the fire had burned itself out by the time it reached the shallow brown water.

But that hadn't helped Leola Parker.

Dimple Kilpatrick experienced a brief surge of satisfaction as she walked past the Presbyterian church where Delia Varnadore played London Bridge with a number of five-year-olds in the grassy area in the building's shade. Good. That should keep her safe for a while. She knew Delia was determined to find out who was responsible for Prentice's death and had been questioning people on her own, but one young life lost was one too many. Prentice's friend Karen James, Delia had reported, was surprised to hear Prentice could have been seeing someone other than Clay and seemed to have no idea who it might have been. Iris was spending part of the summer as a camp counselor in North Carolina, and her parents were withholding the news of Prentice's tragic death until their daughter came home at the end of the session. "I wanted to write and tell her," Delia had explained. "Maybe she would know who Prentice might have been seeing, but her mother asked me to wait. She didn't want her to hear it like that."

"I doubt if she would have access to a radio or newspapers at the camp," Miss Dimple had said. "You can find out more when Iris gets home."

"Her aunt Bertie says she has no idea who Prentice was seeing," Delia added. "Frankly, I don't think she believes it."

"We'll just have to wait and see," Miss Dimple told her, hoping the girl would take her advice. For Delia to try and investigate further could be dangerous, and she trusted she would keep that in mind.

Since Prentice's death, some of the retired men in the community were taking time about helping Knox at the Peach Shed. Delia couldn't bear to even look at the place, and Charlie, who loved peaches almost better than chocolate, confessed that she hadn't been able to drive past since Prentice disappeared over a week before.

When she heard they were looking for helpers at Vacation Bible School at the Presbyterian church, Miss Dimple had offered Delia's name. Charlie and her mother said they would be glad to take care of little Tommy, and all agreed it would be good for Delia to keep her mind and body occupied with something positive. It would also, Dimple hoped, prevent Delia from asking questions of the wrong people, and give her the time she needed to look into things on her own.

Miss Dimple prided herself on being an unerring judge of character, and felt strongly that Clay Jarrett wasn't capable of murder. She had promised his parents she would help clear their son's name by finding the true killer, and now she would start at the beginning. With Leola Parker.

CHAPTER TEN

I'm so glad you dropped by," Chloe Jarrett said, pouring coffee for both of them. "Thank goodness the police decided to release Clay, but I feel like we're walking a tightrope, waiting to see if he'll be arrested."

Miss Dimple had telephoned before stopping by on her early-morning walk, hoping to speak with Clay before he and his father left to work in the orchards, but the two had already gone, and Chloe sounded so distraught, she found herself facing Clay's mother alone. And so they talked of Clay and Prentice and what had brought them to that sad summer morning.

"Clay told me Prentice was having a hard time dealing with Leola's death," Chloe told her. "She was with her when she died, or soon after—awful enough in itself—but Clay got the idea Prentice seemed afraid."

Miss Dimple nodded. Delia had noticed it, too. "Does he think it might have something to do with the way Leola died? That she might have seen or heard something?"

"I don't know. There was that fire right in front of her house. They think it started out near the roadside."

Miss Dimple wasn't so sure about that. "But it seems she would have said something, told someone," she said.

"Maybe she wasn't sure," Chloe said. "Clay thinks she was afraid to say anything about it."

But afraid of what?

Chloe rose and took a pan of cinnamon rolls from the stove. "I bake because I don't know what else to do, and it helps me to keep busy," she said, sliding the buns onto a plate. "Do have one while they're hot, and let me heat up your coffee," she offered, setting the platter on the scarred oak table. Miss Dimple rarely indulged in sweets, especially between meals, and she had eaten one of her wholesome Victory Muffins along the way, but the enticing aroma of yeast bread overcame her. "Perhaps just this once . . ." she said, helping herself.

"You know, I wouldn't put it past that Jasper Totherow to have set that fire," Chloe said, taking a seat across from Dimple. "He's been seen hanging around Leola's property in the past and he'll stick like a tick once he finds a place to burrow in."

If Jasper had ever had a regular job or a permanent place to live, Miss Dimple didn't know of it. He mowed lawns when the mood struck him, picked a little cotton in the fall, and sometimes helped Knox Jarrett harvest strawberries and then peaches, but dependability was not one of his attributes and he showed up only when it suited him.

"This summer, he ate more peaches than he picked," Chloe continued, "and Knox finally ran him off." She sighed. "We have about all we can put up with here with Hattie."

Miss Dimple relished the last bite of her cinnamon roll and washed it down with coffee. "I noticed her at the funeral the other day," she said.

Chloe nodded. "Not one to miss a funeral, our Hattie isn't, or much of anything else, but you can't believe a word she says. She and that Jasper—two of a kind when it comes to stretching the truth."

Miss Dimple frowned. "But why would Jasper want to hurt Leola? What would he gain?"

"Oh, I doubt if he meant to," Chloe said. "Jasper doesn't have the foresight to plan too far ahead, but he might've caused it. Sets those piddling little fires all the time. That's how he heats his beans, or whatever it is he eats.

"Wouldn't hurt to keep an eye on Jasper," she added, "and I've said as much to Sheriff Holland. He's the kind that bears watching."

"Tell me again why we're looking for Jasper Totherow," Virginia Balliew said as they bumped along the narrow, winding road to Leola Parker's place. "I'll have to admit, Dimple, that man makes me feel uncomfortable, especially after what happened to Leola, and now Prentice."

The town librarian, Virginia had reluctantly agreed to use her lunch hour to drive her friend on her quest to find the elusive Jasper. "I'm sure the police have checked out here already," she said, "and if you don't mind my asking, what do you intend to do if we find him?"

Dimple had to admit to herself she didn't know, but Jasper was the only link she had so far with the fire that took place the day Leola died.

Near the main road, weeds were already stretching across blackened splotches of burned earth, but the charred area widened closer to the shallow creek. The grass around Leola's house was higher than a cat's back in spite of the long dry spell, Dimple noticed. And why, she thought, would Jasper have built a cooking fire right in front of Leola's place, where she'd have been sure to see him?

Virginia parked the car under a drooping dogwood and the two picked their way across yellowed grass. Leola would be vexed for sure if she could see the encroaching weeds, the unswept porch.

Shades were drawn inside the silent house, and the only sound they heard was the humming of bees in Leola's weed-choked zinnia bed. Beside the porch, a pink climbing rose, sweet-smelling and dainty, made Dimple think of Prentice. If the police suspected the Rose Petal Killer, they hadn't released the information to the newspapers. Was Prentice's murder made to look like one of the serial killer's in order to mislead the investigation?

"It doesn't look like anyone's been here in a while," Virginia said, stepping cautiously over a fallen limb, "and people will wonder where I am if I don't get back by one o'clock."

If they were smart, Dimple thought, they would rest in the shade of the wide porch that stretched across the front of the quaint log cabin library. Built in the early part of the century with funds from the local Woman's Club, the rustic building was one of Dimple's favorite spots.

"Let me take a quick look in the back," she said, when from somewhere behind the house a metallic clatter like discordant wind chimes made them stop in mid-stride.

With Virginia clinging to her arm, Dimple turned, prepared to bolt for the car, when a large gray cat leapt from the corner of the house and darted into the bushes.

"Well, God bless America, if that cat didn't scare me all the way into next week!" Virginia said, finally relaxing her grip.

Dimple had experienced a moment or two of uneasiness as well but decided she should probably investigate the noise. If the stray cat had somehow managed to get through a back window, she would have to get in touch with Leola's daughter, Mary Joy, to see what damage had been done.

She found instead a rusting pile of empty food cans by the steps and was just in time to see the back door of Leola's house slowly closing.

"Who's in there?" She said it before she had time to think.

"Are you crazy. Dimple? This is none of our business," Virginia reminded her. "Let's get out of here!"

Dimple tended to agree with her friend, but it was too late now.

"It's only me, ma'am." Jasper Totherow, in filthy jeans and shoes that looked as if they'd been chewed by a lawn mower, stood in Leola's doorway.

"Jasper? What on earth are you doing here?" In spite of her revulsion, Dimple wanted to shake him.

And to add to her annoyance, he grinned. "Oh,

hit's all right. You don't have to worry none. Leola's youngun, she asked me to keep an eye on things, see if they's anything missin' and all."

If anything was missing, Dimple thought, it was Jasper's brain if he thought she'd buy that fable.

"I suggest you be out of here by the time the police come, because I intend to call them as soon as I get back to town." Dimple clenched her fist so hard, her fingernails cut into her palm.

Pulling on the straps of his sagging overalls, Jasper stepped into the yard. "Now look ahere, lady, I'm doing a favor is all. That old woman owes me after all the work I done for her." He kicked at Leola's back step with a grimy foot. "I ain't plannin' to hang around here, you can bet on that. Nooosirrree bobtail! Not after what I seen!"

"Exactly what is it you *saw?*" Ever the teacher, Dimple couldn't resist emphasizing the verb.

Of course it didn't do any good. "Seen somebody around here that oughtn't've been. Seen what they did."

"When?" Dimple asked. "You mean the day Leola died?"

"That's right." Jasper nodded, then, probably realizing he'd said too much, started to slink into the pine thicket behind the house.

"Wait!" Dimple called after him. "Who did you see? What was he doing?"

"Didn't say it was a *he,* now, did I?" And with that, Jasper disappeared into the trees.

"I'm glad that's over," Virginia said with a heavy sigh. "No telling what he's been doing in there. I'm afraid Mary Joy's going to have a mess on her hands."

The two quickly made their way to Virginia's car and down the narrow driveway to the road. Both were silent on the drive back to town. A herd of white-faced cattle grazed peacefully in the pasture down the road, and a little farther along, a man and woman, backs bent, made their way down the long rows of cotton, chopping the weeds away. Dimple, who, as a girl, had helped with that toilsome chore on her father's farm, remembered the welcome shade of the oak tree and bucket of icy well water that waited at the end of the row.

Small wooden signs placed at intervals along the route encouraged passersby in the war effort while advertising shaving cream for Burma Shave. They usually evoked a smile, as this most recent one did:

Let's make Hitler
And Hirohito
Feel as bad as
Old Benito!
Burma Shave

They drove past Bertie's small brick home, which sat back from the road in a grove of pecan trees, and Dimple was tempted to stop and see how Bertie was holding up, but she didn't like to drop in unannounced, and, too, Virginia was in a hurry to get back to the library. Delia had said Prentice's aunt had no idea who her niece might have been seeing, and surely the police had asked her that as well, but perhaps, after given time to think . . .

Miss Dimple knew she would *have* to speak with Elberta about this soon, and even though she had expressed her condolences earlier, every part of her agonized about facing such grief again. How can one comfort someone who has lost a child? *Is there anything I can do?* How useless! No one can bring back that precious life.

Dimple fanned herself with an outdated issue of the *Elderberry Eagle*. Because of heavy red dust from the unpaved road, Virginia insisted on keeping her car windows closed, and the interior felt like a hundred degrees.

Finally, relief at last! She rolled down her window as they turned onto the paved street and drove past the high school, which seemed bleak and forlorn behind a row of drooping crepe myrtles. As they entered town, a black-and-white-spotted terrier took its time crossing the street in front of them and two women chatted in the shade of the awning in front of Harris Cooper's grocery. Most people, it seemed, were wisely staying inside during the heat of the day.

Virginia darted a look at the empty streets and sighed. "Don't you miss them?" she asked.

"Miss who?"

"The men, Dimple, *the men*. Since the war, so many of them have gone. . . . It just isn't natural," Virginia insisted. "The town seems so empty without them. I don't like it. I don't like it at all!"

Dimple didn't like it, either, and she knew others who felt their absence even more. Annie Gardner had been so worried about her Frazier lately, she seemed to have lost her appetite, and Charlie, as well as young Delia, were aware of how permanent their loss might be whenever they saw the boy on the black bicycle who delivered telegrams no one wanted to receive.

Years before in an earlier war, young Dimple had experienced such a loss, and no words of comfort, no matter how well meant, had been able to mend her heart.

$\mathcal{C}$HAPTER $\mathcal{E}$LEVEN

A few minutes later at Sheriff Holland's office, Miss Dimple told him what Jasper had said.

"We'll send somebody out there to pick him up, Miss Dimple, but I wouldn't put too much faith in Jasper's tales. Why, I reckon he'd still believe in the tooth fairy if he had a tooth left to trade."

Miss Dimple smiled at the sheriff's jest, remembering his pranks during his early school years. When she'd taught him in the first grade, the child had been so slight, you could've slipped him into an envelope and mailed him first class, but it seemed he had more than made up for that in the years that followed, and he'd proved to be a competent and dependable law-enforcement officer. Dimple had learned by experience she could put her trust in Zeb Holland in a tense situation.

Still, she felt there was some truth in Jasper's claims and hoped they would be able to learn whom he'd seen the day Leola died before that person got wind of Jasper's bragging. "You might want to get in touch with Leola's daughter, Mary Joy. I believe she lives in Covington now," she suggested before leaving. "There's no telling what kind of disarray that Jasper's left behind."

It had been over a week since Prentice's death, and they seemed no closer to finding the person responsible. Dimple remembered Velma Anderson mentioning that the drama coach, Seth Reardon, had directed Prentice and others in the cast of their senior play, and although she doubted if Prentice would have mentioned anything as personal as a love interest to him, there was a chance he might have overheard bits of conversation among the cast. As she hurried back to Phoebe's, Dimple reminded herself to ask

Velma if she remembered who else had taught Prentice during her senior year. Perhaps one of them might have an idea who the girl had been seeing.

Hattie stepped cautiously into the trailer and looked about. Whoever had been here was gone now, but it was obvious they'd been looking for something. To most people, it would seem her place was in constant disarray, but she knew where everything was, and could put her hands on it if necessary. Today, things had been shoved aside, tossed about. The china mug with a bear on it she'd drunk from as a child now lay on its side on the shelf above the makeshift sink. The seashells Chloe Jarrett had brought her from a vacation in Florida were scattered all over the floor. Hattie chuckled to herself. She knew what they'd been looking for, but they would never find it in her special place.

But what was to keep them from coming back? She wouldn't be safe here anymore, at least not for a while, not while the Nazis knew where to find her, but where could she go?

Hattie thought of the old fishing shack down by the river. She could make do there as long as it was warm, and she could always turn in bottles left behind by fishermen to keep her in peanut butter and bread, and maybe a candy bar now and then, until she felt it was safe to come back.

It was almost dark when Hattie trundled her wheelbarrow, piled high with extra clothing, blankets, and the meager contents of her larder, along the edge of the pine thicket that bordered the road, then made her way across the railroad tracks to the bridge that spanned the Oconee River. Stepping carefully over ruts in the road, she turned off right before the bridge, bumping her burden along a narrow trail that followed the river. She heard the dark water rushing below, smelled the dank, muddy odor of its banks. Hattie paused as the moon went behind a cloud. The darkness made it hard to see, but she knew the shack was somewhere up ahead. Not many people used it now, probably didn't even know it was there—so much the better. It wasn't much, but she could make do for a while and no one would bother her here.

Tall grass brushed her ankles and briars clutched at her skirt as Hattie plodded along. She had brought along a flashlight, but the batteries were weak, striping the night with a dim yellow beam that seemed to make shadows loom even larger. But . . . yes . . . there it was just up ahead on that little knoll in the bend of the river.

Hattie froze at the sound of rustling grass behind her. *Someone was here. Someone was following her! Well, she would never tell those Yankees her secret—never! Or maybe it was a Nazi come to carry her away like they did that pretty young girl. Her world wasn't safe anymore. She couldn't trust anybody now. Hattie waited, afraid to go forward, but she would never make it back to the road. What happened to the people who'd loved her, cared for her? What happened to the time when she wasn't afraid?*

After forcing down a piece of dry toast with her morning coffee, Bertie took one look at her silent, empty house and stepped outside. Everything around her reminded her of Prentice: the water pitcher with multicolored stripes her niece had given her last Christmas; the framed crayon drawing of a horse with an unusually large head that Prentice colored when she was six; and, on the back porch, the once brown-and-white oxfords, now caked with dried mud from a not-too-recent rain. How could she bear living here without her? She had to get out of this house!

And where else could she go but to her familiar classroom? Bertie parked in the back of the high school so no one would see her car and let herself inside with her own key. She was one of the few allowed that privilege. The classroom was stuffy and hot, and Bertie turned on the electric fan on her desk and opened some of the windows. The back of the building, where she taught, had no shade except for a small magnolia, presented by Prentice's class, that stood by the back door next to a plaque marking the year of its planting.

Elberta pulled down a window shade to block the view. There seemed to be no escape. By the time she retired, the tree would be taller than the building, and she would pack up her belongings, move out of her sunny, multiwindowed classroom, and go home. But home to what?

She had thought that when the time came for her to leave Elderberry High School forever, Prentice would be out of college and either married or settled in a career of her own. Bertie had hoped for both. She had wanted for Prentice more than she had for herself. Much more. Elberta Stackhouse didn't believe in Prince Charming—hadn't for a long time—but for her niece she'd wished the joy and security of having someone to laugh with, love with. Someone to share her days, her nights, and the years that would come later, when she qualified for the senior discount at Lewellyn's Drug Store.

And what did she have now? *Nothing,* that was what.

A shell of a person walking around with so much sadness festering inside, Bertie felt it might begin to ooze from her pores. And her friends? God help them, they smothered her with kindness; she saw her grief mirrored in their eyes, and longed to run away and hide until she—and they—didn't hurt so much anymore.

Bertie opened her desk drawer and pulled out the roster of upcoming juniors she could expect when school began in a little over a month. This year, she would start with *A Tale of Two Cities* instead of postponing it until after the Christmas holiday—hit the ground running, she thought, with no pause to catch her breath. Or to think. And from now on, she wouldn't require her classes to memorize "Thanatopsis"—such a long, dreary poem, all about death. Most of the students dreaded it anyway, but Bertie had always thought memory work good for the brain, and maybe it was, but this year she would have her classes concentrate on something else. Some of Shakespeare's sonnets perhaps. Something light with a nice rhythm to it.

And for the first time since Prentice died, Bertie almost smiled. That was before she remembered she had agreed to let Adam drop by tonight for cake and coffee. He had been the very soul of patience to listen when she wanted to talk and allowed her time to be alone. Adam Treadway comforted her with his silence as only he knew how, but she knew he was suffering because she was, so when he'd phoned earlier and asked to see her, Bertie had reluctantly agreed. Thoughtful friends and neighbors had supplied her with so much food, she'd finally asked them to stop, and she would have no shortage of sweets to offer him when he came. Louise Willingham had brought over one of her sought-after almond pound cakes the day before, and Bertie had only nibbled at a slice, although she found it delicious as usual.

For the last two of the three years they had been seeing each other, Adam had tried his best to entice her to Clifford, a small town several miles away, where he owned and operated a small bookstore. Widowed for almost a decade, Adam had raised his two sons, now grown, and didn't bother to hide the fact that he had marriage on his mind. Recently, Adam had heard rumors, he told her, that the head of the high school English Department there would soon be retiring and the school board was already looking for a replacement.

It had been only a few days before Prentice died and the two were sipping lemonade on her front porch. "With your experience and credentials, I know you'd have a good chance at the job," he'd assured her. Adam raised his glass to hers. "Why not give it a try?"

Bertie looked down at her glass and took a swallow, touching his fingers as if in apology. "Let's just wait and see," she said.

"Wait until when, Elberta?"

"I don't know." She couldn't bring herself to look into his eyes. Gray like April skies, campfire smoke, kitten fur. Cozy things. Happy things. Her willpower would wilt like a violet, wouldn't stand a chance. Still handsome at forty-seven, Adam appealed to her more than any man she'd known since Knox Jarrett, although there hadn't been many. But did she love him enough for marriage? Bertie wasn't sure.

And the thought of leaving Elderberry . . . well, frankly, it scared her a little. After all, this was Prentice's home, too. She had to think of Prentice, didn't she?

Harris Cooper's grocery wasn't crowded this late in the afternoon when Bertie started for home. It would be refreshing, she decided, to have ice cream on hand to go with Lou's pound cake, so she parked out front and dashed in for a pint of vanilla. It was hard to ignore the fact that Jesse Dean Greeson, who clerked there, went quickly to the back of the store when he saw her come in, and returned weepy-eyed to wait on her. Prentice had been fond of Jesse Dean, since, knowing how much she liked them, he always put chocolate BB Bats—penny taffy on a stick—in their grocery order.

Today, both of them managed to maintain composure under circumstances that wrung out their emotions and hung them up to dry.

Declining Jesse Dean's offer to carry her one small purchase to the car, Elberta tossed her carton of bagged groceries on the seat beside her and backed into the street. She was almost at the end of the block when she saw Hattie McGee, still wearing her black veil of mourning, pushing her wheelbarrow at a plodding pace on the other side of the street.

The voluminous skirts must weigh a ton, and Hattie was still blocks from home. If she had to, Bertie supposed, she could wedge the wheelbarrow in her trunk. Slowing, she waved and blew her horn, but Hattie didn't respond.

Must not be in a sociable mood. Well, that made two of them. Bertie turned toward home for a cold glass of tea and a long soak in the tub. She couldn't pretend she wasn't relieved.

The Elderberry Woman's Club, minus Geneva Odom, who was shopping in Atlanta with her college-bound daughter, and Mabel Rankin, who wasn't speaking to the hostess, met that week on Tuesday afternoon at the home of their president, Emmaline Brumlow. It wasn't their usual meeting day, but Emmaline had wanted to host the meeting, and this was the only day she could do it. "It's only a few days' difference," Emmaline said. "I can't imagine why it wouldn't suit."

It didn't suit Hardin Kirkland, but she was too meek to speak out, as were most of the members. The Elderberry Woman's Club was not a democracy, and Emmaline, as president, was supreme dictator. Her mother had been a Hughes, and her grandmother, Winifred Hughes, had been one of the original members of the club. Hardin knew this because she had been told, first by her

136

mother and then by her husband, and she was also aware that the marker on the courthouse lawn in honor of the Confederate dead had been donated by one of Emmaline's illustrious Hughes ancestors.

Now Hardin sat in the Windsor chair by the mahogany drop-leaf table that had belonged to Emmaline's grandmother and balanced a Limoges plate on her lap. She knew they were all dying to question her about the day Prentice Blair disappeared, but it wouldn't be proper to ask outright. They would have to find a way to lead up to it.

And they did. "I know you must be glad to have your Chenault closer to home," Lou Willingham said as she passed the napkins. "It's refreshing to see young faces about."

"I wish my two lived closer," Ida Ellerby said. "With gasoline being rationed, we rarely get to see our grandchildren."

Back from her recent visit to Atlanta, Lily Moss reminded her, "But you *are* able to see them. Just think of poor Elberta Stackhouse." She lowered her voice, "I hear Doc Morrison had to keep her under sedation."

"She wasn't sedated when I saw her going into Cooper's grocery yesterday," Lou spoke out. "I think she's holding up very well under the circumstances."

"I wouldn't be surprised if they arrested that

Jarrett boy," Bessie Jenkins said with a sidelong glance at Hardin. "Maybe you've heard something, Hardin. After all, weren't you there when they found that poor girl missing?"

Miss Dimple set down her cup with a rattle. She detested going to meetings—especially this one—and was in attendance only at the insistence of her friend Virginia, whose small librarian's salary was paid by the club. "Naturally, they questioned him, Bessie, but it doesn't mean they'll arrest him. I taught Clay Jarrett, and I think I know him as well as anyone. He's simply not capable of doing a thing like that."

"That's what they always say, though, isn't it?" Bessie leaned forward in her chair. "Those people they interview in the newspapers, the ones who live next door to murderers. *Why, I've known little Johnny since he was in diapers and he'd never hurt a soul* . . . and all the while there are six bodies buried in the basement and a bloody hatchet in the attic."

"For heaven's sake, Bessie, we're trying to eat!" Lou said.

Hardin wished they would get on with the meeting so she could leave. She had better things to do than sit here and pretend to enjoy this so-so Scotch shortbread, which wasn't nearly as good as her mama used to make. And her mother would never have served frozen fruit salad without her creamy lemon dressing. It just wasn't the same, but try as she would, Emmaline had never learned to make it. Hardin smoothed the worn linen napkin, which, no doubt, had also belonged to Emmaline's grandmother and probably hadn't been bleached in as many years, and ventured another nibble.

Ida drank the last of her mint punch. "The police aren't saying a word about how Prentice was killed."

"Maybe they don't know," Hardin said.

"Of course they know, but they're not telling. It's none of our business anyway, if you ask me," Lou's sister Jo announced.

Hardin thought Jo was certainly one to talk, since she and Lou were forever making like detectives. She wouldn't be surprised if the two weren't already cooking up some half-baked plan to find out who had killed Prentice Blair.

"Do you suppose it could be the Rose Petal Killer?" Emma Elrod asked. "I heard they were scattered all over her body."

"They aren't saying much about that, are they? I hope it's not anybody from around here." Lily Moss shivered and looked about, as if the murderer might be lurking behind Emmaline's Victorian sofa.

"Atlanta's over an hour away. Why would he come all the way over here?" Emmaline informed her. "Would anyone like more punch?"

Hardin dabbed her mouth with a napkin, and even from where she sat, Miss Dimple could see that she'd gotten lipstick on it. "Maybe he ran out of victims," Hardin said.

Naturally, nobody laughed but Hardin, who covered her blunder with a thin, nervous giggle. Dimple had always suspected the woman had a coarse streak, but surely she wasn't thinking clearly to have uttered such a callous statement even in jest.

Lily passed pastel mints in a silver dish. "I just hope the poor girl wasn't . . . well . . . *defiled*." She whispered the last word, and her hand trembled, so Jo Carr took the candy dish from her.

"Now, Emmaline, you just sit right there and have another cup of punch," Virginia said finally, noticing the time. "We'll take our own plates to the kitchen, and I don't want to hear another word about it."

Miss Dimple smiled to herself, knowing it was probably the only chance her friend would have to boss around Emmaline Brumlow.

Hardin looked at her watch as she left the others standing on the steps, chatting. Maybe they didn't have demands on their time, but she did. The big Labor Day picnic Griffin insisted on having every year loomed alarmingly close, and guess who was in charge of the planning? Of course, hosting the annual barbecue was so familiar to her now, Hardin thought she could probably do it without thinking. But what if something went wrong? What if she forgot something important?

Tonight was their cook's day off and Griffin would expect his supper on time, as usual. She had enough ration coupons for a couple of pork chops if Harris Cooper had any. She would serve them with those tiny parsley potatoes he liked and maybe lemon-glazed carrots.

Hardin glanced over her shoulder. Virginia Balliew lingered on the walkway, smiling at something Lou Willingham was saying. Jo's arm encircled Miss Dimple's shoulders. Bessie Jenkins called out as she made her way down the steps, and everybody laughed. What did they all have to talk about?

Hardin would have given up her membership years ago if Griffin hadn't protested. "You can't buy roots," he'd said. Well, maybe not, but you could damn well buy everything else. And Griffin Kirkland knew it.

Cooper's Store was crowded, but not enough for Hardin to avoid Alma Owens, who cornered her in the produce section, her broken arm still in a sling.

"You bad thing! You promised you'd give me Griffin's recipe for chicken bog. I want to try my hand at it when my niece comes for a visit this summer, if Doc Morrison will ever let me out of this clumsy cast."

The closest Griffin Kirkland came to making

chicken bog was to tell somebody else to do it, and Alma, having known him all his life, probably knew that. "It's in the church cookbook, Alma, but I'll make a copy if you like."

Hardin watched as Jesse Dean weighed a pound and a half of the small new potatoes and put them in a bag. She knew what was coming next.

"Oh, that would be grand. Don't know whatever happened to the copy I had. I'd spare you the trouble if it weren't for this silly old arm, and my knee's been acting up, too. Can't get around like I used to." Alma bent to rub the offending joint. "Just got out of the hospital last week and I've been to three different doctors this summer, and would you believe not a one of them has done me a bit of good?"

Hardin had seen the expression on the woman's face in paintings of the Inquisition. She looked about desperately, but the other shoppers, while nodding politely, ignored them. She was forced to hear about two major surgeries and a bladder infection before she finally wormed her way past the butcher shop in the rear, around a display of canned Spam, and achieved sweet freedom.

It was not until she reached the front of the store to pay for her purchases that Hardin discovered her money was missing.

CHAPTER TWELVE

"Prentice had so many friends, Miss Dimple, I couldn't keep up with them all." Bertie Stackhouse sat at her kitchen table, wearing, under a light seersucker robe, the pajamas she had worn all day. At ten in the morning, this might not be all that unusual for some, but Dimple knew Bertie was not one of those people.

She and Charlie had taken advantage of a gift of bread and butter pickles from Charlie's mother as an excuse to visit, and although they had phoned ahead, Bertie hadn't taken the time to change. The pickles had turned out surprisingly well, Charlie thought, as Jo Carr wasn't known for her culinary efforts. This year, however, their victory garden had yielded an excess of cucumbers and the government continually urged everyone to "use it up, wear it out, make it do, or do without."

Prentice's aunt had made some attempt to comb her hair, Dimple noticed, but she wore no makeup, and her usually pleasant round face might have been sculpted in sand. At any moment, she felt, it might begin to crumble.

Charlie looked at Miss Dimple and Miss Dimple looked at Charlie. One of them *had* to broach the subject.

Charlie took a deep breath. "There might have been someone a little closer than merely a friend."

Bertie shoved aside what was left of her coffee. "So Delia tells me, but the only one Prentice ever cared about was Clay Jarrett. There wasn't anyone else."

Charlie shook her head. "I think Prentice might have broken up with Clay because she was interested in someone else. Do you remember her saying anything about it?"

"We were hoping you might have an idea who it might be," Miss Dimple said.

"I don't remember anybody in particular. It's always been Clay." Bertie lowered her voice. "Dimple, can you believe that boy would do such a thing? Why, many's the time he sat right here at this very table, and now they think maybe he . . . Oh, dear God, I hope it's not true!"

Looking up, she squeezed Charlie's hand and slid a platter of muffins in front of her. "Please eat some of these. Marjorie Mote brought them over last night—apple spice, she said—and I'm sure they're very good, but I just don't have any appetite."

Charlie obediently accepted a muffin, although she wasn't hungry, either, and passed the plate to Miss Dimple, who politely declined.

"Now, Prentice always had a sweet tooth," Bertie went on. She searched for a handkerchief in the pocket of her robe and held it to her eyes like a compress. "I believe that child could have eaten ice cream every day of the week if she could have gotten it."

Miss Dimple hesitated before asking. *It had to be done.* "Do you think Prentice would've told you if she was seeing someone other than Clay?"

Bertie examined her fingers as if to make sure she had the correct number. "I wish I could tell you she would, but I really don't know," she said finally. "Have you spoken with any of her friends?"

Charlie told her the names of the people she and Delia had contacted. "We still haven't heard from Iris, though. I understand she's working at a camp in North Carolina this summer."

Bertie shook her head. "I would think one of them might know if anybody would, but I can't imagine who it could be." Her expression froze as she realized why they were asking, and Bertie slammed both hands on the table, rattling the dishes scattered about. "Is that why . . . Do you think this person had something to do with what happened to Prentice?"

Dimple reached across the table and placed a hand on Bertie's arm. "We're trying to cover all the bases, Elberta. If it wasn't Clay—and I don't believe it was—then who was it? Clay said Prentice had told him she was seeing someone else. Right now, that's all we have to go on."

"But it would make sense for him to say that, wouldn't it? I'll admit that up until now I've been fond of Clay Jarrett, but a person suspected of murder will say just about anything to throw investigators off track."

Dimple sighed. She had to agree that was true.

Velma Anderson, when questioned, had named the teachers who would have had Prentice in their classes. The faculty was small, as was the student body, so with a few exceptions, most of them taught everyone at one time or another. She did say that Prentice seemed to enjoy chorus and drama. Estelle Carnes, who had directed the high school chorus during Prentice's senior year, had since moved with her family to somewhere in Tennessee. A plump jolly woman, she seemed to have a talent for making singing fun without being able to carry a tune herself, and Dimple doubted if she was even aware of the tragedy that had occurred.

"I know Prentice loved being onstage and especially enjoyed being a part of the senior class production," Dimple continued. "Do you know if she was close to anyone in the cast? Perhaps she confided in one of them."

"I suppose she was closest to Iris. She had a leading role as well and the two often went to rehearsals together." Bertie clasped her hands together. "Oh, Dimple! Do you suppose Iris hasn't heard? She's been away at camp for most of the summer and might not even know what happened to Prentice."

"I think her parents want to wait and tell her when she gets home," Dimple said.

"I'm thankful Leola isn't here to know," Bertie said later as she accompanied them to the door. "I suppose it's a good thing she went first, but Prentice wasn't the same after that, you know. It hurt her so, seeing Leola like that. . . . She simply couldn't get past it."

Jasper Totherow counted the money again. Fifty-seven dollars, plus another three dollars and thirty-five cents in change. Why would anybody need all that just to go to the grocery store? Why, he could live off that for months! Still, it wasn't as much as he'd hoped for, but it would have to do. Elderberry, he felt, was not a healthy place for him right now and he knew better than to hang around.

The mosquitoes weren't so bad at the top of the hill, away from the creek, and Jasper rested there under a big blackjack oak and listened to the far-off rumble of thunder. At least he thought it was thunder; couldn't be sure, with his hearing as bad as it was, but the skies were boiling gray, like dirty dishwater. Storm couldn't be far away, and what if he got caught in it? That policeman had locked up Leola's place tighter than a banker's fist, and he didn't know who might be waiting for him back at his shed.

He knew he shouldn't have said what he did to those women—the ones who came poking about Leola's—about seeing somebody there the day Leola died. He knew better than to tell what it was he saw, and if that Miss Pimple . . . Temple . . . whatever her name was, were to blab that to the wrong person, he might as well say his prayers. *Now* where was he to go?

In most of the movies he'd seen, the one who was in danger waited until dark to leave town, but Jasper didn't want to wait. Some innate sense of survival warned him to get out now and he wasn't going to argue, but his granddaddy's watch was back at that old shed, along with a photograph of his mama, an extra pair of shoes, and every stitch of clothing he owned. He had rolled them up in his jacket and hidden the bundle in the rafters of the shed when they'd thrown him out of that shack he'd rented back in the spring. He'd have to watch the place for a while to be sure nobody was around. With a storm coming on, they wouldn't hang around long.

Getting to his feet, Jasper took the money from the purse and jammed it deep into his pants pocket. Funny she should be the one he'd stolen it from. Made it easy, really, standing there talking to that mouthy woman, pocketbook gaping open like that. Well, there was more where that came from. Jasper remembered when her mama had taken in sewing, baked cakes to make ends meet. He tossed the change purse aside as he made his way to the other side of the hill.

Damned if every step he took didn't sound like a stampede in all this dry grass. Even *he* could hear it, and him half-deaf. Jasper squatted behind a sumac and watched the shed. Nothing moved, only the clouds rolling in dirt up there, getting blacker, meaner. He stuck a twig in his mouth and settled down to wait. There were worse things than getting wet.

Jasper didn't know who owned the shed. Empty now, it had once been used for storing fodder. About halfway between Leola's property and an old tumbledown church, it had come in handy when he needed a place to sleep. He'd hoped for better before winter came, but had a plaguing deep-down feeling the person he saw at Leola's that day had seen *him,* so he reckoned it would have to be somewhere as far from Elderberry, Georgia, as he could get.

Atlanta came to mind. Jasper had never seen Atlanta; heard about it, though. A person could get lost there. If he was lucky, he might be able to catch a ride, be in Atlanta before dark.

Now pine trees bowed in the wind in the open field before him. The old gray shed crouched under a sweet-gum tree, its sagging door banging against the wall. Jasper strained to listen, but all he could hear was the slapping of limbs above his head, the measured whack of the shed door.

He cringed as lightning cracked across the sky, then stood slowly, eyes on the shed. If he got his belongings out now, he could get a head start. Spend the night on the road if he had to, but Lord, he hoped he wouldn't have to. Jasper paused to listen at the door of the shed, then braced himself before stepping inside. He wondered how long his money would last in Atlanta.

And that was the last thing he wondered.

"Help me, Miss Dimple! Save me!"

Miss Dimple clutched to her chest a small package containing a pad of notepaper and a bottle of Scripto ink she had purchased in town and held out an arm to ward off the oncoming collision with Willie Elrod, racing toward her at full speed. At eleven, Willie had grown almost as tall as she, and Dimple didn't care to end up sprawling on the sidewalk in front of God and everybody.

The boy took one look at her face and stopped short, barely in time. With breathless gasps, he darted behind her.

"For heaven's sake, William Elrod, what on earth has gotten into you? You almost made me fall, and if it's all the same to you, I'd rather remain vertical."

"I'm sorry, Miss Dimple, but you've got to protect me, please! She's after me, and I'm much too young to die."

"Who's after you? Now, stop that this minute." Miss Dimple grabbed a skinny shoulder and held him at arm's length.

"It's Marguerite! Mama makes me take her everywhere, and she's ruining what's left of my summer. I wish she'd hurry and go home."

Dimple knew Willie's cousin Marguerite was visiting next door for a few weeks with her mother, and since the two were close in age, Willie was expected to entertain her. "Why don't you take her to the picture show?" she asked. "Abbott and Costello are playing at the Jewel."

"We saw that yesterday." Willie made a face. "And I had to sit with her, too."

Dimple was about to tell him that most girls liked to play Tarzan and roller-skate and build forts in the woods just as boys did, but she was interrupted by a bloodcurdling screech as the dreaded Marguerite raced up with danger in her eyes and murder in her heart. "Prepare to die!" she announced, reaching for Willie.

"Just a minute!" Miss Dimple eyed them both with her most severe "I mean business" expression. "Now, young lady, what's this all about?" Of course she knew before the girl even answered that whatever it was must be Willie's fault, but one had to try to be fair.

Marguerite recognized a voice of authority and stepped back an inch or two. "He keeps singing that awful song," she said. "He sings it all the time—especially when we're around any of his friends." She stuck out her tongue at Willie. "If he *has* any friends!"

"And what song is that?" Miss Dimple asked, but Willie found something of keen interest to look at in the window of Total Perfection and didn't answer.

Marguerite gave him a quick jab with her sandaled foot, as if to say, *Tell her, Willie!*

The boy sighed. "Oh, Marguerite, go wash your feet! I smell them clean across the street!" he chanted, and then had the nerve to burst into giggles.

"When you get home, William, I think it would be a good idea to ask your mother to please invite some of the girls in your class over to visit with Marguerite. But right now, I believe I'll treat myself to an ice-cream cone at the drugstore. Would the two of you like to join me?"

They would, of course, and that was when she heard about Jasper Totherow.

"I imagine Ruthie Phillips or Lee Anne Stephens would be happy to have someone new to play with," Miss Dimple suggested as the three sat with chocolate cones at a small table in Lewellyn's. She was certain the beleaguered Marguerite would welcome female company after her cousin's constant badgering.

"Aw, you can't believe a thing neither one of those girls says," Willie said, licking a chocolate trail from his wrist. "That crazy Ruthie told me she and Lee Anne found a dead man in this old shed the other day, and Lee Anne—she was so scared, she almost wet her pa—"

Miss Dimple cleared her throat. "And where was this shed?"

He shrugged. "Out in the country somewhere. She said they were riding their bikes when it started to storm and they ran in this shed to get out of the rain. Lee Anne—she swears she almost stepped on him."

"Stepped on who, Willie? Did the girls know who it was?"

"Ruthie thinks it was that old man who looks like a scarecrow and never takes a bath—Jasper somebody—but you know what, Miss Dimple? I think they made it all up, 'cause when the police-man came, there wasn't nobody there."

CHAPTER THIRTEEN

H ow do they know it was Jasper?" Virginia asked.

"I spoke with Ruthie's mother soon after I got home," Miss Dimple said, "and it seems the police found some of his clothing in the rafters. It looks as if he'd been sleeping there."

Virginia was taking advantage of an afternoon lull at the library to visit with her friend, and the two sat in rocking chairs on the rustic porch, shaded by wisteria vines and screened from passing traffic.

"This isn't the first time Jasper's passed out somewhere," Virginia said. "He gets ahold of some liquor and doesn't know when to stop. It's a wonder it hasn't killed him."

"Maybe it has," Dimple said. "Seems something did. Or somebody."

"Then where's the body? Dead people don't just get up and wander away. Maybe he stumbled and hit his head. He might've been unconscious when those girls found him."

Miss Dimple rocked faster, her feet tapping with the rhythm of the chair. "Or . . . whoever killed him was interrupted before he could get rid of the body. He might have been hiding somewhere close by when Ruthie and Lee Anne came along."

"Why, Dimple Kilpatrick, that's a comforting thought! I do believe you're getting to be down-right gruesome!" Virginia gasped in mock horror. "I'll admit I'm not fond of Jasper, having run him off from sleeping on this very porch whenever he gets a chance, but what makes you think somebody would want to kill him?"

Dimple stopped rocking abruptly. "I can't be sure, but I think it has something to do with what happened the day Leola died. Remember, Virginia, what Jasper said the other day when we found him at Leola's?"

"And what was that? My goodness, he carries on so, I didn't pay much attention to him."

"He said *he knows who killed Leola!* He as good as admitted he saw what happened out there that day," Dimple reminded her.

"And you believe he was telling the truth?" Virginia shooed away a fly with a cardboard fan with *The Last Supper* on the front and an advertisement for Riley's Funeral Home on the back.

"I can't be sure, of course, but there was something going on, and I think Prentice might've seen it, too."

"Good heavens, Dimple! What makes you think that?"

Dimple reminded her about the fire. "Delia had a feeling Prentice was holding something back,

155

that she was afraid of something, and Clay told me the same thing. He said at first he thought it was because Leola died—the *way* she died. Prentice seemed to get upset when anyone mentioned it. She didn't want to talk about it."

Virginia rose to help little Peggy Ashcroft, who had arrived for a new supply of Bobbsey Twins books. "Have you spoken to Bertie about this?" she whispered.

Dimple shook her head. "Not in so many words, but Elberta told me Prentice just couldn't come to terms with Leola's death. I think there might be more to it than that."

"Then I think you should go to the police," Virginia said. "When she was here earlier, Emmaline Brumlow told me she'd heard they'd arrested somebody for those murders in Atlanta— the Rose Petal Killer, they call him. He might've had something to do with what happened to Jasper, and possibly Prentice, as well."

The courthouse clock whirred as it always did before striking the hour, but at five o'clock sidewalks still sizzled on the sunny side of the street, and the faded purple umbrella Miss Dimple carried to ward off the sun was of little help in the heat. Even the soldier on the recruiting poster in front of the post office looked miserable in his heavy uniform as she passed by on her way to the police station.

Bobby Tinsley had stepped out, she was told, but Officer Warren Nelson welcomed her into a small cubicle of an office where an electric fan stirred hot air, ruffling papers on his desk.

Miss Dimple had not taught Warren, as his family hadn't moved to Elderberry until he was in the third grade, but his younger sister Eugenia had been in her class, so she spent the first few minutes of her visit catching up on Eugenia's experiences as an army nurse in Liverpool, England, where they struggled with blackouts, air raids, and the constantly cold, rainy weather. Miss Dimple thought fondly of the shy little girl who tucked a tongue in her cheek as she labored over her letters and wished she could send a hug along with a warm blanket.

"I wondered if you'd had any word on what happened to Jasper Totherow?" she asked finally.

Because that area came under county jurisdiction, Sheriff Holland's department had been called to the scene of the shed where the two frightened girls had stumbled upon Jasper, Warren told her, but he understood they undertook a thorough search of the area.

"No telling where that fellow's gotten to," he added, shaking his head. "Probably sleeping it off somewhere. I reckon he'll turn up sooner or later."

Miss Dimple pulled her chair closer and leaned forward. "I believe there might be more to it than that," she said, and told him what Jasper had claimed to see.

Officer Nelson listened intently, nodding his head from time to time. He knew from experience that it was not customary for Miss Dimple Kilpatrick to jump to conclusions.

"If he saw whoever set that fire, he should've reported it then and there," he told her. "Do you know if anyone else was aware of this?"

"It seems Prentice Blair might have noticed it, as well. Several people have commented that she seemed to be worried about something— something she was reluctant to talk about."

"And you think this might have had something to do with her death?" Warren Nelson gripped the sides of his desk until his knuckles were white and his face crimson.

Miss Dimple gathered her purse and umbrella and prepared to leave. "I think it's something you certainly need to investigate . . . and I hope you won't waste any time."

She hesitated at the door. "I heard they arrested someone for the rose petal murders. Could there be a connection there?" Her question sounded like an afterthought, although, of course, it wasn't.

The officer stood politely. "They got a confession from him this morning. Wish we *could* tie this thing up, but this man had nothing to do with killing Prentice Blair."

"Are you sure? How do you know?"

Warren Nelson glanced at the closed door behind her and lowered his voice. "This guy was in jail over in Gainesville at the time that young woman was killed. Police caught him trying to break into somebody's house. Actually, that's how they finally got him. Man has a record for assaults against women. Been in trouble before."

"But the rose petals . . ." Miss Dimple began.

Warren sat on the desk and crossed his arms. "I'm going to let you in on something before the newspapers get ahold of it, so please keep this confidential. We've known it all along, but now that this guy's confessed, it will all come out in the open. . . ." Officer Nelson paused, his expression grave. "The Atlanta Rose Petal Killer used only white petals. Whoever killed Prentice Blair covered her in petals of every color."

When she reached home, Dimple found Annie in the kitchen, helping Phoebe put together a fruit salad for supper, Odessa having gone home for the day.

"We're having cold fried chicken and potato salad left over from dinner, and I thought some fruit would go well with that," Phoebe said, mixing a marinade of lime juice, mint, and honey. "It's just too hot to cook." She paused, acknowledging Dimple. "Don't suppose you've heard any more about what happened to that Jasper fellow.

159

Doesn't make sense, him disappearing like that."

"Well, they're going to take a closer look around that old shed where the little girls found him," Dimple told them, "but we might never know what happened to that poor soul."

Miss Dimple told them about her visit with Warren Nelson, except for the information about the rose petals. She wanted to ask Annie if she had heard from Frazier, but from the young woman's downcast expression, she already knew the answer.

Phoebe added strawberries to her bowl, along with the contents of a small can of diced pineapple and a pinch of powdered ginger. "There's no way around it," she said, frowning. "It's not the same without peaches."

Suddenly, Annie found the two of them looking at her. "Well, I guess I'll have to go back there sometime," she said with a shrug. "Might as well get it over with."

Miss Dimple wasn't looking forward to a trip to the Peach Shed again, either, but she volunteered to go along. After all, she thought, Annie needed a bit of distraction, and how long did it take to buy a basket of peaches?

Phoebe looked up with worried eyes. "Are you sure?"

Dimple had learned that as a rule it was best to face unpleasant memories and do her best to deal with them. "Perhaps it will give me a chance to speak with Clay," she said. It had been a while since she'd seen him and she wanted to discuss with him what Jasper had said.

But Clay wasn't minding the Shed.

Asa Weatherby, who was helping out that day, told them Clay had gone across the road to Grady's for a cold drink. "Be right back if you want to wait," he said, filling a bag with the heady-smelling fruit, but Miss Dimple knew Phoebe was waiting for the peaches, so they hurried over to Grady's on the chance they might have a quick word with Clay.

They found him in conversation with Grady Clinkscales at the cash register, but neither noticed them enter. "Don't reckon you've seen Hattie lately?" Grady asked as he scooped up the dime for Clay's RC Cola and ice-cream cup and tossed it into the cash drawer.

"Yeah, she was picking up bottles over near the high school. Had that old wheelbarrow," Clay said.

"Well, she didn't turn 'em in to me. When was this?" Grady slammed the drawer shut with a beefy hand and leaned on the counter.

"Hasn't been too long—a few days maybe. Why?" Clay dipped up a bite of ice cream with a tiny wooden spoon, savoring the sweet vanilla rush.

"I don't know, but I've got a feeling something ain't right."

"What do you mean?" Clay wondered when *anything had* been right lately.

"Hell, Clay, you know how Hattie comes in here every so often—couple of times a week at least. . . . Oh, sorry, Miss Dimple. Didn't see you ladies come in."

"I heard you speaking of Hattie," Miss Dimple said. "I hope she's not sick."

"Wouldn't be surprised, hot as it's been," Grady said. "She never asks for anything, you know, just wants to cool off some, she says, but I usually treat her to a cold drink or some of them cookies she likes." He ran a hand over thinning red hair. "Hasn't been in here in about a week now."

Clay frowned. "You think something's happened to her?"

"Maybe. That old woman is scared, and who can blame her?" Grady nodded toward the Peach Shed through fly-specked windows, where a display of canned tomatoes gathered dust.

Across the road, car doors slammed as two women got out of a gray Plymouth red with dust. Probably from the next county, Clay thought; he didn't know them. He tossed his empty ice-cream cup into a trash can as he watched them buy peaches from Asa. They ought to put up a marker, he thought: *Something Terrible Happened Here!* Those women probably had no idea that almost three weeks before someone had snatched up Prentice, *his* Prentice, from this very place.

And then they had killed her. Clay still thought of her as his, even though she'd given him back his ring, told him she didn't want to see him again. But he didn't want to remember that. He would think of her as she was before, as *they* were before.

"I think Hattie's afraid of the police," Grady was saying. "They questioned her, you know."

Annie frowned. "Why would she be afraid?"

"It's the blue uniforms," Clay explained. "She thinks they're Yankees." He took a box of cheese crackers from a display on the counter and dug in his pocket for money. "Told me they were after her. She was hiding something, she said. Some kind of gold thing." He shook his head. "We've all heard that tale before."

Grady gave him back his change. "When was this?"

Clay could never forget. It was the morning of Prentice's funeral, he told them. He'd worked all day, until it was time to get cleaned up and go. *Climbing, picking, itching, sweating. Not thinking.* The Shed had been closed for the day, but it would be open first thing in the morning. Peaches didn't wait for death; didn't wait for anything. Hattie was there when he went to unload the baskets. Must've been waiting behind the Shed. Like to have scared him to death, he said, coming out at him like that, all dressed in black and yelling like a banshee about Nazis and Yankees and no telling who else. Said she *saw* what they did.

"Saw what who did?" Annie asked.

Clay shrugged. "Who knows? But you're right," he told Grady. "She *was* afraid. Seemed even crazier than usual, but I was going through hell myself. Didn't pay much attention to her."

"But somebody might have," Miss Dimple said. "What if they believed her?" *And what if she was telling the truth?*

"Do you think Hattie might be in danger?" Annie asked.

"I know the police questioned her, or tried to. Doubt if they learned much." Grady went to the window and stared out as a truckload of pine logs rumbled past. "Who knows what that old woman sees. Or knows. She's been telling folks she *found* something. . . . Well, maybe she did, but God knows what, or where she is now."

"Maybe she went somewhere. She might be staying with somebody." Annie spoke softly. As soon as she said it, she knew it didn't make sense.

"And where would that be? Would you want Hattie McGee for a houseguest?" Clay asked.

Grady inspected the cans in the window as if he might rearrange them, then decided against it. "No, I think something happened, and I'll tell you why," he said.

"The other day, I looked out the window there, and here comes Hattie, plodding down the road, pushing that old wheelbarrow, and dressed head to toe in some kind of flappin' black outfit. Looked for all the world like a witch. And hot! Remember how hot it was? Close to a hundred in the shade and it barely past sunup, too." Grady pulled out a dingy handkerchief and mopped his face, as if the thought of it made him ooze.

" 'Hattie!' I yells. 'Why don't you come in here and cool off a spell? Got a Co-Cola with your name on it.' And you know what? That old woman didn't pay a bit of attention to me. Just went on past like she didn't hear, and I reckon I hollered three or four times. I swear she heard me, too, but she never looked back or nothing. I watched her turn in there where there used to be a road to that trailer she lives in. I tell you I felt like a damned fool!" Grady slammed a fist onto the counter so hard, it jumped two packages of cheese crackers and a package of Beeman's gum out of the display box.

"And I'll tell you something else," Grady said. "She didn't walk like Hattie, either. I'm tellin' you, something ain't right!"

CHAPTER FOURTEEN

Y ou mean you think it wasn't Hattie, but *somebody else?* Maybe you ought to call Chief Tinsley," Clay suggested, but he hoped Grady would wait and call after he left. He'd had enough dealings with the Elderberry police.

Grady flicked a dead fly off the counter and thought about that. "Tell you what," he said. "Why don't you go over and check it out first? Hate to bring in the law if there's no call to. I'd go with you, but I can't close up here just yet. You can spare a few minutes, can't you?"

"Sure, I guess so." Clay didn't relish the idea of what he might find over there, but he didn't want to appear chickenhearted.

Noticing his reaction, Miss Dimple looked at Annie and Annie looked at Miss Dimple. "I'd like to use your telephone, Mr. Clinkscales, if you don't mind," she said. "We should let Mrs. Chadwick know we're going to be a few minutes late."

Across the road, Clay led them through knee-high undergrowth, pausing every few steps while Annie picked beggar-lice off her skirt. "I'll have to admit I'm glad of the company," he told them. "I've had enough surprises this summer to last

166

me a lifetime." He picked his way carefully through the brush until they came to Hattie's worn little path, barely perceptible in a carpet of pine needles and yellowing grass. Hazy splotches of fading sunlight filtered through the trees and spread in patches on the ground. Everything was still.

Miss Dimple stopped in a spot of shade to breathe in the musty smell of the woods, the sweet scent of honeysuckle, and for only a second, wished she were ten again.

In the clearing ahead, white-painted stones marked a path to Hattie's trailer home, and on either side bloomed roses of just about every color, all mixed up together. Clay had been here many times before, but he never got used to the magic of it. He had never admitted this to anyone, not even Prentice, but coming upon Hattie McGee's rose garden was like stepping into a fairy story. Even Miss Dimple stopped wide-eyed in mid-stride and let out a delicate gasp of astonishment.

"The door's not quite shut," Clay said, moving closer. "She must be here."

"Hattie! Hattie! It's me, Clay. You in there?"

There was no answer. Clay stepped back on the path, swept clean except for shattered petals, and wished he were somewhere else. "Maybe we ought to leave her alone," he said. "She doesn't like to be bothered."

But Dimple had no such reservations. Stepping forward, she banged repeatedly on the dented door with the palm of her hand. "Hattie, it's Dimple Kilpatrick. If you're in there, answer us, please. We want to know if you're all right."

When Hattie still didn't answer, Clay opened the door wider and poked his head inside. Annie tried to look over his shoulder, but she couldn't see much. *Charlie's going to hate missing out on this,* she thought. The adventure of helping to solve a mystery seemed to have become an integral part of their lives since the two friends began teaching in Charlie's hometown of Elderberry.

"Perhaps we should take a look out back," Miss Dimple suggested, and the women followed Clay single file, edging around rosebushes shoulder-high to a hard-packed area of red clay behind the trailer. Stooping, Clay pointed to the crawl space beneath it. "There's her wheelbarrow, still heaped with empty bottles she's collected." He frowned. "Grady's right. She never turned them in, and you know as well as I do Hattie would never go off and leave that behind."

"Then where could she be? I think we should call somebody. . . . Grady should still be open." Annie turned and started back up the pathway, but Miss Dimple put out a hand to stop her. "First let's be sure she's not inside," she said, speaking softly, and the others knew then what she expected to find.

Under normal conditions, Hattie McGee didn't smell like the roses she collected, Clay thought as he stepped inside. If the woman had been dead for even a few hours in this heat, they would know it as soon as they walked in the door, but if something had happened to Hattie, it had happened somewhere else. He breathed a silent "Thank you" as they made their way to the back of the trailer, where Hattie apparently slept. The place was dingy and close. Hattie wasn't much of a housekeeper, but it wasn't as bad as he'd expected, although a good scrubbing with disinfectant wouldn't hurt. Clay thought of his mama in her bleach-splattered cleaning clothes, sleeves rolled up above her elbows.

"Looks like she got rid of the funeral clothes," Annie said, calling attention to a mound of black garments spilling over the narrow bed, with the veiled hat like a garnish on top. The niche that served as a closet in the corner of the tiny room held only a nubby winter coat, a pair of muddy galoshes, and a worn red velvet dress trimmed in lace, with dried mud weighing the hem.

"Looks like she took her other clothes with her," Clay said. He certainly hoped so. The thought of Hattie McGee running around naked made the ice cream he'd just eaten squish around in his stomach. "What now?" he asked, turning to the others.

Miss Dimple dug in her large purple handbag and brought out a letter she'd received from her brother. "I think we should leave a message just in case," she said, and carefully tearing off the back of the envelope, she wrote a note in her elegant Spenserian script. "If she sees this, at least she'll know we're looking for her, and if we don't hear something from her in a day or so . . ."

"It will be time to get worried," Clay said. He anchored the note under an empty fruit jar in the space that served as a kitchen, and the three of them hurried out, shutting the door firmly behind them.

Clay took the pathway in long strides, stopping now and then to see if the others were keeping up. They were, of course. Clay never thought he'd be glad to get back to grading peaches, but he couldn't get away fast enough.

Annie was eager to curl up after supper to read for about the tenth time her most recent letter from Frazier and know that at least at the time he wrote it he was still alive, but it had been several weeks since she had heard from him last.

Miss Dimple was thoughtfully quiet. *If Hattie McGee wasn't in her makeshift trailer home, where in the world could she be?*

Charlie stood for a minute before Clay noticed her, and when he did, he merely raised a hand in acknowledgment and turned back to what he was doing. Drag-assed glum, an expression her father use to use, came to mind.

She didn't want to be here, especially alone, but there had been no word from Hattie for the last few days. After Prentice was killed, Delia's work at the Peach Shed came to an end; Miss Dimple was volunteering at the Red Cross blood drive that day, and Annie had gone along to donate, claiming she'd rather they'd take every drop than have to go near that trailer again. "You don't have to go in," Annie'd promised. "Just drop by the Shed and see if Clay's around. Maybe he's heard something."

Charlie had been tempted to invite her mother and her aunt Lou to come along today, but if those two became involved, they would probably stir up more trouble than she could deal with right now. They meant well, bless their hearts, but Charlie cringed to think of some of the frightening close calls the women had experienced.

Asa Weatherby, who was minding the Shed, had said he thought Clay was somewhere out back, but Charlie hadn't seen him anywhere. Calling to him, she'd walked hesitantly down the stone-bordered path, half-expecting to meet the Tin Man or the Wicked Witch.

"Whaddaya want?" Clay called out to her now as he moved from a yellow hybrid to a pink climbing rose near the trailer door. She couldn't see his face.

"To tell you you've won a million dollars! What do you think I want? What are you doing?" she asked, noticing the gallon milk jug in his hand.

He shrugged. "Watering Hattie's roses. Seems like somebody ought to. Shame to let 'em die."

Charlie sniffed a crimson blossom. If she picked it, would a horrible beast appear and order her to leave? "Need any help?" she asked.

"Thanks, but I'm about through." Clay paused to mop his face and set the empty jug on Hattie's single step. "The note's still inside, where we left it the other day. Doesn't look like she's been back here."

"What note?"

"The one Miss Dimple wrote to let her know we were worried about her. Doesn't look like she's coming back."

"Miss Dimple thinks something's happened to her," Charlie said. "Do you?"

"Looks that way. Grady has the police looking for her. They were here earlier, poking around."

"Did they find anything?"

"The police don't let me in on their little secrets," Clay told her. "Since that nut in Atlanta confessed, they're more convinced than ever that I killed Prentice. That guy was *in jail* when Prentice was killed."

Clay went inside to fill the jug and emptied most of the contents on the bush with velvety red blossoms. "What about Miss Bertie?" he asked. "Do you think she might know who Prentice was seeing?"

Charlie shook her head. "Not according to Miss Dimple. Her friends didn't know, either. Delia and I have spoken to all of them except Iris."

"She's working at some camp." Clay poured what was left in the water jug over his sand-colored hair.

"I know. We'll just have to wait till she gets home.

"Guess you heard about Jasper Totherow."

"A little. Fill me in."

Charlie did. "Maybe he and Hattie eloped," she said in an attempt to make him smile.

It didn't. "Something stinks," Clay said. "What's going on, Charlie?"

"I wish I knew. Do you think more than one person could be involved? Jasper claims he saw somebody out there the day Leola died. Maybe Prentice did, too. Delia says she seemed to be nervous . . . worried about something. Now Prentice is dead, Jasper's missing . . . and nobody knows what's happened to Hattie. Where does the boyfriend come into this?"

He frowned. "You don't believe me about the boyfriend?"

"That's not what I said, but we have to find him, Clay. Maybe there's a connection, but right now, I can't see it."

"Don't give up on me, Charlie. *Please*."

Swallowing tears, Charlie turned away. There were too many things to cry about: The man she hoped to marry was in danger's way every day, as was her brother Fain, Delia's Ned, and oh so many others. She couldn't afford to break down now. "I'm not giving up on you," she said, facing him, "but I don't know where else to look. I've thought of everybody it might possibly be, but none of them makes any sense."

"You think I haven't?" Clay set the milk jug inside the trailer and slammed the door. "I make lists in my sleep. *When* I sleep."

Charlie hesitated before speaking. "There's a possibility, you know, that Prentice made that up. Delia said she was upset with you over your objection to her going away to college this fall. . . . Well . . . *more* than upset really. She might've said that just to hurt you, Clay."

He stiffened. *"No!* Prentice doesn't—didn't lie. Wish to hell she had, but she was telling the truth. I know it."

Charlie looked at the empty trailer, the bright mass of roses; water dripped softly from the foliage. "Clay, do you know where Hattie is?" *Now what made her ask that?*

Clay must have wondered, too. *"What?"*

"She could know something important, Clay."

In answer, he climbed into the cab of his truck, slammed the door shut, and started the engine. Silently, Charlie walked back to her car and followed him out to the road. He never did answer her question.

"I'm afraid I might've made a mess of things with Clay," Charlie told Annie when she stopped by Phoebe's later. She found Annie on the back porch, adding another coat of white polish to her sandals.

"I don't know why in the world I said that," she added, explaining what she'd done. "I've known Clay Jarrett all his life, but sometimes it's hard to know what he's thinking."

Annie set the sandals aside to dry. The polish had covered most of the worn places and they would have to do for now. "I wouldn't worry about it," she said, and sighed.

Charlie frowned. "Oh, Annie, have you still not heard?"

Annie shook her head. "Something's happened. I know it, and Frazier's right in the middle of it. I've read all about what's going on over there, heard it on the news. They're trying to push past the Normandy beaches, take all those towns away from the Germans. It's been *weeks* now, Charlie, and I haven't heard a word. I know he would write if he could—even if it's only a few sentences—just to let me know he's all right."

"Maybe his parents have heard something. Do you know how to get in touch?"

Annie wiped away a tear with the back of her hand. "Well, I have their names and address. They live in this little town in north Georgia, somewhere up near the Tennessee line."

"Then *call* them! Maybe they've heard something. At least you'll know."

"Okay, but I'll wait until the mail comes tomorrow. Maybe I'll hear something then," Annie said.

Charlie smiled. "Good! Now, let's go drown our problems at the drugstore. I've been thinking about a root beer float all day."

Charlie asked Delia to join them, hoping it might help to cheer her up as well, and they took little "Pooh" along to gnaw on his usual cone— minus the ice cream—having learned from experience that otherwise the baby and everything within several feet of him would have to be scrubbed down afterward. "We're going to be in trouble when he learns the difference," Charlie said as they settled into a booth at Lewellyn's.

Annie scooped a spoonful of vanilla into her mouth and glanced at the young man in uniform approaching them. "Who's that?" she whispered, trying not to stare. He was exceptionally good-looking, so it was hard to look anywhere else.

Delia concentrated on stirring her chocolate soda with a straw. "Chenault Kirkland," she whispered, flushing.

She looked up as he stopped by their booth. "I'm so sorry about your friend, about Prentice," he said, speaking softly. "I still can't believe that happened."

Delia nodded and thanked him, her eyes

welling with tears. Thank goodness right at that moment Pooh decided he wanted to climb onto the table and everyone scurried to move everything out of his way as Delia secured him safely in her lap.

Chenault Kirkland belonged in an advertisement for beachwear, with a towel over his shoulder and a girl on his arm—a blond girl with large breasts, Annie thought.

They were interrupted by a greeting from Bobby Tinsley, who had stopped in for his customary afternoon ice cream. "Chenault—glad I ran into you. The sheriff tells me they've found your mother's purse. They tried to call your home but couldn't get an answer."

Chenault shrugged. "Probably out running around as usual. Is that the one that was stolen at Cooper's grocery?"

"Sheriff's pretty sure it is. Says she can claim it at any time."

Chenault frowned. "Who took it? Or do they know?"

"Probably Jasper Totherow," the chief said. "They found it on the hill near that old shed he used to sleep in."

"*Used* to sleep in. You think he's dead?" Charlie asked.

"Either that or he's disappeared somewhere. Nobody's been able to find him," Bobby Tinsley said.

Chenault shook his head and frowned. "Jasper Totherow. Isn't he the man those little girls found? I thought they said he was dead."

Bobby sighed. "Frankly, I think the old scalawag took that money and went on a spree. He's holed up somewhere; you can bet on it."

"I don't think I've ever seen anybody with eyes as blue as that," Charlie said after the two men left.

"I assume you're speaking of Chenault," Delia said, "and may I remind you that you're an engaged woman?"

Charlie laughed. "I may be engaged, but I'm not blind! It's hard to ignore somebody who looks like that."

Delia smiled. "Prentice and I used to make up stories about him. Both of us had a terrible crush—as if he would bother to look at two pitiful teenagers."

Charlie drank the rest of her float, but she couldn't help thinking that Prentice Blair at eighteen hadn't been pitiful at all.

A letter from Will Sinclair was waiting when Charlie reached home. Snatching it up, she went immediately to her room. Hitler was using V-1 flying bombs to wreck havoc on England, with horrible losses, especially in the London area. And from the news, she knew Will's unit had participated in bombing oil fields and protecting Allied bombers in Germany and Romania, but he didn't write about that. She didn't know how he managed to keep his letters light, sometimes describing the friends he had made and how they passed the time, usually including some kind of joke about the food. But there was an undercurrent of tenderness in every line. Charlie held the thin paper to her lips and kissed the scrawling signature. Although there was an ocean between them, she could feel his love as if he were right beside her in this very room. She hoped Annie had heard from Frazier, as well. Surely she would telephone if she had. Charlie was reading Will's letter for the third time when her mother tapped on her door.

"When you can stop smiling long enough, you might want to phone Iris Ellerby," she said. "She got home from camp this afternoon and seems eager to talk with you."

$\mathcal{C}$HAPTER $\mathcal{F}$IFTEEN

M ama said you wanted to talk to me about Prentice," Iris said when Charlie called, and her voice didn't sound eager at all, but weighed down with the sadness of the news that had awaited her.

Charlie glanced at the clock. It was almost five and Delia was upstairs giving Pooh his bath. After contacting most of their close friends after Prentice disappeared, her sister found it difficult to talk about her death and lately had avoided discussing it whenever possible.

"Would it be all right if I dropped by later?" Charlie asked. "It's important," she added, noticing Iris's hesitation. "We're trying to piece together everything we can to learn who's responsible for this and you're the only one we haven't been able to get in touch with."

Iris sighed. "I don't know what more I could tell you, but . . . sure, come on if you think it might help."

"Iris just got home from camp and I'm going by there in a few minutes to see if she has any idea who Prentice might've been seeing," Charlie called to Delia from the top of the stairs. "Do you want to come with me?"

But her sister wasn't interested. "You go on. I'm gonna feed Pooh an early supper and try to get a letter off to Ned."

Although she would've welcomed the company, Charlie understood Delia's reluctance to delve into questions about her friend's death. Iris would probably be more likely to share a confidence with a close friend like Delia, but she would just have to do the best she could.

"She's out back in the glider swing," Iris's mother told Charlie when she arrived a short while later. "Maybe I should've told her earlier about what happened to Prentice. . . . She's taking it pretty hard. I'm so glad you've come. I think it might help to have someone to talk to."

The glider swing rested under a tulip tree and Iris sat in the spotted shade with one leg curled beneath her, mechanically turning the pages of her high school yearbook. "I still can't believe this has happened," she said, looking at Charlie as if she expected her to tell her it was a cruel lie.

Charlie wished with all her heart that she could. She climbed into the opposite seat and wasted no time explaining to Iris that they suspected Prentice had been intimate with someone other than Clay.

"What?" The swing jiggled as Iris sought to stand, but then she abandoned the idea. "Where in the world did you get a notion like that? She wasn't even going *that far* with Clay, and you know how long they'd been together!"

Charlie waited for her emotional reaction to level off before telling Iris that Clay Jarrett himself had shared that information.

"Well, naturally he would!" Iris said, flushing. "How do you know he isn't making that up to save his skin?"

"I don't know . . . but what if he's telling the truth? Prentice broke up with Clay a couple of weeks before she was killed, and according to him, she admitted she'd had sex with somebody else. You knew her better than most of us, Iris. Why would she have said that?"

Iris shrugged. "*If* she said that, it was probably because he was so selfish about not wanting her to go away to college. I guess he pushed her too far and she wanted to get back at him."

Charlie didn't answer, and Iris correctly read her silence to mean she disagreed. "You know how Prentice was," Iris protested. "There was never anybody but Clay. I can't believe there was anything going on with somebody else."

Her last statement wasn't convincing, however, and Iris shifted her gaze to the yearbook in her lap, then looked quickly away.

"Iris, are you *sure? Think, please.* Do you remember her mentioning *anybody*—even in jest? Someone she admired or thought good-looking?"

Iris smiled slightly. "You mean other than Clark Gable or Tyrone Power? The only person I can think of would be Chenault Kirkland, but that was back when we were in the ninth grade. I think most of us had a crush on him then, but she hadn't said anything about him lately."

Charlie nodded. Her sister had, too, but Chenault Kirkland was rarely home on leave, and besides, she'd heard he was serious about some girl from Savannah. Prentice would've been much too young for Chenault, but she *was* beautiful, and it would be hard to believe he wouldn't have noticed her. She reminded herself it certainly wouldn't do to disregard him.

Charlie wished Miss Dimple were here. She sensed that Iris wasn't telling her everything, and there was something about Dimple Kilpatrick that made others put their trust in her hands. "If you think of *anybody,* please let me know," she said. "The longer Prentice's murder goes unsolved, the greater the chance we'll never know who did it. . . . And what's to keep him from doing it again?"

Iris didn't answer but continued to grip the yearbook in her lap, and it was obvious she wasn't going to say anything more. Charlie said good-bye and started across the yard. She could see Iris's mother watching from the kitchen window and felt sorry that not only had she been useless in comforting Iris, but she had made her feel even worse.

She had reached the corner of the house when Iris called to her from the swing. "Charlie . . . wait!

"There was *somebody,* but it's . . . crazy to even think of it. I'm sure there's nothing to it." Iris glanced down at the unopened annual. "I used to tease her about him—just joking, naturally—and she'd get all flustered and turn as red as a beet. Honestly, I didn't think there was anything going on—not with Prentice. Who would believe she'd—"

"*Who,* Iris?" Charlie tried not to scream. "Tell me who!"

"Look, I'm not sure about this, but maybe she really did have a thing for him. Got kind of mad when I teased her." Iris lowered her voice. "It was Mr. Reardon. Seth Reardon, the drama coach."

Seth Reardon. Charlie tried to picture his face and couldn't. The drama teacher wasn't someone who would stand out in a crowd. Dark-rimmed glasses, brownish hair, medium height—not someone she would expect. She drew a blank when it came to his face. Seth Reardon was just sort of there. She'd worked with him some her junior year when he was adviser to the annual staff, and remembered him only slightly. Pleasant enough. Kind of low-key. And much too old for Prentice.

Good Lord, Prentice! Why?

Although it was still sweltering in late summer, Charlie felt the need of a cup of tea. When she reached home, her mother looked up from her ancient rolltop desk, where she wrote her weekly society column for the *Elderberry Eagle*, and acknowledged her daughter with a wave of her hand. Delia was nowhere around. Probably upstairs writing to Ned, Charlie thought as she waited for the kettle to boil.

Iris Ellerby was only guessing about Prentice and Seth Reardon, and it wouldn't do to blow it all out of proportion with nothing to go on but secondhand gossip. Miss Dimple would know best where to go from here, Charlie decided. It was too late to phone her tonight, but she would talk with her first thing tomorrow.

Her mother glided past her to put her coffee cup in the sink and yawned. "How did you find Iris?" she asked. "Poor girl! It's hard for her, I know, to lose a friend like that, and then have to leave for school right away. She goes to Wesleyan, doesn't she?"

"Uh-huh. Sophomore year." Charlie didn't look up. She wished she could confide more in her mother, but there were some things she'd learned not to share with Jo Carr or her sister Lou. The two liked nothing better than to latch onto the trail of a possible suspect, and Charlie didn't want to be responsible for them putting themselves in danger. *It was different, of course, if she did it herself . . . but she wasn't going to think about that.*

Her mother leaned on the edge of the sink. "So . . . did she have anything to say—about Prentice, I mean?"

"She was still in shock, I think. I don't believe Iris has had time to come to terms with what happened. She's pretty broken up."

"I'm not surprised. Well, bed for me. I've had

enough for one day." Sighing, Jo kissed her daughter's cheek. "Don't stay up too late."

"I won't." Charlie smiled. Her mother always said that, and Charlie always answered in the same way, and then went to bed as late as she pleased. It was a ritual. "By the way," she added, "did Annie phone while I was gone?"

But Jo shook her head. "I sat on the porch for a while to cool off, but I would've heard the phone ring, and of course Delia was inside to answer it. Now, don't forget to turn out the kitchen light."

Before she went to bed, Charlie pulled out her high school yearbook, the *Eagle's Eye*. In addition to advising the annual staff, Seth Reardon coached the debate team and directed most school productions. He was nice-looking enough, she thought, examining his faculty photograph, but nobody who would make you do a double take. Delia had mentioned once that she thought he had a droll sense of humor. Maybe that was what had appealed to Prentice.

If he had appealed to Prentice. That was something they would have to find out.

When Charlie dropped by Phoebe's the next morning, she found Dimple at the kitchen table with her usual cup of ginger mint tea and one of her unappetizing Victory Muffins. She had returned earlier from her customary morning

186

walk, and aside from Odessa, who was hanging out clothes, and Phoebe, out watering her drooping begonias, Dimple was the only one up. Annie was still asleep, she was told, and if she had received a letter from Frazier, Miss Dimple wasn't aware of it.

Naturally, Miss Dimple practically insisted Charlie have one of her muffins, proclaiming their value in aiding digestion, and, she added, "in keeping one regular." But Charlie had been led down that path before and found that one sample of foul-tasting sawdust was more than enough. "Thank you, but I just had a big breakfast and can't eat another bite," she said, then wasted no time telling Miss Dimple about Seth Reardon.

"Hmm . . . it says here he lives on Oglethorpe Street," Miss Dimple said, thumbing through the thin volume of the Elderberry telephone book. "Must be that large Victorian house on the corner. I believe it's been made into apartments."

"I wonder who else lives there," Charlie said. "It would be better if we had a reason to drop by."

"Alma Owens rents an apartment downstairs," Phoebe told them when she came in to fill her watering can, "and I believe Florence McCrary lives on the other side. That used to be the old Douglas place."

"*Florence McCrary!* Well, no need to ask any further," Charlie said. "That woman knows *everything* about *everybody* in this town!"

187

Most people suspected that Florence, as the local telephone operator, frequently listened in on private conversations, but Miss Dimple was willing to give her the benefit of the doubt.

"Did I hear somebody mention the old Douglas place?" Velma Anderson, still in robe and slippers, helped herself to coffee, making a point to bypass the offending muffins. "Mary Edna Sizemore and her mother rented the upstairs there until they moved into that place in the north end of town. You all know Mary Edna—teaches home ec at the high school."

Everyone acknowledged that they did. "I believe Seth Reardon's living there now." Velma rustled cornflakes into a bowl, added milk, and sat at the table with Dimple. "Wouldn't be surprised if he moved on to other things soon, though. He's getting married, you know."

Charlie didn't. She waited.

"Girl from Virginia," Velma continued. "Think they went to school together. Heard she was an actress or something. Good Lord! What would she do *here?*"

"He hasn't resigned, has he?" Miss Dimple asked.

"Not yet. Wedding's not till December. He showed me her picture once. Seems right attractive, but she's no spring chicken. . . . Of course, Seth isn't, either. I think he's been taking classes at the university this summer—working on his master's."

Charlie glanced at Miss Dimple, who pretended not to notice. This complicated matters. A fiancée made the situation even more unlikely. Could Iris have imagined this? After all, she never actually witnessed anything that might be compromising.

"How are we going to manage this?" she asked Miss Dimple after they moved to the front porch. Annie joined them there, silently shaking her head to let Charlie know she still hadn't heard from Frazier, and both Velma and her roommate, Lily Moss, had left for errands in town. Phoebe and Odessa were bustling about the kitchen, making watermelon-rind pickles, and the house was soon filled with the tart smell of vinegar and spices, which quickly became overwhelming. Charlie thought longingly of the preserves her aunt Lou made of watermelon rind, but that would take too much sugar. The pickles would have to do until after the war.

"I think we should all confront him together," Annie said, having been informed of Iris's suspicions. "There's not much he could do to the three of us. How do we know he didn't kill Prentice to keep her from telling his fiancée?"

Charlie agreed. She had thought of asking Clay to accompany them, but if the rumor about Prentice's involvement turned out to be true, there was no telling what his reaction might be. "But we still need a plausible reason to visit him, and I can't think of a thing," she admitted.

"I believe I can," Miss Dimple said after a few moments of silence. "If you'll remember, Prentice had one of the featured roles in the school production of *H.M.S. Pinafore*. It seems to me her aunt Elberta might like to have a copy of that script to remind her of happier times, and who else would we ask to help us find another than the person who directed it?"

The morning was half gone by the time the three women walked the several blocks to the house on Oglethorpe Street, having decided it was best not to telephone in advance. On the way, Annie confided that she would put in a long-distance call to Frazier's parents if she didn't hear from him in the afternoon mail. The opportunity to confront Seth Reardon would at least help to distract her friend for a while, Charlie hoped.

A gray Plymouth coupe, which they assumed belonged to Seth Reardon, was parked in the narrow gravel driveway, and Miss Dimple didn't hesitate as she led the way inside and up the stairs.

They found his name on a card attached to his door and waited for what seemed like an eternity after Miss Dimple knocked. *What do we say now?* Charlie wondered, and for a brief minute, she found herself hoping Seth Reardon wouldn't be at home.

"Just a minute!" someone called from inside,

and the sound of hurried footsteps drew nearer.

Naturally, he recognized Charlie right away, since it had been only a few years since she was a student at Elderberry High. "Why, it's Charlie, isn't it? Charlie Carr. You're Delia's sister, aren't you?" Puzzled, he looked about. "And Miss Dimple—how nice to see you. What can I do for you ladies?"

You can tell us if you had anything to do with Prentice Blair's murder! Charlie thought, but she wisely let Miss Dimple do the talking.

"We've come asking a favor," Miss Dimple began. "I'm sure you're aware of what happened to Prentice Blair. . . ."

The man's face turned doughy white and he grasped the door frame as if he were afraid his legs wouldn't hold him up. "Yes . . . yes, of course . . . but what—"

"Is it all right if we come in?" Miss Dimple barged past him without waiting for an answer, and the others followed meekly.

But not before Charlie heard Annie whisper behind her, " 'Yond Cassius has a lean and hungry look.' "

CHAPTER SIXTEEN

L eave it to Annie to quote Shakespeare at the most inopportune times, Charlie thought, but she welcomed the lighthearted respite, however brief.

The room they entered was large, sunlit, and practically bare, with a daybed in one corner, two shabby overstuffed chairs, and a radio on a small table. An electric fan whirred in the window and books lined two walls and overflowed onto the floor.

"Oh—here, sit down, please." Seth Reardon grabbed a handful of papers from one of the chairs and brought a straight chair from the adjoining kitchen. Charlie and Annie sat on opposite ends of the daybed; Miss Dimple chose one of the armchairs, and the drama teacher perched uneasily, Charlie thought, on the one from the kitchen.

He looked from one to the other as if he expected them to say something, but nobody spoke. "That was a horrible thing that happened to Prentice," he began finally. "Have they learned anything more? I thought it might have been connected to those killings in Atlanta, but now they say no."

"I'm afraid not," Charlie mumbled. Somebody

had to say *something,* she thought. She looked at the bookshelves, the walls, searching for a photograph of the man's fiancée, but she didn't see one. Annie, on the other end of the daybed, looked as if she might explode at any minute.

"We came to see if we might get a copy of Prentice's script from her last play," Miss Dimple said at last. "The role was important to her, and I believe her aunt Elberta would like to have it as a reminder of happier times."

"That would be *H.M.S. Pinafore.*" He frowned. "I'm afraid I mailed those back. Have to pay a fee, you know, if you don't return them on time. Some of the leads paid for theirs, didn't want to give them up, but I'm almost sure Prentice turned hers in." He started to say something more, then shook his head. "She was wonderful in that role," he whispered finally.

"Oh," Miss Dimple said. She looked as if she might burst into tears at any moment. "Well, that's a shame. We were hoping—"

"Look, I won't be able to get the same script Prentice used, but I can order one if you like," Seth said. "At least I'd like to try."

"That's very kind of you," Miss Dimple said, standing. She paused. "You knew Prentice, well, didn't you, Mr. Reardon?"

He flushed. "Of course . . . yes . . . I directed Prentice in several productions. She was a talented young lady."

Seth Reardon had started for the door and now he stood in the middle of the room, waiting for them to follow him and leave.

"I wonder," Miss Dimple continued, "if you might have noticed any interest she may have taken in a particular young man . . . an interest of a . . . well . . . a romantic nature, I mean."

If their mission hadn't been so serious, Charlie would have been tempted to laugh at the older teacher's demure act as Dimple fumbled in her purse for the familiar lavender-trimmed handkerchief and held it to her lips.

He attempted a smile, and it was easy to see he was searching for a reply. "It's been over a year since Prentice graduated, you know, but during that time I believe she was going with Clay Jarrett."

Looking him steadily in the eye, Miss Dimple tucked her hankie away. "Prentice admired you, Mr. Reardon, and shared your enthusiasm for the theater. I thought perhaps she might have stayed in touch."

His smiled vanished as he moved toward the door. "Other than running across her in town now and then, I haven't maintained a relationship with Prentice Blair," he said curtly. "I'll see what I can do about getting the script you wanted, and will let you know when it arrives."

This is not going the way we planned it. Letting the others start downstairs ahead of her, Charlie turned when she reached the landing, to see Seth Reardon watching them from his doorway. "I wish you'd just tell us the truth," she said. "Was there something going on between you and Prentice?"

The man looked as if he'd been slapped. She wasn't surprised when he didn't answer.

"Because if there was, Clay Jarrett's getting the blame for something he didn't do," Charlie continued. "How long do you mean to let it go on?"

Charlie gripped the stair railing. What had she done? Did she really expect the shock of her accusation to jar the man into confessing? The others stood at the foot of the stairs, mutely looking up at her. Now she'd done it for sure! She turned back to apologize, to try to explain her irrational behavior. For all she knew, the man could sue her for what she'd said.

Seth Reardon stood silently crying.

"Believe me, I had nothing to do with what happened to Prentice," he explained as they regrouped in his apartment a few minutes later. "I was attracted to her, I'll admit. She was like someone out of a poem—so beautiful. . . . I don't think she realized how beautiful she was. And kind." Again he sat in the kitchen chair, his head in his hands. "And, too, we shared a love of the theater, so naturally I was drawn to her."

"So you were the one." Charlie spoke without thinking, but it was too late to care.

" 'The one'?"

He raised his head and she saw that his face was flushed and streaked with tears. Miss Dimple looked at her with a warning glint, but Charlie continued in spite of it. "*The one* Prentice went all the—the person Prentice *slept* with," she told him. *Slept* wasn't exactly what she meant, but she wasn't going to mention the word *sex* in the presence of Miss Dimple Kilpatrick.

Seth Reardon sat straighter. "I came close to falling in love with Prentice Blair—and would have if I hadn't stopped myself." He spoke calmly, with a tinge of sadness in his voice. "Because of the age difference, you see . . . it would've been unfair to her. I had to come to terms with that."

Charlie looked at Miss Dimple, expecting her to speak, but Miss Dimple simply eyed him silently, as if she might be examining every molecule in the man's body. Her expression didn't change.

"But not before you had your fun," Charlie said. From what Clay reported, it had been fun for Prentice as well, but that wasn't the point. "Isn't there a rule against that sort of thing between teachers and students?"

The man had the audacity to appear offended. "You are referring, I believe, to something that took place when that was no longer the case."

Annie leaned forward. "So *when?*" she asked.

He looked from one to the other, as if deciding whether or not to reply, and finally took a deep breath and sighed. "Prentice asked for my help last spring while she was assisting with an Easter pageant for the children at her church," he began. "It felt comfortable working with her again, and it all began on friendly terms. I assure you I had no intentions of it developing into a more personal relationship. After the pageant, our contact mainly took place by phone, and that's when I learned she and Clay were having problems about the college issue. She needed someone to talk to, and I guess I made a sympathetic sounding board . . . and . . . well, after a time the two of us became intimate. I honestly didn't mean for it to go as far as it did."

"When did you end this relationship?" Miss Dimple asked, her expression unchanging.

He almost smiled. "Soon after it began. We were on the verge of becoming serious—too serious— and both of us agreed it was the right decision. Prentice looked forward to going away to college and I wanted her to enjoy the opportunities that accompany that—including dating. You may have heard I'm engaged to be married in December and I want you to know I do care deeply for Deborah. Now I suppose this will all come out. . . ."

Miss Dimple's words were swift and cold. "Surely you don't expect us to be concerned about your marriage prospects when a young woman is dead. How are we to know *you* didn't kill Prentice when she objected to your ending the relationship? Perhaps she threatened to tell your fiancée what had taken place."

The chair tottered as Seth Reardon jumped to his feet. "Prentice would *never* have done that! You must understand it was a mutual agreement, and I would never have hurt Prentice—never! It made me physically ill when I heard what happened. . . . I can hardly sleep for thinking about it. Believe me, I want to find the person responsible as much as, or even more than, most. Surely you don't think I had anything to do with her death."

Silence hung like a dark, hovering cloud as the three faced him in accusation.

"*No!* You don't understand! I couldn't have killed Prentice. I wasn't even here when that happened. Ask—" He looked about, as if searching for a name. "Ask Florence McCrary downstairs— or Alma. They saw me leave. Ask anybody who knows me and they'll tell you I was in Virginia visiting Deborah and her parents.

"Here . . . wait a minute. . . ." Seth left the room abruptly and returned a few minutes later with two ticket stubs. "These were still in the pocket of the suit I wore on the bus. You can check with Clyde Jefferies at the Feed and Seed. He's the one who sold me the ticket."

What could you say to that? Charlie found herself waiting for Miss Dimple to speak and noticed that Annie did the same.

Dimple stood slowly. "Then *who?*" she said, and without looking to the left or to the right, walked sedately to the door.

"He could've gotten off the bus somewhere and come back without anyone seeing him," Annie suggested as they walked slowly back to Phoebe's. But Miss Dimple shook her head. "He had the return ticket as well. He's telling the truth. I noticed the dates."

"I suppose he could've gotten those tickets from somebody else," Charlie said, "but he knows we could check out his story with Clyde Jefferies."

"He did seem genuinely upset," Annie mumbled almost to herself. "But of course that doesn't excuse what he did," she added after a look from Miss Dimple.

"That's not to say May-December romances are always a mistake." Miss Dimple spoke almost as an afterthought, thinking of her own parents. Although in that case, her mother was a good bit older than her father. "I would imagine it depends on the people involved. It saddens me, though, that Prentice didn't get the chance to go away to college."

"Or for anything else," Annie added.

• • •

Later that evening, Annie and Charlie sat in deepening twilight on the Carrs' large front porch, discussing what had happened that day. Earlier, Annie had attempted to get in touch with Frazier's parents, but no one had answered the phone. Taking that as a positive sign, the two had spent the rest of the afternoon at the picture show to see the musical *Girl Crazy* with Judy Garland and Mickey Rooney, hoping it would take their minds off the troubles of war and the perplexing tragedy of Prentice's death.

For a while, it did exactly that, and afterward the two had danced all the way home, humming the music to "Fascinating Rhythm."

"I don't think anybody can match Judy Garland's voice," Annie said later.

"Prentice had a sweet voice," Charlie commented. "Not in the same league as Judy Garland's, of course, but she did have talent. I wonder what she might've done if she'd had the opportunity."

Annie reached out to touch her friend's shoulder. "Well, *don't* wonder," she advised, speaking softly. "It only makes you sad and it won't do any good."

"You're right." Charlie drank the last of her iced tea and set the glass on the floor with a thump. "It's driving me crazy that we keep hitting a brick wall at every turn. There's a murderer running around right under our noses, Annie, and you know as well as I do that the longer it takes, the fewer the chances they'll ever find out who did it."

Annie watched their neighbors Bessie Jenkins and Marjorie Mote meet at the corner for their customary after-supper stroll around the block. "Leola must've seen something—or somebody thinks she did—and whoever it was probably suspected Prentice saw it, too, or that Leola told her about it right before she died."

Charlie nodded. "Thank goodness the creek stopped that fire before it got close to Leola's. I think the police think it probably started when somebody threw a cigarette out of a car window, but I don't know about that."

"What do you mean?" Annie asked.

"I'm not sure, but you can bet your boots Miss Dimple has given it some thought. I'll ask her about it tomorrow."

The screen door slammed as Jo Carr stepped onto the porch. "There's pimento cheese in the Frigidaire if you two want to make sandwiches, and I think Delia left a few pieces of your aunt Lou's chocolate meringue pie."

"What are we waiting for?" Charlie jumped to her feet. Her aunt was a fantastic cook, and with rationing, her pies were a rare delicacy. "Race you!" she challenged.

Her mother waited until they were safely inside before she hurried down the street to her sister's house in the next block. She'd thought all along that fire hadn't been an accident, and since she and Lou didn't have to work at the ordnance plant tomorrow, it would be as good a time as any to see what they could find out.

CHAPTER SEVENTEEN

I don't know about this, Josephine," Lou Willingham said the next morning when her sister climbed into the car beside her.

"Don't know about what? Didn't you say just the other day you wished you knew what Dimple Kilpatrick was planning? You know very well she's up to her knees digging into that awful thing that happened to Prentice Blair—and your own niece and Annie Gardner right along with her."

Lou shifted gears to back into the street and stuck her arm out the window to signal a right turn at the corner. "But the police have already searched Leola's place several times, haven't they? What makes you think we can find out anything new?"

Jo Carr gave her sister a bewildered look. "Oh, for heaven's sake, Louise! They're *men,* aren't they? When have you ever heard of a man finding anything? All I want to do is take a look around with a fresh eye so to speak."

Lou had to admit Jo had a point and she guessed it wouldn't do any harm to take a quick look. "Well, I hope we don't run into that weasel Jasper Totherow. Wasn't it somewhere out there those two children stumbled onto what they thought was his body? And now it appears he just up and walked away. I don't want anything to do with that one, dead or alive!"

Jo agreed. It did seem Jasper had a habit of turning up like a bad penny when you least expected him. "I wonder how Bertie Stackhouse is doing," she said as they passed the home she had shared with Prentice. "I wish there were something we could do for her, but nothing can ease the pain of losing a child." Jo could empathize to a certain degree with that kind of grief, as her son Fain had been reported missing in action for several months earlier in the war. Later she learned he was recuperating from his wounds on a British hospital ship before returning to his unit in Tunisia. Now Fain was fighting in the European theater with Charlie's Will, Delia's young husband Ned, Frazier Duncan, and countless others, and she counted as a blessing every day without a visit from the boy on the black bicycle who delivered the dreaded telegrams.

"She should sell that place and go on and marry Adam Treadway," Lou muttered. "He's waited long enough and I think it might be a good idea for her to get a fresh start somewhere else. Elberta's only in her forties, isn't she?"

Jo nodded. Now in her mid-fifties, the forties didn't seem so old anymore. "I think Bertie was reluctant to make any major changes until Prentice was more or less on her own. After all, this was her home, too."

"But that's not all that's been holding her back," Lou said. "You know as well as I do there's more to it than that."

And Jo did, but neither of them was going to say it aloud.

"It looks sad, doesn't it?" Jo said as they approached Leola Parker's place a few miles down the road. "Forlorn, and it's only been a little over a month since Leola died."

"It looks like somebody's cut the grass," Lou said, sniffing the fresh green smell as they turned into the long dirt road leading to Leola's place. "Mary Joy's husband must've been here, or else they paid somebody to take care of it." She parked beneath the dark green canopy of a blackjack oak and glanced at her sister beside her. "Well, we're here. What are we supposed to do now?"

Jo didn't answer, but climbed out onto the hard-packed red earth and looked about. Leola's small white cottage stood closed and shuttered at the top of a low hill with a series of stepping-stones leading to the front door. A crow cawed from somewhere in the woods behind the house and a blue jay scolded from a limb above them. It was such a peaceful place, she thought, and it saddened her to think something bad had happened here. *Something like murder.*

Jo said as much to Lou, who, with great reluctance, had joined her. "What makes you think it was murder?" Lou asked. "From what I've heard, they seem to think Leola slipped and hit her head."

"But don't forget about the fire," Jo reminded her. "I overheard Charlie telling Annie that it might have been deliberately set, and they're planning to look into it with Dimple Kilpatrick. In fact, I wouldn't be surprised if they aren't on their way here now."

"And you want to beat them to the punch?"

Jo shrugged. "Something like that."

"Well then, what are we waiting for?" Lou moved quickly past her to see if she could find anything suspicious near Leola's closed-up house.

Jo Carr waited patiently while her sister circled the house, poking behind bushes and attempting to peek into shuttered windows. "I wish I knew what I was looking for!" Lou exclaimed at last.

"Well, you're not going to find it here. If somebody meant to set that fire, he obviously did it closer to the road. The fire never reached as far as the house," Jo pointed out. "I think we should look in the other direction."

Walking slowly down the long drive that led to the road, Jo searched the area on one side and Lou covered the other. After crossing a narrow bridge, they discovered a wide splotch of scorched grass bordering the shallow stream that ran across the property. "This looks like where it might have been set," Jo said. "See . . . it burned this patch here and then trailed off along the creek bank in one direction and meandered along the driveway to the main road in the other. I wonder if there's anything under the bridge." Climbing down from the road, she made her way through blackened singed grass where tender green blades were already beginning to peek through and shoved aside a head-high stalk of pokeweed to look underneath.

"See anything?" Lou knelt on her hands and knees on the bridge above her.

Jo shook her head. "Nope, but I don't see how this fire could've been started by somebody tossing a cigarette from a passing car when this is the spot that received the most damage and it's way too far from the road. It's obvious the fire began here and then spread in two directions." She looked about to see if anyone had left behind what would now have been the charred remains of a torch, but if that was what was used, it had been consumed in the fire.

Frowning, Lou climbed down to join her. "I think you're right, Jo. I wonder if Leola surprised someone setting the fire and the person dropped the match or whatever he was using and ran."

"Or it might've been started with kerosene," Jo said. "I guess the smell would've washed away by now, wouldn't it? Remember, we had a heavy rain not too long after that happened, so a lot of it probably would've run off into the creek."

Her sister didn't answer, but stood studying the narrow brown stream that moved sluggishly over rocks and between eroded banks before twisting out of sight under the main bridge at the road.

"What is it?" Jo demanded. Lou was seldom this still and quiet.

"I don't know, but I think I see something. It's caught on a tree root downstream."

Jo looked where her sister was pointing. "Just looks like a stick to me. . . ." But Lou had already plunged ahead, and, breaking off a fragrant limb of sassafras that hung over the bank, she fished the blackened object in question from its muddy enclosure. The top part of the vertical stick had been burned to within an inch or so of where it was lashed to a crosspiece and the part that remained was wrapped in strips of cloth, now soggy and stained with ashes and mud.

Lou held it up for her sister to see, wishing for all the world that she could scrub away the awful significance of what she had found. "It's a cross,

Jo. That's what it was meant to be before part of it burned away. Somebody tried to burn a cross on Leola's property. *Why would anybody have done that to her?*"

Jo Carr didn't know. She only knew she wanted to cry, and to get as far away from this hateful place as she could. Leola had owned the land she lived on for as long as she could remember. Why had somebody objected to that all this time later and attempted to frighten her away?

Lou shivered and tossed the hateful thing aside. "We've got to tell the sheriff about this, Jo. This should prove that fire was no accident."

Jo agreed, and reluctantly picked up the remains of the charred cross. "I don't want to take a chance on leaving this here. You can show him later where you found it."

Neither spoke until they were on their way back to town, when Jo turned to her sister and smiled.

Lou frowned. "What do you find so amusing?"

"I was just thinking how surprised Miss Dimple and the others will be when they learn what we found out."

But Dimple was busy for most of the day, heading up a scrap-metal drive, and didn't learn of the sisters' discovery until she returned for supper at Phoebe's, where Annie told them of the news.

This was met with stunned silence all around until the horror of the discovery struck home. "I find this hard to believe," Phoebe uttered under her breath in case Odessa might overhear from the kitchen. "I don't know of anyone who didn't think the world of Leola Parker. Whoever's responsible must be mean to the core!"

"Add stupid and ignorant to that," Velma Anderson sputtered. "It takes a special kind of idiot to do a thing like that."

"Oh dear!" Lily Moss clutched a napkin to her lips and looked about, as if she expected someone to tell her it wasn't so.

"Does this kind of thing happen very much around here?" Annie asked. "I thought all that Klan business was a thing of the past."

Miss Dimple spoke at last. "Unfortunately not. But I haven't heard of any recent activity, and frankly, I wonder if someone else might be behind this."

"But who?" Phoebe asked. "And for heaven's sake, *why?*"

Dimple helped herself to the pineapple-carrot gelatin salad and passed the mold along to Velma. "That's what we have to find out," she said, "and the sooner, the better."

"I wonder why Sheriff Holland and his bunch didn't notice that before?" Velma asked. "They've been out there several times now, haven't they?" She shook her head. "It must've been embarrassing to have two women show them up like that."

"Charlie said her mother told her he got kind of flustered and turned as red as a strawberry," Annie said. "He told her it was probably lodged under the bridge or something until a heavy rain washed it downstream, but Charlie's mother believes it was tossed onto the grass on the other side of the bridge from the house. She said it looks like that's where the fire began to spread."

"So what do they plan to do now?" Phoebe asked. "I hope it's not too late to find out who's responsible."

"I imagine Sheriff Holland's familiar with the hoodlums associated with the Klan," Miss Dimple said. "I would think he'd begin there."

But she doubted if it would do any good.

After supper, everyone gathered around the radio in Phoebe Chadwick's parlor to listen to the war news on the radio. Sometimes the commentator would be H. V. Kaltenborn or gentle-voiced Gabriel Heatter, who often began his broadcasts with "Ah, there's good [or bad] news tonight." Tonight's announcer was Edward R. Murrow.

Phoebe's young grandson, Harrison, had been part of the taking of Kwajalein Atoll in the South Pacific with the Seventh Division of the 111th Infantry Regiment the winter before and was still somewhere in the Marshall Islands. Annie's fiancé, Frazier, had been among those landing on Normandy beach on D-day in June and was now with the troops attempting to break out of the beachhead and push on to Paris. Her brother, Joel, was a bomber pilot somewhere in Europe, and for Annie, the most difficult part of her day was listening to the news. Sometimes she wanted to cover her ears and hide, but for days on end it was the only link she had to two of the most important men in her life.

Others felt much the same. Phoebe usually found something to do with her hands, such as mending or crocheting, but even so, she listened with a statuelike countenance until the broadcast ended. And Annie knew that everything came to a standstill in the Carr household as Jo Carr and her daughters paid strict attention for any mention of the areas where Fain, Ned, or Will might be fighting.

Dimple sat silently, so as not to miss a word, and prayed that the children she had watched become men would make it safely home. The names of those who hadn't were already written on her heart.

The dreadful violence and the resulting grief that came with this war could not be avoided, but the needless death of a young woman and the hurtful incident directed at Leola Parker stirred an innate longing deep inside her that yearned to put things right.

Phoebe tucked her mending away in her basket when the broadcast came to an end, and Lily and

Velma went outside to sit on the porch after Edward R. Murrow signed off in his customary manner, wishing everyone "Good night and good luck." Dimple had little doubt they were going to need it. Annie, she noticed, seemed so restless, it was almost painful to watch her.

Dimple approached her as she stood by the window. Outside, a lawn sprinkler swish-swished in the grass, showering the pink impatiens in the side yard with glistening drops. "Why don't you try to speak with your young man's parents again," she suggested. "They're sure to be at home by now, don't you think?"

Annie turned with a startled look, and Miss Dimple could see she was trying to hold back the tears. "I'm afraid of what they might tell me," she admitted in a voice so low, Dimple could hardly hear her.

Sooner or later, you'll have to know the truth, Dimple thought, but it would have been cruel to speak it aloud, so she said nothing and remained where she was.

"Will you go with me? I mean, stand there with me while I make the call?" Annie said at last.

Dimple slipped her arm through Annie's. "Of course I will," she said.

It seemed to take forever for Florence McCrary to connect them with Frazier's parents in the little town of Ringgold, Georgia, and Annie felt herself stiffen as the telephone rang two . . . three . . . four times before someone picked up the receiver. Watching her, Miss Dimple started to move away, but Annie motioned for her to stay.

"Oh, Annie dear, it's so good to hear from you," Frazier's mother said after Annie told her who was calling. "We all can't wait to meet you! Why, from all Frazier has told us, we feel like we know you already."

Annie smiled, relaxing a little. If the Duncans had received bad news, they would be having a different conversation.

"No, we haven't heard in several weeks," his mother said, answering Annie's question, "but we have to keep in mind he probably hasn't had an opportunity to write with all that's going on. I expect we'll hear something before too long. Sometimes we even receive several letters at once." Her words were warm and comforting, and they embraced Annie like an enveloping hug. "I'll telephone when we hear," Mrs. Duncan assured her, "and, Annie, I hope you'll do the same."

Annie turned to Miss Dimple, smiling. "She sounds so nice, Miss Dimple. I think I'm going to love Frazier's mother."

"Now, aren't you glad you called?" Dimple said. "I hope you'll be able to get a good night's sleep."

Annie agreed, and went upstairs to bed with a

lighter heart, but in spite of her assurances, something Frazier's mother had said haunted her still: ". . . he probably hasn't had an opportunity to write with all that's been going on."

She knew what was going on over there and it wasn't encouraging.

CHAPTER EIGHTEEN

L et's play war," Willie Elrod suggested to his friend Junior Henderson. "We can pretend to be soldiers and Ruthie and Lee Anne will be the enemy. We'll take 'em prisoner and lock 'em in your garage."

"Oh no we won't! The last time we did that, Lee Anne broke all the fruit jars in there that my mama was saving to put up all that stuff out of the garden."

"Okay, then, let's pretend like it's D-day and I'll be one of our soldiers landing on the beach. You can be the Japanese—you can even be Tojo if you want to," Willie promised.

Junior groaned. "Don't you know *anything?* Old Tojo resigned the other day. He's not chief minister anymore. He might not even be a general."

Willie frowned. He knew he should keep up with the war better than he did. He always paid attention when they showed *The March of Time* at the picture show, but when the rest of his family gathered around the radio for news broadasts, he was always outside somewhere, it seemed.

That morning, however, Willie had overheard his mama and Mrs. Sullivan from across the street talking about something that had happened a few days before in Prussia.

"Well, I'll bet I know something you don't, Mr. Smarty!" Willie looked around and dropped his voice. "Couple of days ago, some of Hitler's own men tried to do the old devil in. They were gonna get rid of him for once and all, but I guess he got wise to them, and—" Willie made a schlepping noise and drew his finger across his throat. "I reckon that's the end of them."

"That's too bad," Junior said. "They would've done us all a favor."

Willie grinned. "Hey, I know! You can be Hitler and I'll be one of the—"

But Junior was having none of it. "How come *you* always get to be the good guy and *I'm* the enemy? Besides, I'm tired of playing war all the time. Let's play something else."

The day before, the two had been to see the film *Tarzan Triumphs*, in which Tarzan fights the Nazis, and Willie agreed that would be the next best thing to playing war. They found the two girls dressing paper dolls on Ruthie's front porch, and armed with stout sticks to make their way through the jungle, the four started out for their favorite Tarzan setting, since their school principal, "Froggy" Faulkenberry, forbade them to climb in the big oak tree on the playground.

"I wish we had some alligators," Willie said as they neared the bridge over the Oconee River. "Seems like Tarzan's always fighting alligators."

Lee Anne shivered. "Well, I'm glad we don't. You'll just have to fight pretend alligators."

Turning off the road, they picked their way single file along the path beside the river. "My mama told me I wasn't to go close to the water," Ruthie announced. "Even if you're a good swimmer, that current can catch you before you know what's happening and sweep you away."

"Aw, I'm not afraid of any river!" Willie's mother had told him the same thing, but he wasn't going to admit it.

"Then let's see you go down there and stick your foot in the water," Junior dared.

"You'd better not, Willie." Lee Anne clutched at his sleeve. "Really. You might fall in and drown."

Of course that was all Willie needed—that and the fact that Lee Anne actually cared if he drowned or not. Lee Anne Stephens was pretty, with light brown hair that curled around her face, and her pink cotton halter top concealed small buds that would soon become breasts. Although Willie had learned to swim at Boy Scout camp, he had a deep respect for the river. It was swift and dark and deep, and far too wide for him to swim across it.

"Well . . . what are you waiting for?" Junior urged. "I double-dog dare you!"

There was no way he was going to back down from a double-dog dare. Gingerly, Willie plunged down the steep bank, stopping short at the water's edge. *What was that awful smell?*

He grabbed a slender sapling to keep from sliding farther. Something that looked like a sack of old clothes was bundled at the foot of a sycamore tree whose branches hung over the rushing water. The odor of rotting flesh was almost suffocating in its intensity.

Willie stumbled backward. "Gah!" he shouted, turning away in an effort not to throw up.

"What's the matter, chicken?" Junior taunted. "I thought you weren't afraid!"

"There's something down here—*somebody*. I think they're dead." Willie scrambled up the bank to join the others. He had come across decaying animals before and knew the smell of death, but never anything like this, never a *person*. "We've got to go find somebody. . . . We've gotta get help." Willie clamped his hand over his nose and mouth to shut out the smell. He wanted to go home and scrub with Octagon soap from his head to his feet, and then do it all over again.

"How do you know they're dead?" Ruthie asked. "I think you're just making that up."

"Aw, that's only a bunch of old clothes," Junior persisted. "You're just scared to get near the water."

"Okay, go see for yourself if you're so brave," Willie challenged. "*I'm* going to call Chief Tinsley."

"Huh! Just wait and I'll prove it," Junior said, and not to be outdone, he made his way down to where the pathetic bundle lay. The smell was worse than his grandpa's outhouse, but he held his breath and gave the pile a hasty poke with his foot.

The mound of garments shifted, exposing a grinning skull. Spiders scurried from the empty eye sockets and the claw of a skeletal hand slid from a shredded sleeve.

Junior's scream echoed in his head and continued until his throat hurt so much, he couldn't scream anymore. The others had been hollering, too, but now the only sound he heard was his own sobbing breath, and Junior realized he was still standing barely two feet away from a horror he had never imagined even in his worst nightmares. And his friends had left him there.

Somebody tugged at his shirt and he turned and struck at the air. "Leave me alone! Stop it! Leave me alone!"

"It's just me, dummy! Come on, let's get outta

here!" Grabbing Junior's hand, Willie half-pulled, half-shoved him the rest of the way up the steep hill and back along the path to where the two girls waited, trembling by the bridge.

"What *was* that?" Ruthie gulped between sobs. "I've never been so scared in my life!"

"A dead body," Lee Anne said, and she suddenly felt cold in the heat of a Georgia summer. "I wonder how long it's been there." She had seen a dead person before—but not one like that. Her great-grandma had been laid out properly on a lace pillow, with her hands all folded in front of her like she was done with all her work on earth and ready to rest.

"How you reckon it got there?" Junior asked, now that he could get his breath. "Oh gosh! What if it was a *murder?*"

"Oh, hush, Junior," Lee Anne said, racing on ahead. "You always make things sound worse than they are. It's probably just a tramp who was passing through and got sick and died there."

Willie thought he knew who the dead person was, but he wasn't going to say anything. Chief Tinsley would know what to do, and since they were the ones who'd found the corpse—or what was left of it—maybe the chief would let them in on the investigation.

"It *might've* been a murder," Junior persisted as they hurried back to town. "And whoever did it *might even have come back* to see if the body has been discovered. They could've been watching us the whole time! Did you ever think of that?"

Nobody had, and nobody answered, but everyone ran just a little faster.

Willie Elrod didn't even think of crying until he spied Miss Dimple Kilpatrick crossing the street on her way back from town and he ran right up to her and buried his head in her middle. She was his bastion, his refuge, and the two of them had been through trying times together.

"Why, Willie, what in the world is wrong? You look like you've seen a ghost." With a calming hand, she brushed his strawlike hair from his brow and held him at arm's length, although she would have liked nothing better than to hold him close. It wouldn't do to show favoritism to one child above another, although he would always have a special place in her heart. It made her smile to remember six-year-old Willie's gift to her of a small box of Valentine candy when he was in her first-grade classroom. "Now, if you don't like candy, Miss Dimple," he'd said, "you can give it back to me—but you can keep the box!" Of course she had shared the chocolates with him.

"It's worse than a ghost, Miss Dimple. We just saw a *dead person*—nothing left but a bunch of bones!" Junior told her. "No tellin' how long it's been there."

And bit by bit, the others filled in the necessary—and sometimes unnecessary—details.

Later at the police station, the four gave the particulars to Chief Bobby Tinsley, who thanked them for the information and told them he would get in touch if anything further was needed.

"Maybe we'll get our pictures in the paper," Ruthie said when the interview was over. But Willie was disappointed. Having read just about every book in the Hardy Boys mystery series, he had expected to be included in the actual investigation.

"Are they sure it was Hattie's body they found?" Annie asked Miss Dimple when she reported the news. The two sat at the kitchen table with Phoebe after supper that night, cutting up apples to make applesauce from the tree by the back steps.

"It seems so from what remained of the clothing . . . and of course the size." She didn't want to go into details about how animals and insects had destroyed most of the flesh, but Bobby Tinsley had conveyed as much when she'd questioned him earlier about the dead person's identity.

Phoebe frowned. "Oh, that poor thing! How long do they think she's been . . . er . . . I mean, can they tell when this might've happened?"

"Not exactly, but they believe she's been dead for at least two weeks—possibly three," Miss Dimple told her. "In this hot weather and with all the humidity, it wouldn't have taken long."

Annie added a handful of apple slices to the pan on the table. "But didn't Grady Clinkscales say he *saw* Hattie pushing her wheelbarrow not too long ago? Remember? He said he called to her but she acted like she didn't hear him."

Miss Dimple nodded. "And Clay claimed to have seen her, too. She was collecting bottles somewhere near the high school."

"But she didn't turn them in," Annie added. "We found the wheelbarrow still full of bottles behind her trailer."

Phoebe frowned as she sliced an apple into fourths. "Then somebody must've been pretending to be Hattie. Why in the world would they do that?"

"I suppose they didn't want anyone to know when she died," Dimple said. "There doesn't seem to be any doubt she was killed intentionally."

"Do they know how?" Annie asked.

Together, Dimple and Phoebe lifted the full pan of apples to the stove, where they added lemon wedges and water. Dimple clamped a lid on the pot and paused to dry her hands on her apron. "Dr. Morrison said she probably died of a broken neck. He believes she either fell or was pushed from the ledge above the place where she was found. There's a steep incline there and it must've been dark, as they found a flashlight beneath her." She hesitated before telling them that investigators had also found what once had been rose petals scattered near the body.

"Well, she couldn't have been killed by the Rose Petal Killer," Annie pointed out. "He was already locked away by then."

"I suppose whoever killed her didn't know that," Phoebe said. "It wouldn't take much of a fall to break those brittle old bones." She shook her head. "Bless her heart, the town won't seem the same without her. I'm going to miss that old bird, even if she did help herself to my Queen of Denmark rose. Remember, Dimple? I had it out by the corner of the house, and then one morning I looked out and it was gone. Nothing left but a hole in the ground!"

Annie admitted the old woman had acquired quite a collection. "Maybe you could go over there and dig it up," she suggested. But Phoebe made a face and shook her head. "No, thank you. The very idea would give me nightmares. I think I'll just leave well enough alone. What I can't understand," she added, "is what she was doing down there by the river in the first place, and it must have been dark, since she had a flashlight with her."

"Chief Tinsley seems to think she was headed for that old fishing shack down there," Dimple explained. "She's used it some in the past, and he said she'd go there to collect bottles from time to time."

"But the wheelbarrow wasn't with her when she was found," Phoebe began. "So . . ."

"So whoever took it was the one who killed her," Annie finished.

But why? Why would anyone want to kill harmless Hattie McGee?

The pleasant smell of stewing apples filled the kitchen. When they were tender, they would put them through a food mill, add sugar and cinnamon, and simmer them a little longer. A cheerful late-summer task shared with friends. Dimple would have liked to bask in the comfort of it, but something was very wrong in this town, and she couldn't rest until she learned the reason behind it.

CHAPTER NINETEEN

Virginia Balliew stamped the return date in the mysteries Dimple had selected from the library and nuzzled the big orange cat in her lap. Cattus meowed a complaint and jumped to the window ledge behind her, almost knocking over a bud vase with its one yellow blossom from the bush by Virginia's front steps. "Ungrateful wretch!" Virginia mumbled.

The flower reminded Dimple of Hattie and her strange passion for other people's roses and she frowned as she accepted the books, stacking one on top of the other. The walk to the library that morning had refreshed her, and for a few minutes she had put the gloomy puzzle of Hattie's death and the murder of young Prentice Blair from her mind.

Virginia looked up at her and smiled. "Why so sad and wan?" She knew, of course, that Dimple would be fretting over what had happened to Hattie McGee. "You must know, Dimple, that you can't cure all the ills of the world. As much as you would like to, you can't make all the bad things go away."

Dimple sighed. "Well, at least I can try. I don't understand this, Virginia, and I'm concerned about Chloe Jarrett and Clay, and . . . well, Knox, too. They've had to deal with this awful thing that happened to Prentice, and now Hattie has—"

"Well, from the look on your faces, I see you must've heard the news." Lou Willingham, her arms full of books, bustled inside and bumped the door shut with her ample rear.

Virginia looked up. "Right. We were talking about Hattie McGee."

Lou deposited her books on the return table and shook her head. "Poor Hattie! What a terrible way to go. . . . Makes me sick to think of it, but I was talking about Clay Jarrett. Did you know they arrested him this morning for Prentice Blair's murder?"

Dimple reached out and gripped the corner of the desk in front of her. "Then they've made a big mistake," she said. "Whatever led them to come to that conclusion?"

"It doesn't look good, Dimple," Lou said. "The police found Prentice's high school class ring in the glove box of that old truck Clay drives."

"What kind of evidence is that?" Dimple Kilpatrick came close to sputtering. "The two were a couple for over two years, weren't they?"

"Whoa! Don't shoot the messenger." Lou held up a hand. "Bertie had planned to bury Prentice with that ring, but Prentice wasn't wearing it when she died and Bertie was sure she'd had it on the morning she disappeared."

"So why wait this long to mention it?" Virginia asked.

Lou shrugged. "I suppose she thought it would turn up, but after she searched through Prentice's jewelry box and practically turned the house upside down looking for it, with no luck, Bertie finally called in Bobby Tinsley."

Virginia frowned. "How can they be sure how that ring got there? It seems to me Bobby Tinsley's looking for easy answers."

"There aren't any easy answers," Dimple said. "As I've said before, I believe this all hinges on what happened to Leola Parker."

Lou pulled up a chair and dabbed her moist face with a pink-flowered hankie. "Law, it's as hot as Hades already out there. . . . But that's just the point, you see, now the police are beginning to think Clay Jarrett started that fire because he was upset with Leola.

"Listen, I know it doesn't make sense," she added when the others protested. "I can't for the life of me imagine Clay doing anything so downright mean and underhanded. It's simply not in him. It looks to me like somebody was trying to frighten Leola off her land."

"But why would they do that?" Virginia asked.

"Perhaps her daughter can give us some answers," Dimple suggested. "I think Mary Joy still lives in Covington. I'll try to get in touch."

But first she must go, she decided, and lend her support to the Jarretts.

"Thank goodness you're here," Knox Jarrett said as he greeted Dimple when she arrived later that day. "Chloe's sitting in the parlor. It's dark as pitch in there, but she won't let me open the shades and I can't get her to talk to me. I don't know what to do."

"I'll speak to her," Miss Dimple said softly, taking his hand in hers. She noticed he had at least two days' growth of beard and his eyes were red and bleary with worry, and no doubt lack of sleep, as well. She left him there in a front porch rocker with an old Collie dog for comfort and company and was glad to see Walter Dunnagan, the family minister, arriving right behind her.

Chloe Jarrett sat rigidly in a Victorian chair that looked uncomfortable, but if it was, she didn't seem to notice or to care. She wore a light cotton housedress and blue bedroom slippers—or at least Dimple thought they were blue. It was hard to see in the dimness of the room. Chloe's hands were clasped on her lap and she didn't seem to notice when Dimple entered the room, although Dimple made a point to close the door firmly behind her and walked with steady steps to approach her.

She chose a straight chair and moved it to sit facing the woman. "Chloe," she began, "why are you sitting in here in the dark? Preacher Dunnagan is here with Knox. Why don't you come and join them on the porch?"

But Chloe didn't answer and she didn't change her expression, and for a few seconds, Dimple found herself thinking of Brer Rabbit's conversation with the Tar Baby, a favorite tale of her schoolchildren.

Miss Dimple took a deep breath, asked her Creator for patience, and sat with the woman in silence until Chloe began to fidget ever so slightly, first by shifting one foot a half inch or so, then raising a couple of fingers.

"How is this helping Clay?" Dimple persisted. "He needs your support now more than ever, and so does your husband." Reaching out, she took

Chloe's slender hand, worn and freckled with all the cooking, scrubbing, and canning from her years on the farm. "You're bigger than this, Chloe Jarrett, and you're not in this alone."

A shiver went through Chloe's frail body and then a sigh and a gasp. She began to cry, softly at first, and then the floodgates opened. Miss Dimple was glad she had thought to bring an extra handkerchief, as both were pressed into service.

"Oh, Dimple, you should've seen my boy when they took him away! I felt so helpless, like we had abandoned him, and there was nothing we could do." Chloe pressed the first hankie to her mouth and reached for the second.

"He knows very well you haven't abandoned him, and neither have we," Dimple assured her. "We have to be strong for Clay, for each other." Dimple went to the window and raised the shade to let sunlight stream across the floor.

"We've known Bobby Tinsley all his life and he's known us. How can he possibly think our Clay did all the things they say he did? He swears he doesn't know how that girl's ring got in his car. Why won't they believe him?" Chloe blinked in the sunlight and shifted in her chair. "Whoever put that ring in there is the one who killed Prentice Blair!

"Now they're claiming he might've had something to do with what happened to Hattie

McGee! Clay was fond of that crazy old woman, Dimple. He really cared about her. Why would he have wanted to hurt Hattie?" She sniffed and looked about for another handkerchief, but Dimple hadn't brought another backup, so she made do with what she had.

"Of course he wouldn't," Dimple assured her. "We all know that."

Chloe rose and went to the window, twitched at the lace curtain hanging there. "Did you know the only prints they found on that wheelbarrow were Hattie's? Somebody brought it back here, Dimple, somebody dressed like Hattie. It was left behind her trailer—not far from the Shed. . . . Anybody could've done it."

Through the open window they heard low voices from the porch, where the Methodist minister was consoling or attempting to console Knox, and Dimple took inspiration from it. "You must know, Chloe, that the community is behind you. We *know* Clay and we believe in his innocence."

"So why did they arrest him?" Chloe asked, facing her.

"I assume it's because the evidence—what there is of it—points to Clay. And there's nobody else in the picture—at least right now. But I told you in the beginning I would help find out the truth, and I will."

She was relieved to see a glimmer of hope in Chloe's eyes. "The phone has been ringing all day, but I just didn't have the courage to answer it," Chloe said. She smiled as she held out a hand. "Knox and I will be mighty grateful, Dimple, for anything you can do . . . and now, I guess I'd better go out and speak to Walter."

Dimple Kilpatrick straightened her shoulders. Like John Paul Jones, she had not yet begun to fight.

"I wonder who might have the telephone number for Leola's daughter, Mary Joy," Dimple remarked to Phoebe when she reached home that afternoon. "I suppose I could ask Elberta, but with Clay being arrested for what happened to Prentice, I don't think that's such a good idea right now."

"Odessa might know," Phoebe suggested. "I think a cousin of hers married one of Leola's nieces, or something like that," and she hurried to the kitchen, where Odessa was chopping vegetables for a pot of soup for supper.

"Odessa doesn't know," she said upon returning. "Her cousin moved to Detroit a couple of years ago and she doesn't have his number, but she said Leola's preacher might have it. It's the Reverend Abraham Lincoln Hamilton and I think he lives over on Blossom Street. He should be in the phone book."

Dimple smiled. She knew the Reverend Hamilton. The two had worked together on a paper drive back in the spring, but the preacher wasn't in and his wife said she knew they had that number somewhere but she just couldn't put her hands on it.

Miss Dimple went to the porch and sat in the rocking chair in the lengthening shade of the willow oak in the front yard. Clay had been arrested and the truth wasn't going to wait. She needed to get in touch with Mary Joy *tonight*. Surely *somebody* would know how to help her. It would have to be someone Leola had trusted to get in touch with her daughter if trouble arose or if she became ill. She could try the Reverend Hamilton later and hope he still had the number, and of course there was Elberta, but only as a last resort. *Who else might Leola ask to contact Mary Joy in case of an emergency?* Miss Dimple rocked a little faster . . . and then the answer came.

Inside in the hallway, she picked up the telephone. "Florence, get me Dr. Morrison, please." And after a few minutes' wait, the good doctor picked up the phone. Yes, of course he had the number, he said. He would never forget the dark day he'd had to call Mary Joy to tell her about her mother, and after a period of paper shuffling, he gave Dimple the information she wanted.

"I know it's none of my business," he said before hanging up, "but do you mind telling me just what you have in mind?"

"I'm hoping Mary Joy might have some idea about why anyone would want her mother off her land," Dimple told him. "And remember, this is between the two of us, Ben."

Ben Morrison smiled to himself. "And *you* remember, I'm very good at keeping secrets, Dimple Kilpatrick." Never in this lifetime would he let anyone know she had a bright pink birthmark in the shape of a rabbit on the outside of her right thigh.

Mary Joy's husband, Luther, answered the phone when she finally got connected almost ten minutes later, and Dimple could hear Florence McCrary's loud breathing as she listened in from her switchboard. Florence had a touch of asthma and the rasping gave her away every time.

"Thank you, Florence!" Dimple spoke loudly before identifying herself to Luther and was gratified to hear a dead silence on the operator's end. But Mary Joy, she learned, had left the day before to take care of Luther's elderly mother after some kind of surgery he was reluctant to discuss, and he expected her to be away for at least a week.

"Do you have a phone number or some way I can get in touch?" Miss Dimple asked. But Luther's mother didn't have a telephone and lived several miles away, out in the country, not too far from Griffin, Georgia, he told her.

Determined now, Dimple persisted. "Just which side of Griffin? Can you give me some directions? I really need to see her and I don't have much time."

"Well . . . it's between Zebulon and Orchard Hill, only you turn left before you get there. There's a little old store on the right—has a rooster painted on it—and you'll see a silo right before you turn, but don't go past Robinson's Mill. Road's awful bad there and you'll have to turn around and backtrack. Her name's on the mailbox—Maisie Hodges. Can't miss it," Luther added.

Miss Dimple thanked him and, feeling thoroughly confused, went in search of pencil and paper to jot down the directions.

Annie eagerly agreed to go with her the next day, hoping it would keep her from dwelling on the weeks that had elapsed since she'd heard from Frazier. The night before, she had reread his letters until the words blurred together. She knew he had survived the D-day invasion of Normandy and was literally crawling inch by inch and foot by foot to help drive the German army out of France; and on July 28, American forces had captured the key town of Coustances. *So where was Frazier Duncan?*

Charlie was willing to drive if the others would share their gas rations, as gasoline was still in short supply. She hoped Mary Joy would be able to tell them something, as there didn't seem to be any other leads.

Later in her room, Charlie sat down to write to Will and told him in her letter about the children finding what was left of Hattie McGee, but she didn't tell him the authorities had determined it wasn't a natural death. Although Will was entertained by her tales of adventures with Miss Dimple and Annie, he was concerned they were taking chances with their own safety after he learned of the danger they had encountered only a few months before. But it was nothing, she thought, to the perils he faced every day. He never mentioned his time in the air or the close calls she knew he'd had. She did know he had lost several good friends and she lived in fear the next one would be him.

Instead, she told him how fast Delia's little Pooh was growing and what fun she was having being around a baby, as one day she hoped they would have some of their own. The thought made her long for him even more. A part of her was missing and Charlie wished she could climb into the envelope and mail herself to him in England—or wherever he was now. It only made things worse to dwell on all the things that might have happened since she'd last heard. He probably just hadn't had time to write.

She had lost count of the times she had read his last letter, and now she read it again.

My own Charlie,

Do you know how very much I love you? Miss you? I'll bet you didn't know you go with me everywhere, as I keep your picture in the cockpit, and all the fellows who've seen it are jealous of my good luck—although they don't understand it one bit. I don't, either, but I'm darned grateful for it and for having you in my life.

This is the greenest place I've ever seen and the countryside, except for the bombed areas, is beautiful. I'd love to bring you here someday when this blasted war is over. We listened to Bob Hope on BBC radio the other night and it made me think of home and how lucky we are to live in the good old USA. It's a country worth fighting for and I'm proud to do my part.

Keep writing and keep on loving me and pray it won't be long until I hold you in my arms once again.

Yours always,
Will

Charlie put the thin, wrinkled letter under her pillow and went to sleep, dreaming of their last time together. He'd had a few days' leave at the end of February, before being shipped overseas, and on the last night she had gone to sleep in his arms on the sofa in front of the living room fire. And that was the way she wanted to go to sleep for the rest of her life.

CHAPTER TWENTY

"Of course you can use the car today," Jo Carr told Charlie over breakfast the next morning, "but you won't get far on the few gas rations we have left."

"Annie and Miss Dimple are helping out with that," Charlie said, noticing an immediate gleam in her mother's eyes at the mention of those two names. "And we won't be driving all that far," she continued, trying to make the prospect sound as dull as possible.

"Oh, and what are the travel plans for today?" Jo asked. She concentrated on spreading margarine on her toast as she spoke, as if she wasn't all that interested, but she didn't fool her daughter for one minute. Charlie knew she might as well tell her mother the truth and deal with the consequences.

"We thought we'd try to talk with Mary Joy Hodges—you know, Leola's daughter. She lives in Covington, but her husband said she was taking care of his mother for several days. She's had some kind of operation, I think. Anyway, his mother lives somewhere close to Griffin, and she doesn't have a telephone."

Jo bit into her toast and chewed thoughtfully. "I suppose this is all about that fire at Leola's."

Charlie busied herself slicing a peach onto her cornflakes, and with a shrug she told her mother Miss Dimple thought it would be worthwhile to find out if Mary Joy might have an idea why anybody would do something like that.

"Somebody wanted Leola Parker off that land." Jo faced her daughter and spoke in a matter-of-fact voice.

Charlie nodded. "It would seem that way."

"Hmm . . ." Jo sipped her coffee and let the steam waft into her face. "I wish Lou and I could go with you. I just have a feeling we could find out *something*—and I used to be fairly familiar with that area, you know. My old college roommate lived on the other side of Griffin. . . . You remember Olivia, don't you? Married a lawyer and moved up north. I never could see what she saw in him . . . had an Adam's apple as big as a baseball and talked through his nose."

Charlie smiled. She remembered Olivia and thought she was probably lucky to have landed the lawyer who talked through his nose.

"But Mama, aren't you and Aunt Lou supposed to work at the ordnance plant today?" Of course they were, and Charlie knew it very well. That

238

was why she felt safe in telling her mother about today's mission.

Jo Carr frowned. "You're right, but I do wish we could go along. That fire didn't start from the road, you know, and if it hadn't been for Lou and me, who knows how long it would've been before they figured that out?"

Charlie laughed and hugged her mother. "You're right. They'd probably still be in the dark, but Miss Dimple doesn't feel like we can afford to wait on this now that they've arrested Clay." She planted a kiss on Jo's cheek. "I promise I'll give you a full report tonight when I get home."

"It's not that I don't want them to come," Charlie explained to the others later as they drove past the courthouse on their way out of town. "It's just that they always end up putting their lives in danger, and I'd never forgive myself if anything happened to those two."

Beside her in the front seat, Dimple frowned over her bifocals. "And don't you think your mother might feel the same about you? It's not as if you haven't given her good reason."

Charlie sighed. She had to agree Miss Dimple was right. "Okay. Maybe next time," she said.

It was half past nine before they left, and already the sun scorched the streets with a bold yellow light. The statue of the Cherokee Indian that marked the town's limits looked as if he would welcome a cooling shower or at least a tall glass of iced tea.

"How far is it to this place where Mary Joy's mother-in-law lives?" Annie asked from the backseat.

"You remember Griffin, don't you?" Charlie reminded her. "We went there with Will and your brother, Joel, soon after we started teaching together—had lunch at that little place right outside of town."

Annie laughed. "Oh my gosh! How could I forget? That seems like a million years ago. Is this place close to there? Does anybody have directions?"

Miss Dimple took a folded paper from her purse. "I have this for a start, if I can decipher it. At least it should give us an idea of where to begin."

"Look! Isn't that a new rhyme?" Annie said, calling their attention to a series of small Burma Shave signs placed at intervals along the roadside. She read them aloud as they passed:

> *Maybe you can't shoulder a gun*
> *But you can shoulder the cost of one*
> *Buy defense bonds*
> *Burma Shave*

Miss Dimple smiled. "That must be a new one. I don't think I've seen it before." The verses not only livened up what might be a monotonous drive but often carried a patriotic message.

"Tell us again where we're headed," Charlie asked Miss Dimple as they left Elderberry several miles behind them.

Dimple unfolded the small paper she had taken from her handbag and frowned as she read it aloud. "According to Mary Joy's husband, Luther, it's between Zebulon and Orchard Hill, *only you turn left before you get there.*"

"Turn left before you get *where?*" Charlie asked.

Dimple examined her notes again. "To tell you the truth, I jotted this down so quickly, I'm really not sure. I suppose we'll just have to wait until we get close and try to find our way."

Annie shook her head. "Sounds like an adventure—oh, wait! Slow down, Charlie! There's a soldier up ahead. Looks like he needs a ride."

The young figure in khaki, duffel bag by his side, stood by the side of the road in the partial shade of a sweet-gum tree and his slender tan face broke into a wide smile when Charlie stopped beside him.

"Where to, soldier?" she asked, smiling.

Climbing into the back beside Annie, he hoisted his bag in behind him and leaned forward to thank the driver. "Anywhere near Sparta, thanks. I wasn't looking forward to standing out in that sun for long," he said with a grin. "We get enough of that at camp."

"Have you been waiting very long?" Annie asked.

"Only a few minutes. I've never had any trouble getting a ride. Most folks are glad to stop if they have room—and some even if they don't." He laughed. "On my way home on leave the other day, my buddy and I rode part of the way on the back of a truckload of chickens."

Charlie laughed. "And where's your buddy now?"

"Oh, he went on back to Fort Benning, but I have an extra day, so I'm stopping to see my girlfriend in Sparta."

"I don't think that's very far out of our way," Miss Dimple said with a questioning look at Charlie. "Perhaps we can take you there."

"I don't see why not," Charlie agreed, thinking someone would have probably done the same for Will and Fain. After introductions, they learned that Pvt. Jack O'Donnell from Rockmart, Georgia, was returning from a visit with his parents after completing his basic training at Fort Benning, in Columbus. "I saved a day of my leave to stop and see my girl before I have to go back to base," he explained. "It might be the last time I get to see her, as it looks like we might get shipped out sometime soon."

Miss Dimple tried to ignore the lump in her throat. "And what's your girl's name?"

The young soldier grinned. "Beth—well, it's

really Elizabeth, but nobody calls her that." He took a worn black-and-white photo from his wallet to show them, and everyone took turns telling him how pretty she was. They didn't have to exaggerate. Fair hair framed the oval face of the smiling young woman in the photo, which was signed, *Love you forever, Beth.* Miss Dimple hoped she meant it.

"We met at the university," Jack explained. "Both of us finished our freshman year before I signed up. I decided I might as well go on and get it over with. Beth has promised to wait."

"I hope she doesn't have to wait long," Miss Dimple told him.

Less than an hour later, the three women watched silently as Jack jumped from the car, tossed his duffel bag aside, and ran to embrace the smiling young woman who greeted him with outstretched arms. No one spoke until they had driven several miles down the road.

Finally, Annie, remembering the reason for their trip, blinked away her tears and asked if anyone had spoken to Clay.

"Delia went to see him yesterday," Charlie told them. "She said it was pretty grim."

Miss Dimple shook her head. "Losing someone you love is tragic enough, but to be *blamed* for her death! I can only imagine the turmoil he must be going through. Somebody *planted* that ring in there, but it won't do any good until we find out *who*." She eyed the road ahead as if she could will the car to speed up the miles in front of them. "Let's hope some good will come of today's efforts."

"It shouldn't be long," Charlie said. "It's not that far to Griffin."

"But shouldn't we turn at this other place first—what is it, Zebulon?" Annie asked.

Charlie glanced over her shoulder and frowned. "Okay, everybody, start looking for a sign."

"There's supposed to be a store on the right with a rooster painted on it." Miss Dimple examined her notes again. "And you'll see a silo just before you turn. . . . Where are you going, Charlie? I don't see any store."

"And I don't see any silo," Annie added as Charlie swung abruptly into a narrow side road and began to drive faster. "I don't think this is where we're supposed to turn, Charlie."

"Thought I'd try a shortcut," Charlie mumbled as they bumped over ruts in the road.

"Well, I suppose we can always turn around," Miss Dimple said, casting a quizzical look at the driver. She glanced at the darkening sky. "Oh, dear, it looks like it's coming up a storm."

"And a bad one," Charlie said as black clouds loomed overhead and the day that had begun bright and sunny turned dark and threatening. She increased her speed as she continued down the deserted country road, finally slowing as rain descended in sheets and the road became awash in water.

Charlie gripped the wheel and leaned forward. It was hard to see in the distance and the surface of the unpaved road was becoming mired in mud. "Good! Looks like some kind of building up ahead. I'm turning around before we get hopelessly stuck."

Dimple wondered why it wouldn't be just as easy to get stuck going the other way, but she withheld her opinion for the time being. "I believe it's a mill," she said. "Or it used to be. Seems to be abandoned."

Charlie glanced in the rearview mirror and took the next curve in a burst of speed. "Good! It couldn't come at a better time," she said, and turned quickly into the weed-covered entrance and circled behind the weather-washed building. "Keep down," she said as she parked behind a screen of scrub pine and turned off the engine.

Soon a dirt-spattered vehicle, slinging mud in its wake, sped past and disappeared over a hill. Immediately, Charlie turned back onto the road and started back the way they had come.

Annie leaned forward in her seat. "What in the world was *that* all about?"

"I didn't want to scare you, but this car has been following us since we left Sparta," Charlie told them. "Even when I made a couple of stops— remember when we bought cold drinks at that filling station back there, and circled the block to look at that pretty old church? It kept behind us. I thought I'd find out for sure by turning off here."

"Why would anybody be following us?" Annie asked.

Charlie slowed as she turned back onto the main road, then accelerated. "I don't know, and I don't want to find out."

Miss Dimple finally leaned back in her seat and allowed herself to relax. "I didn't want to mention this," she began, "but now that we're well on the way, I suppose it's all right to tell you. . . . That old mill back there was Robinson's Mill. The sign was faded, but I could still make out the letters. That was the road Luther advised us to avoid."

Charlie laughed. "Good thing I didn't know that earlier."

Miss Dimple was quiet for a few minutes, and then she said, "I wonder who knew we were coming here today."

"Do you think somebody followed us from Elderberry?" Charlie asked. "I told Mama, but that's all, and who would *she* tell . . . except Aunt Lou?"

"And I mentioned it to Ben Morrison and Phoebe, and I believe I might've said something to Virginia, too," Dimple confessed.

"I can't see what difference that makes," Annie said. "Who cares how many people knew where we were going today? Why would anybody want to follow us?"

Charlie concentrated on the road ahead. "I don't know, unless somebody wants to find out if we've talked to Mary Joy."

"But how would they know Mary Joy wasn't in Covington?" Annie asked.

They would learn the answer to that question when they finally arrived at Luther's mother's home a short while later.

$\mathcal{C}$HAPTER $\mathcal{T}$WENTY-ONE

The brief thunderstorm passed as quickly as it had come up, and by the time they noticed the sign to Zebulon, sunlight again sparkled on the grassy verges on either side of the road.

"I think I see the store Luther was talking about," Miss Dimple said a few minutes later, pointing out a small gray building ahead, and if one looked closely, you could barely make out the faded red rooster on the side.

Soon after that, Charlie turned onto a rutted dirt road immediately past the silo that Mary Joy's husband had mentioned.

Maisie Hodges lived in a small farmhouse set back from the road, and it looked like it had been there almost as long as the ancient oaks on either side. The house, although unpainted, looked neat and welcoming with bright red geraniums in tin-can planters lining the front porch railings. An elderly Negro woman sat in a rocking chair, shelling field peas into an enamel pan, and chickens strutted around a bare-swept yard.

"Hello! You must be Maisie." Miss Dimple stepped from the car to greet her. "I'm—"

The woman's face lit up in a broad smile. "I reckon you be Miss Dimple. My Luther said you was comin'." She started to rise. "Mary Joy, she out back hangin' out the wash again. Had to bring it all in when it started to rain."

"Ma Maisie, you sit yourself down and behave now, you hear?" Mary Joy, apron flapping, hurried around the side of the house and smiled at the newcomers. "Luther told us to look for you today. Come on up on the porch and have a seat. I'll bring us some iced tea."

Odessa had packed a Thermos of tea in their lunch basket, along with ham-salad sandwiches and a few tea cakes left over from Phoebe's last meeting of the Jolly Jonquils Garden Club, but it would have been rude to refuse refreshment, so they all trooped onto the porch and sat in the welcome shade.

Mary Joy introduced Luther's mother to everyone, explaining in a low voice that she was recuperating from *a female operation*.

Miss Dimple murmured appropriate sentiments.

"It feels twenty degrees cooler out here," she said. "You must enjoy this nice shady porch.

"But tell me," she added, addressing Mary Joy, "how did you know to expect us if you don't have a telephone?"

"Oh, Mr. Mule Blackstock tell us when he come by with the mail," Maisie said.

Annie smiled. *"Mule?"*

Mary Joy laughed. "Well, his real name's Thomas, but everybody calls him 'Mule' because he used to make his living selling them. He has a telephone and lives right down the road, so he doesn't mind bringing messages when he can. I reckon Luther's daddy worked for Mr. Mule forever, didn't he, Ma Maisie?"

Maisie Hodges smiled and nodded. "More'n thirty years, I reckon."

Luther, they learned, had received another call soon after Miss Dimple's, from someone asking how to get in touch with Mary Joy.

"Man wouldn't give his name and Luther didn't know who he was or what he was up to," Mary Joy said, "so he told him he didn't know how to get in touch with me."

The three visiting women exchanged glances. "So *that's* why that car was following us," Charlie said, and told the others what had happened.

"Did you recognize the car?" Mary Joy asked. But Charlie shook her head. "It was covered in mud and hard to see through all that rain, but I think it was black."

The others hadn't been able to see the car well, either, but as Annie pointed out, at least three-fourths of the automobiles made before the war were painted black. Manufacturers hadn't been making many since, as the country needed those materials for the war effort.

Mary Joy frowned. "Do you think the person who called was the one who followed you here?" she whispered to Charlie.

"We turned off the road and waited behind this old mill until the car passed, and didn't come out until it disappeared over the hill. I hope they're still looking in the wrong direction. I didn't notice anybody following us after we left it behind," Charlie assured her.

"Among those we told about coming here, who would've passed the information along?" Miss Dimple said. "I can't imagine who it would be."

"It would only take two," Charlie told her.

"And who would that be?" Annie asked.

Charlie shrugged. "Someone we told and Florence McCrary."

Mary Joy sighed. "You mean that woman who works the switchboard at the telephone company? Oh, law! I reckon the whole town knows by now!"

"But they don't know how to get here. If they did, they wouldn't have been following us," Charlie told her.

Miss Dimple sipped her tea. Mary Joy had garnished the drinks with a sprig of fresh mint, and that and the tinkle of ice almost made her forget it was over ninety degrees.

"There must have been a reason someone wanted to frighten your mother off her land," she said to Mary Joy. "Has anyone approached you about wanting to buy it?"

She shook her head. "Not me, but I think there was somebody bothering Mama for a while."

Miss Dimple frowned. "What do you mean?"

"She didn't say much about it, but I remember her getting several phone calls. I think it was back in the spring or the first part of the summer. You know, Mama was pretty patient, but this was getting on her nerves. She finally told them to leave her alone."

"Did she receive anything in writing?" Dimple asked.

"No, I don't think so. Mostly it was just phone calls, but a man came out one time to talk to her about it."

"What man?" Charlie asked.

Mary Joy shook her head. "Mama didn't know him. Said she never saw him before."

Miss Dimple paused to stroke a gray-striped cat that curled about her ankles. "And did he come back after that?" she asked.

"I don't think so. At least not that I know of," Mary Joy told her.

"He will," Annie said. "You can count on it."

"I think he already has," Miss Dimple said.

Mary Joy leaned forward in alarm. "Do you think *he set that fire?* That it was deliberate?"

Dimple nodded. "Either *he* did or he told someone to do it."

"I always thought we'd go back there one day—Luther and me," Mary Joy said. "It was only Mama and me after Papa died, and that place is home to me.

"That little piece of land between the house and the road isn't big enough to farm. Mama put in soybeans a couple of times, and once in a while she'd plant a little corn. You could put a few head of cattle on it I reckon, but other than that, I don't see what anybody would want it for."

"How many acres?" Charlie asked.

Mary Joy shrugged. "About fifty, I guess, or close to it. Papa bought it from Mr. Claude Keever. He's dead now, but he owned the farm next to us. His son Bo has it now, and I know he's not gonna let go of any of his.

"What makes you think somebody set that fire on purpose?"

Dimple explained that it looked like the fire had started away from the road, closer to the house. "Fortunately, the creek stopped it from going any farther."

"And that's not all," Annie began. "Charlie's mother and her aunt Lou found—"

"Found the place where it looks like it might have started." Miss Dimple spoke up, shooting a warning look at Annie. It was tragedy enough to lose one's mother, but she couldn't bring herself to tell Mary Joy that Leola might have been frightened to death.

As they were leaving, Miss Dimple remembered to ask Mary Joy if she had any idea what might have been bothering Prentice or if she knew whether the girl was seeing someone other than Clay.

Mary Joy smiled. "Why, Mama wouldn't have mentioned it to me if she was," she said as she followed them to the car. "They kept their secrets, those two. I didn't get back home as much as I wish I had, so I really didn't see much of Prentice this summer—or Mama, either," she added sadly.

Although they had parked in the shade, the car felt like a furnace as they left Maisie Hodges's place behind, and even Miss Dimple admitted discomfort as she blotted her face with a lace-trimmed handkerchief.

Everyone was hungry, but they agreed it would be best to wait until they were clear of the area to stop and eat the sandwiches Odessa had packed with a container of ice.

"Let's stop for a minute," Miss Dimple suggested before Charlie reentered the roadway. "If someone did follow us here, they could be waiting nearby."

But no other cars were in sight as Charlie nudged cautiously onto the road.

"Didn't we see another mailbox on the way in?" Dimple asked, looking about. "There should be a neighboring house close by."

"Right. I noticed it when we passed," Charlie said. "Do you want to stop there?"

Dimple nodded. "I think perhaps it would be a good idea. What if someone *did* follow us here or succeeded in locating Mary Joy on his own? I don't like leaving those two women out here by themselves without anyone to keep an eye out for them."

Olin Frix and his wife, Lila, agreed when they spoke with them a few minutes later. The couple, who looked to be in their fifties, had just finished their midday meal and invited the visitors into their small, dark parlor, where they sat on equally dark, scratchy upholstered furniture. And this time the offer of tea was politely declined as the three thought, no doubt, of the quickly melting supply of ice meant to keep their lunch chilled.

"We see most everybody who comes down this road," Lila told them, fanning her moist red face with a current copy of *The Saturday Evening Post*. "I hadn't noticed anybody today but the Hicks boys, who live up the road apiece—and you all, of course."

Her husband stood in the doorway, obviously

eager to get back to work. "We'll keep an eye out," he said, frowning, "but to be on the safe side, Maisie and her daughter-in-law oughta go back and stay with Luther until whatever this is blows over."

Miss Dimple looked at Charlie and then at Annie. "I think you could be right. I'll phone Luther tonight."

"I wish you luck getting Maisie Hodges to leave that house," Lila said, smiling. "That woman's more stubborn than any mule."

Her husband jammed on his hat and made for the door. "You should know," Olin told her, and with a grin, he hurried outside.

"They might be perfectly all right," Miss Dimple said as they walked back to the car, "but I'd feel better if they were with Luther in Covington."

" 'Love all, trust a few, do wrong to none,' " Annie said, quoting from Shakespeare's *All's Well That Ends Well*, and Miss Dimple reminded her that *she* was more concerned about those who had already done wrong and meant to do more.

They stopped for a brief lunch under a shade tree on the way home, narrowly avoiding another quick shower, but aside from that, the trip was uneventful.

"What now?" Charlie asked as she turned into Phoebe Chadwick's driveway.

Annie paused with her hand on the door. "Don't you think we should say something to Leola's neighbor? Maybe someone has been interested in his land, too."

"Bo Keever. I think you're right. I taught his sister, but I know him only to speak to," Miss Dimple said.

"I'll bet I know someone who does," Charlie told them. "Elberta Stackhouse. They're practically neighbors. She lives right down the road."

"Good. I'll phone Luther tonight, and you can speak with Elberta," Miss Dimple said. "It should be obvious to anyone now that someone set that fire at Leola's to frighten her off her land. All we have to do is find out who."

"And *why,*" Annie added.

*C*HAPTER *T*WENTY-TWO

The skies were overcast when Charlie drove out to the tidy brick bungalow on the outskirts of town, where Prentice Blair had lived with her aunt. As she approached the house, Charlie blinked back tears as she recalled the July day not long ago when they had come here expecting Prentice to have returned home early from her job at the Peach Shed.

"Well, of course I know Bo Keever," Bertie Stackhouse said. "Known him all his life." The two sat in Bertie's kitchen over a plate of muffins neither of them touched while Charlie explained what they suspected about the fire at Leola's.

Bertie frowned. "I remember her mentioning something about somebody wanting to buy her land—said it was aggravating—but she didn't take it too seriously." Bertie's eyes misted. "Leola didn't complain a lot. She was a very private person. Why, I doubt if she would've even let on if she'd felt threatened." She found a handkerchief in her pocket and blew her nose. "God, how I miss her! Miss them both!"

"School will be starting soon," Charlie said gently. "It should help to keep your mind occupied with other things. I hope you're planning to continue teaching."

Of course she was. That was who she was, what she did. For the first time, Elberta Stackhouse allowed herself to think about her future, a future without Prentice. Did she really want to stay here? Adam Treadway wasn't going to be patient forever. Was she willing to face life without him, as well?

But first she would have to face the ghost of a tragedy and the man who was responsible for it.

"You know Bo Keever better than I do." Charlie's voice brought her back to the present. "Would you call him for me? If he's had the same offer, maybe he can tell us who was interested."

But instead of contacting her neighbor by

phone, Bertie decided it might be best to visit him in person, and a few minutes later they found him mending a pasture fence when they turned in from the main road.

Mopping his red face, Bo welcomed the two and invited them into the shade of a large red oak where watercress grew in a clear spring. There he offered his visitors a seat on a makeshift bench, then knelt and splashed cold water over his face, shook his head, and sputtered.

"Bertie," he began, and the old plank creaked as he sat beside her, "not a day goes by that Maggie and I don't think about you. What can I do for you, sugar? Just say the word."

But he shook his head when Bertie asked him if anyone had expressed an interest in buying some of his land.

"I reckon anybody around here would know they'd be wasting their time there. Why, this farm's been in our family for over a hundred years. My daddy would whirl in his grave if I let so much as an inch of it go." He frowned. "Why you askin' me that?"

Bertie told him what they suspected about the fire at Leola's place, and Bo jumped to his feet. "The hell you say! Why haven't I heard about that before?"

Charlie explained they hadn't been sure but it was looking more and more likely that the fire had been deliberately set, especially after her mother and aunt found the remains of a charred cross.

If a storm could begin in a man's eyes, Bo Keever's would have been flashing lightning. "That woman was like a second mother to me, and I remember when my daddy sold that little parcel of land to Leola and Floyd," he said. "Floyd Parker had worked side by side with him for Lord knows how long, and we were glad to have them as neighbors." He sat and put his head in his hands. "Why in the world would anybody want that place bad enough to do a thing like that?"

"That's what we're trying to find out," Bertie told him. She spoke in a low, steady voice. "And if anybody approaches you, I hope you'll—"

"I'll sure let you know, Elberta," he said, frowning. "You know I will."

But Bertie shook her head. "Don't let *me* know. Call the sheriff."

"If Bo should hear from whoever's trying to buy that land, the sheriff better get here quick," Charlie said as they started back to Bertie's.

"Why is that?" Bertie asked.

"From the look on Bo Keever's face, I don't think that fellow would stand much of a chance," Charlie told her.

"I think you'd better come over right away," Miss Dimple said. The telephone had been ringing when

Charlie got home and she'd dashed through the house to answer it, hitting her shin on the cedar chest in the hall in her hurry. "Has something happened to Mary Joy?" she asked. "Were you able to get in touch with Luther?" What if the person who had been following them had waited until they left Maisie Hodges's place, and then . . .

"No, Mary Joy's all right—at least as far as I know. Just come," Miss Dimple repeated, and Charlie did.

Frazier. It had to be Frazier . . . or Joel, Annie's pilot brother and Will's friend. Or maybe it was Phoebe's young grandson, Harrison, who was serving in the South Pacific. Charlie raced across Katherine Street, took a shortcut through a neighbor's backyard, and arrived breathless and panting on Phoebe Chadwick's porch. Phoebe, Velma, and Lily sat in a group at one end of the porch, talking quietly together, and when Phoebe saw Charlie, she hurried to meet her. "They're in the parlor," she said. "Annie and Miss Dimple . . ." And she gave Charlie an encouraging pat on the shoulder.

Charlie's breath came fast and her mouth was so dry, she could hardly swallow. "Who? What is it? What happened? Did Annie get a telegram?" *Please God! Don't let it be the boy on the black bicycle!*

Phoebe held open the screen door. Her voice was gentle. "I'll let them explain."

She found Annie sitting ramrod-straight on one end of Phoebe's worn velvet love seat. Miss Dimple sat next to her in a mahogany Sheffield side chair with the flowered needlepoint seat Phoebe had stitched years before. Only their hands were touching.

Charlie dropped to her knees in front of them. "Oh, Annie, I'm so sorry! Is it Frazier?"

Annie looked up and without a word put a letter into Charlie's hands. It was written on the thin tissuelike paper issued to servicemen and women, and Charlie paused to get control of her trembling hands before reading it. At least, she thought, it wasn't the horrible yellow telegram.

The brief message apparently had been scrawled hastily with a pencil and addressed to *Miss Annie Gardner, Elderberry, Georgia.* Glancing at the signature at the bottom, Charlie didn't recognize the name. She glanced up. "Alex Carpenter?"

"Just read it," Miss Dimple urged her.

Dear Annie,
I remembered you lived in a little Georgia town called Elderberry, so I'm hoping this will reach you okay. Frazier was in my unit, but we got separated after bombs killed several of our men. I couldn't find Frazier among the dead, but we've been under fire and I haven't seen him since

that happened over a week ago. Knowing him, I reckon he'll come out just fine, but it's hard to send word from here with the Germans out to get us as much as we're out to get them. He talks about you all the time and I know he'd want me to tell you how much he loves you. I hope by the time you get this you will have heard from him.

Lt. Alex Carpenter, U.S. Army

The letter was dated July 27, 1944.

Charlie felt relief wash over her, but her hands still shook as she read the note once again. "Annie, this is a *good* thing. He said he couldn't find Frazier among the dead, and surely you would have heard by now if he'd been . . . if something had happened."

Annie nodded and Charlie could see she was trying to smile. "You should call Frazier's parents," Charlie suggested. "Maybe *they've* heard something more by now."

"I already have." Annie held out her hand for the letter and folded it; then, as if thinking better of it, she opened it in her lap and stroked the paper lightly with her fingers.

"What did they say?" Charlie asked.

"His mother cried." Annie seemed to disregard her own tears. "They haven't heard from him, either."

"*And also* no telegram from the War Department," Miss Dimple reminded her. "I believe Frazier's friend was attempting to reassure you— at least as best he could."

"But that was written weeks ago, and Frazier had been missing a week already . . . and he said they were *under fire* from the Germans. We all knew that, of course. They're having to fight their way inland a little at a time. . . . I don't even want to think about it. Anything could've happened to him!" Annie stood suddenly and went to the window, as if she were hoping to see Frazier rounding the corner at the end of the block. *"Why doesn't he write?"*

"Probably because he doesn't have the opportunity, or the means to send anything just now." Miss Dimple spoke in a firm voice. "Until he does, I believe he would want you to try to go on with your life as best you can."

Charlie gripped the back of Miss Dimple's chair and looked away. How awful to live in limbo like this! This continued *not knowing* was eating away at everyone. But it could be worse, much worse. She wiped away tears with the back of her hand and took a deep, calming breath.

Although Miss Dimple had never discussed it, those close to her knew from the Elderberry grapevine that the older teacher had endured the loss of a loved one in an earlier war, and Annie wished with all her heart she could shake off the worry that gnawed at her until she could think of nothing else.

Well, she decided, this wasn't helping Frazier or anyone else. She gave herself a few minutes to get her emotions under control before turning to face them. "Okay then, getting back to this other problem, tell us what you learned from Leola's neighbor. Has he had an offer for his land?"

"Bertie and I went by there this afternoon," Charlie told them, "but Bo hadn't heard from anybody about it, and didn't expect to. That property's been in his family for over a century and he has no intention of letting any of it go."

Dimple frowned. "And how is Elberta?"

"I guess she's getting along about as well as she can," Charlie told her. "She seems sort of . . . well . . . unsettled, but who could blame her after what happened to Prentice and Leola?"

Miss Dimple confessed that she hadn't had a chance to telephone Luther Hodges but that she would do so immediately.

Charlie glanced at Phoebe's porcelain clock on the mantel. "Uh-oh! It's after five o'clock! Time for Mama to be home from the ordnance plant. I'd better hurry and help Delia with supper." With practice, her sister had become a better cook than when she first came to live with them when her husband shipped overseas, but Charlie hadn't quite managed to forget the Spam and rice casserole with canned peas the size of marbles

Delia had presented her first month back home.

"I'll let you know what he says," Miss Dimple promised.

It wasn't until the next day that they learned Luther had taken the neighbor's advice seriously and brought his mother and wife (the former protesting audibly) to Covington in case the person who had attempted to buy Leola's land found his way to Maisie Hodges's.

Charlie was washing dishes after supper that night when the telephone rang in the hall. Jo Carr was enjoying a relaxing soak in the tub after a long day at the ordnance plant, and Delia, busy coaxing little Tommy to eat "just a little more" of his *yummy* dinner, shook her head, displaying a hand smeared in mashed potatoes. Hastily drying her hands on her apron, Charlie hurried to answer the phone.

"Well, I guess you've heard," her aunt Lou began.

Charlie hadn't, but she knew she was about to find out. "Heard what?"

"They're burying poor old Hattie McGee tomorrow, or what's left of her," her aunt said, and then added the obligatory, "Bless her heart.

"It's to be a graveside service and I thought I'd try to go. Ed won't be able to get away, but I thought you all might want to come. Walter Dunnagan's going to take care of the service, I hear. Hot as it is, hope he'll keep it short. That man can pray till the cows come home!"

Charlie wondered who was going to cover the expenses, since Hattie hadn't had two nickels to rub together, but she didn't have to wonder long.

"Ed says Knox Jarrett's paying for the casket and all that—and him with all that worry over Clay, too, but then, who else is going to do it? I thought I'd bring some of my Portland roses from that bush by the cellar door. You know how Hattie loved roses, and this one's bloomed for most of the summer in big old pink clusters. I'll take some up there in a bucket and we can put them in a vase after everybody leaves the cemetery."

Charlie said she would join her and was pretty sure her mother would, too. A phone call to Annie assured her that most of Phoebe's guests would be there, as well.

The service was scheduled for midmorning, probably so those attending could get on about the business of living as soon as it was over, Charlie thought. She was surprised to see a large crowd gathered at the cemetery when they arrived in Uncle Ed's Studebaker with the bucket of roses sloshing around at her feet in the backseat. The day promised to be hot, although clouds hid the sun now and then, and by the time they walked to the grave site at the end of a narrow graveled drive, she was glad to see the familiar blue canopy under the welcoming shade of a sycamore tree.

Miss Dimple and Annie stood outside the canopy with Phoebe, Velma, and Lily. Others congregated in small groups, waiting for the service to begin. Dora Delaney of the Total Perfection Beauty Salon whispered to Grady Clinkscales of the Gas 'n Eats, and Hardin Haynesworth Kirkland, handbag under her arm, made her way painstakingly up the hill behind Marjorie Mote and Emma Elrod. No one, it seemed, wanted to claim the few seats underneath where the casket waited beside the open grave and where Knox and Chloe Jarrett and their daughter, Loretta, sat alone in the first row.

With a nod from Miss Dimple, Charlie followed her and some of the others to fill the empty seats behind the Jarretts. There was no music and the Reverend Dunnagan's words were surprisingly brief, but not brief enough for her not to be aware of the grief and worry etched on the faces of Knox and Chloe Jarrett. The tragedy of Hattie McGee's death was overshadowed by the obvious suffering Clay's family was enduring.

The single spray of red roses that had been on Hattie's casket was set aside before her remains were lowered into the grave, and as soon as the minister gave his benediction, many people dispersed, but at her aunt's direction, Charlie followed her back to the car to retrieve the bucket of roses while the grave was being filled. Later, as her mother and aunt arranged the bright pink roses and anchored them in place over the fresh red earth, her eyes burned with tears as one by one others followed suit until the raw mound over Hattie's grave was covered in roses of every hue.

CHAPTER TWENTY-THREE

I guess you noticed how many people went to Hattie's funeral yesterday," Charlie mentioned to Annie as the two walked to town the next morning. Both needed to mail letters to their fiancés, and Charlie wanted another look at that yellow-striped blouse she'd noticed in the window of Brumlow's Dry Goods. School would be starting soon and it would boost her spirits immensely if she had just *one new* thing to wear.

"Do you think Hattie realized she had so many friends?" Annie said. "To be honest, I was surprised at the number there."

Charlie shrugged. "I hope she did. But who knows what Hattie knew? Obviously she knew too much, or she wouldn't have been buried up there on Cemetery Hill yesterday."

"Do you really think that's why she was killed—that is, if she *was* killed?" Annie asked.

"If she *wasn't* murdered, why would somebody throw rose petals over her body and then dress like Hattie and show up in town with her wheelbarrow? *Somebody* wanted us to think she died later than she actually did," Charlie explained. "I wonder if the person who killed her was at the cemetery yesterday."

"Oh my gosh, Charlie! You're giving me chills! Do you really think they were?"

Charlie shrugged. "Who knows? I tried to look around when it was over, but several people left after the benediction, and Aunt Lou practically dragged me away to get those roses. Were you able to see who was there?"

But Annie didn't answer. She was staring at a war bond poster in front of the post office showing a helmeted soldier preparing to throw a grenade. It read:

GOD HELP ME IF THIS IS A DUD
His life is in your hands!

Charlie threaded her arm through Annie's and stood with her as people passed on the street; a truck with a load of chickens on the back stopped at one of the town's two traffic lights, and two blocks away, the train whistle blew as the NC & St. L chugged through town. If she closed her eyes, she might pretend there was no war, no heartbreak, no worrying.

"We went through this when Fain was missing,

remember?" Charlie began. "I'm not telling you not to worry. That would be impossible, but you have to try to find something to occupy your interest to get you through each day as it comes. Focus on that and what's going on around you."

Annie groaned. "Charlie, I'm sorry. I know I'm not easy to be around right now. It's just that I feel like I'm at the bottom of a deep well and I can't get out."

Charlie knew how she felt, but right then she couldn't think of a thing to say that would make either one of them feel better.

"Why don't we do something for Clay?" she suggested. "Can you imagine how he feels locked away from everyone he cares about in that little cell with barely enough room to do more than turn around?"

Annie smiled, and Charlie was relieved to see a glimpse of her friend's good humor return. "Well, sure, but I doubt if the authorities would take kindly to our giving him a file."

"But they probably wouldn't mind if we took cookies. I'll ask Clay's mother what he likes best. How many sugar ration coupons can you spare?"

"He loves those chewy molasses cookies with black walnuts," Chloe Jarrett said when Charlie phoned later, "but our walnut tree didn't bear last year, and I don't know where you're going to find them this early in the season."

Charlie promised they would do their best. "How is he?" she asked. "And how are you?" She knew Miss Dimple had been concerned about Clay's mother and had made a point to speak with her on a regular basis.

Chloe didn't reply immediately. Finally, she said, "I just have to keep reminding myself that the good Lord knows my boy is innocent and the truth is on our side."

Charlie assured her that many of their friends were on Clay's side as well and that she had no doubt his name would soon be cleared.

But she wished she could feel sure of that herself.

"I asked Odessa where she got those black walnuts she used in that 'poor man's fruitcake' she made last Christmas," Annie reported later, "and she said there's a woman who lives somewhere on the edge of town who sells them, but she's not sure if she has any now."

But Minnie Prescott, Phoebe told them, didn't have a telephone. They would either have to drive or walk to her place out on River Bend Road to find out if the walnuts were still available.

Annie groaned. "Won't pecans do as well? Sounds like an awful lot of trouble to me."

Charlie agreed. "And then you have to crack them with a hammer or a rock, and they're the dickens to pick out."

Miss Dimple, who had been listening, was

visibly perturbed. "For heaven's sake, I walk out that way once in a while. I'll be glad to get the walnuts if she has any." She paused just long enough to fasten attention on Annie and Charlie. "And with three of us shelling them, it shouldn't take long to have enough for a batch of cookies. If that boy wants walnuts in his molasses cookies, then he should have them."

Charlie longed to be able to slip through a crack in the floor. Dimple Kilpatrick rarely lectured and would be aghast if she thought she had unintentionally made anyone think less of herself. However, she realized, this *was intentional*. She and Annie were meant to feel ashamed, and they were. At least enough to agree to accompany Miss Dimple on her walk the next morning when everybody but the milkman, and possibly Count Dracula, was hours away from waking.

Fortunately, Miss Dimple delayed starting out until a more suitable hour, but it was still cool enough to enjoy an early-morning breeze as they turned into the oak-laced shade of Katherine Street. Marjorie Mote paused to speak as she swept her front walk. She had lost her son Chester earlier in the war and the other, Jack, was now serving in England.

The stores hadn't opened yet in town, but Arden Brumlow waved at them from across the street while rearranging the window of the family dry goods store, where Charlie had purchased her blouse the day before; and a glimpse into the dusty confines of the *Elderberry Eagle* revealed the silhouette of Linotype operator, Thad Autry, busily setting words in lead.

The fountain in the park trickled onto lily pads under which goldfish languidly swam, and the two magnolias on either side of the pathway cast Virginia's log cabin library into deep shadow.

"Oh dear!" Miss Dimple paused to take a second look as they passed. "I hope that's not who I think it is. And I heard he'd been doing so well lately."

"Who? Where?" Charlie shaded her eyes to see where Miss Dimple was looking.

"There, on the porch of the library. It looks like someone's sleeping there on the bench." Miss Dimple pursed her lips. "I suppose Virginia will just have to run him off. Well, it won't be the first time."

"Run *who* off?" Annie asked.

"Delby O'Donnell, of course." Everyone knew his wife locked him out when he'd had too much to drink.

"Wait a minute!" Charlie ventured a few steps down the path. "I don't think that's—it doesn't look like Delby from here."

Miss Dimple followed, shoving aside a low-hanging magnolia limb with her umbrella. "You're right. It isn't Delby. . . . My goodness, I do believe that's *Jasper Totherow!*"

Hearing remnants of their conversation, the

person in question raised his head from the bench where he'd been sleeping and looked about. Seeing he'd been discovered, he shook his head, rubbed his eyes, and bolted, grabbing a bundle— probably clothing—at his feet. Then, to their astonishment, Jasper cleared the camellia bush at the edge of the porch in one leap and disappeared behind the building.

"Jasper Totherow, you come right back here!" Miss Dimple demanded, but of course he ignored her and kept right on running. When they followed, there wasn't one sign of that man in sight.

"I suppose we should report this," Charlie said after they had looked in every possible hiding place, "but I doubt if they'll ever catch him now."

Crossing the street, they found the door of the *Elderberry Eagle* unlocked, and Thad pointed out the telephone without even asking why they seemed so eager to use it, then went back to his Linotype.

"Well, I guess that means the scalawag isn't dead," Chief Tinsley said when Charlie told him whom they'd seen. "I figured Jasper was too slippery to stand still long enough for somebody to catch up with him."

"Then why did Lee Anne and Ruthie *say* he was dead?" Charlie asked.

"I reckon he could've been sleeping, but it seems more likely he got stunned by lightning,"

274

the chief explained. "That was a pretty bad storm and there was a big scorch mark on a pinc tree not three feet from where they said they found him."

Miss Dimple and Annie had chosen to wait on the sidewalk to avoid the dense fog of cigar smoke inside, and after telephoning, Charlie hurried to join them. "The chief said he'd send somebody over here to try to round Jasper up," she told them. She was hoping the delay would encourage Miss Dimple to forget about the walnuts, but of course it didn't.

The courthouse clock was striking ten by the time they returned from Minnie Prescott's with a paper bag filled with black walnuts, and the two younger teachers sat on Phoebe's back steps and cracked them with a hammer while Miss Dimple picked out the nut meats. When the cookies were ready, the three went together to deliver them to Clay at the city jail.

They were relieved to find him playing checkers with Dickson Perry, who delivered meals to the jail from Ray's Café, and the tantalizing smell of fried chicken wafted from a covered container on the counter. Miss Dimple took comfort in the knowledge that at least Clay wasn't going hungry.

When the others arrived, Dickson made excuses to leave, and it was a good thing, Charlie thought, as there was barely room for the four of them in Clay's tiny cell. She thought Clay looked thinner in spite of Ray's famous fried okra, cream gravy, and biscuits, and his healthy tan seemed to have paled, even though he had been locked away for only a short time.

"How are you, Clay?" Miss Dimple asked.

He shrugged. "I'm all right."

"No, *really*. How *are* you?" she repeated.

"Have you ever wished you would wake up and discover you'd been dreaming? I keep hoping that will happen to me. It's all like a horrible nightmare, and the worst part is, I know I'm *not* going to wake up," Clay said. "I was working in the orchard all morning the day Prentice was taken, but unfortunately, nobody saw me there to prove it."

Miss Dimple sat in the chair Dickson had vacated so that Clay, who had stood when they entered, would take the other seat on his bunk. Charlie and Annie lingered close to the barred door, which had shut with an echoing clang behind their backs.

Now Dimple leaned forward in her chair. "Clay, are you *certain* that you saw Hattie McGee as recently as you say?"

"Hattie or somebody dressed like Hattie. Grady saw her, too."

"I wonder if anyone else did," Miss Dimple said. "It's obvious that whoever was posing as Hattie wanted to be noticed."

Charlie spoke up suddenly. "Miss Bertie saw

her, too. Remember when she went with me to talk with Bo Keever the other day? When we were driving back, I said something about finding Hattie's wheelbarrow with bottles still in it in back of her place, and Miss Bertie told me she'd seen her in town not too long ago. It was a hot day and she called to her to offer a ride, but Hattie acted like she didn't hear her."

Clay spoke in a monotone. "Because it wasn't Hattie," he said.

"Then who was it?" Annie asked. "And why would anybody go to all that trouble when he or she knew Hattie was already dead?"

Clay looked from one to the other. "I think somebody was looking for something and wanted more time to search."

"Looking for what?" Charlie asked.

Clay shook his head. "I wish I knew, but whoever it was didn't take time to put things back the way they were. That trailer's in a mess."

"Whoever it was certainly wasn't thinking clearly if the intention was to get everyone to believe Hattie died later than she did simply to throw the investigators off track." Miss Dimple rose to leave. "That might have some effect in the cold of winter, but . . ."

She didn't have to finish her sentence. Everyone understood what she was trying to say.

CHAPTER TWENTY-FOUR

Well, that was a close one! He wouldn't be sleeping on the library porch again, but it had been so dark, and he had been so tired, he just couldn't go another step farther. Jasper Totherow groaned as he rose from his rumpled bed of tow sacks and rubbed his aching back. That blasted bench at the library had been as hard as granite, but at least he would've been out of the rain. He was going to have to find a better place to sleep than this drafty old shed. It had rained some during the night and enough water had blown through the cracks to dampen his clothes and his spirits. He was getting too old to live like this. If he got chilled by a little rain in August, what would it be like in the colder months ahead?

Jasper rubbed his arms and shivered. He knew the shed where he'd spent the night was used as a temporary storage place for cotton before it went to the gin, and in a few short weeks, the fields around him would be dotted with pickers—mostly women and older children now that most of the men were in the armed services. A lot of the county schools let out for that purpose. If he could just get by until then, Jasper was sure they would take him on to help, maybe even give him a place to stay, at least until the crop had been picked.

And then what? He stretched and relieved himself behind the shed. He would worry about that when the time came. Right now, he was hungry. Last night, he'd eaten tomatoes and cantaloupe he'd taken from a garden down the road, and he needed something to hold him, something solid. Jasper thought of his grandma's biscuits, fluffy white inside and crusty gold on top. He'd give anything for one right now— steaming hot, with butter and honey—but Grandma was long gone and laid to rest in an overgrown churchyard. Jasper wiped a couple of tears away with a grimy hand, unaware himself if he shed them for the biscuits or for his grandmother.

If he couldn't have biscuits, loaf bread would have to do, and there was a little store about a mile or so down the road. The fact that he didn't have any money didn't concern him.

Jasper waited until a couple of customers had the attention of the store clerk. One, an older woman in a skirt down to her ankles, wanted a can of Garrett sweet snuff, which the clerk had to stoop and look for underneath the counter. At that moment, Jasper took the opportunity to help himself to a loaf of bread, and if he had stopped there, he might've gotten away with it, but a couple of cans of Vienna sausage would taste mighty good with that bread, Jasper thought, and he might as well treat himself to a Nehi orange to wash it all down.

It was the drink that got him into trouble, as one of the cans of sausage slid from beneath his shirt as he lifted the bottle of orange drink from its ice-water bath, and it startled him so that he grabbed up the other items and bolted, not even taking time to pry the cap from the bottle of Nehi with the opener on the ice chest.

"Hey! Come back here! You haven't paid for that!" the clerk yelled after him, and a tall bearded man standing on the front porch of the store, who happened to be the husband of the woman buying the snuff, reached out a giant hand, grabbed Jasper by his shirttail, and swung him around, pinning him against the wall. And there is where he stayed while the clerk telephoned the sheriff, and Deputy Peewee Cochran came out to collect him in his 1931 Model A Ford truck.

The deputy's wife told Jesse Dean Greeson about it when she went to Cooper's Store to get some pinto beans for supper, and Jesse Dean told Emma Elrod, who told Emmaline Brumlow, who told everybody at that afternoon's meeting of the Elderberry Woman's Club.

"Well, I'm not surprised," Miss Dimple said to her friend Virginia after the meeting, and neither was Virginia, who had been told earlier about

Jasper's recent nap on the library porch. "At least he'll be given something to eat and a place to stay for a while," Dimple said.

"I don't understand why he disappeared so suddenly," Virginia said. "Not that I didn't appreciate his absence." The two had put the folding chairs away after the meeting, and now Virginia swept crumbs from the floor. How could grown women make such a mess with a few cookies and a handful of peanuts? she wondered.

"I believe he was frightened," Dimple said. "Jasper saw something or *someone* around the time Leola Parker died and that suspicious fire was set."

"I'd like to know what it was. Maybe Sheriff Holland can get to the bottom of it," Virginia said.

Miss Dimple didn't answer, but she was thinking it might not hurt to have a little visit with Jasper herself.

There's no time like the present, Dimple thought, and leaving Virginia, she set out to walk the mile or so to the county jail on the outskirts of town. The August afternoon was sultry, and for a few minutes she wondered if perhaps she should have waited until morning, but if a visit with Jasper would help clear up who was behind the dreadful things that had been going on, she didn't want to wait another minute.

The owner of the store where Jasper had

attempted to take the food had declined to press charges, saying if Jasper had merely asked, he would have *given* him something to eat, Peewee told her. But at Jasper's request, he preferred to remain a guest of the county, at least for a few days.

"I don't know why he wants to stay here," the deputy told her, "but Sheriff Holland says it's okay. I reckon he's just glad to have a place to sleep and three meals a day."

Miss Dimple agreed, but she also thought Jasper wanted to be safe. If anyone planned to harm him, it would be unlikely for them to invade the county jail to do it.

She found him asleep on his bunk, his mouth wide open and a scattering of bread crumbs in his beard, but at least he wore a clean jumpsuit of worn blue denim. He sat reluctantly and rubbed his eyes when Peewee opened the door of his cell to tell him he had a visitor. It was obvious he wasn't at all happy to see her.

Miss Dimple accepted the only chair and got right to the point. Using her usual method of dealing with first graders, she faced him directly, forcing him to meet her eyes. "Jasper," she began, "I want you to tell me what you saw the day Leola Parker died that frightened you into running away."

"Didn't see nothin'." Jasper hung his head and looked away.

"Someone set that fire—set it deliberately," she continued. "Did you see who it was?"

He shrugged. "I *told* you I didn't see nothin'! Wasn't even there."

"Then you have a short memory," Dimple said. "You must have forgotten that not too long ago you told my friend and me that *you saw somebody that day and you knew what they did.*" Dimple rose and looked down at him. "Three people have died because of what happened that day, Jasper Totherow, and an innocent person has been arrested for it. *Now, tell me what you saw!*"

"It ain't got nothin' to do with me." He shifted on his bunk and looked around as if he hoped to find some way for a quick escape, but Jasper was in a jail cell and he wasn't going anywhere.

"Then why did you run away?" Miss Dimple persisted. When he didn't answer, she took a deep breath and sat again. "You were afraid you'd said too much." She spoke softly. "Isn't that right?"

He looked up, his eyes wide with fear. "I don't want nobody comin' after me."

"No one's going to come after you here, Jasper. Don't you want to put the person who did this away? Just think of it—you wouldn't have to run anymore. You wouldn't have to worry."

He thought about that for a minute. Sighing, he finally spoke. "See . . . the thing is, I really don't know who it was."

Miss Dimple frowned. "Were you too far away to recognize the face?"

He shook his head. "Couldn't see his face, or much of the rest of him either 'cause he was covered by a sheet. Could've been a woman, for all I know. Had on some kind of white pointy thing. Looked kinda like a ghost."

"You mean he had on a hood like people wear in the Ku Klux Klan?"

"Yeah, I reckon. I ran when I saw him set that fire. No tellin' what he might do if he saw me watchin'."

He could've helped Leola, might've even saved her life! "Did you see what happened to Leola that day? Did he attack her, too?"

Jasper shook his head violently. "*No!* I saw her run out of the house—I reckon she must've seen that smoke; then all of a sudden like, she stopped and ran back toward the house. I don't know if that man in the hood scared her or if she meant to get inside to the telephone, but she tripped on that step and fell. Right soon after that, that little gal showed up, come runnin' from them woods behind the house.

"Heck, at first I didn't even know the old woman was home. She keeps—kept—her car, that old Plymouth she drove, in the garage out back."

"Then what were you doing there?" Miss Dimple asked.

"I come to get me some tomaters—she told me to help myself— and radishes, too. Them was the best radishes!" Jasper smacked his lips, remembering.

Dimple thought of the garden Leola kept behind her garage, and knowing Leola, she didn't doubt that this time Jasper spoke the truth. Leola Parker was always glad to share what she had. Clearing her throat of a lump that threatened tears, she asked if Jasper had seen a car.

This time, she was rewarded. He nodded eagerly. "Sure did, but I don't know what kind and didn't stick around to find out."

Miss Dimple frowned. "Do you remember what color it was?"

"Uh-huh. It was black." Jasper stretched and yawned, obviously eager to get back to his nap. Dimple thanked him and left.

"You had a telephone call while you were out," Phoebe told her when she got home. "It was a long-distance call and I wrote down the number. Leola's daughter, Mary Joy, asked if you would call her back."

"Well, Miss Dimple, you were right," Mary Joy told her when they were finally connected. "Some man came out here yesterday and asked if I was interested in selling Mama's place."

"What man?" Dimple asked.

"Never saw him before. He didn't give his

name and I didn't ask. I told him I wasn't selling, but he gave me a card with some company name on it—in case I changed my mind, he said. Luther wasn't here and I didn't let him in."

"Good for you! Do you still have the card?"

"Just a minute and I'll get it," Mary Joy said.

"Here it is," she said when she came back to the phone. "It's something called Bold Victory, Incorporated."

"Hmm . . . does it say what it is?"

"No, and there's nobody's name on it, either. Only a phone number and some kind of fancy initials."

"What kind of initials?" Miss Dimple asked.

"Looks like a *B* on top of a *V*," Mary Joy said.

"And that's all?"

"Yes, ma'am, except for Bold Victory and the phone number, and it's not a local number, so it must not be anybody from around here."

Miss Dimple wrote down the number Mary Joy gave her, but she didn't recognize the exchange. "I'll ask Florence McCrary," she said. "She should be able to tell us where it's located." Of course Florence would also be curious about why she wanted to know, but that couldn't be helped.

"Is Luther's mother still with you?" she asked.

Mary Joy's sigh was barely audible, but it was a sigh all the same. "Yessum, but she's rarin' to go home."

Dimple hated being the bearer of discouraging

news, but she advised Mary Joy to play hostess to Maisie a little longer and not to unlock her door for anyone she didn't know. "I don't want to frighten you, but this person might come back and try again." *And this time, he could be more persuasive.*

"Why, that's an exchange way down in Florida," Florence said when Dimple spoke with her the next day. "You planning a vacation?"

Miss Dimple told her she was trying to get in touch with her brother, Henry, who had called and left a message, but she wasn't sure if whoever answered the phone had written the number down correctly. It surprised her that she was getting so good at lying, and it shocked her even more that her Victorian conscience didn't even raise an eyebrow.

"You want me to connect you, then?" Florence asked.

"Yes, please." She might as well dive in headfirst, Dimple thought.

"It might take a few minutes. I'll ring you when I get an answer.

"Dimple, I don't think that's your brother," Florence told her when she called back. "Some woman answered and she talked so fast, I couldn't understand a word she said. Must've been a Yankee. I asked if Henry Kilpatrick was there, and she got all huffy—just plain rude—so I didn't think you'd want any dealings with *her*. It's someplace in Jacksonville. I'll call her back if you want, but it's gonna be expensive."

Long-distance calls cost dearly and few people could afford them. Dimple wasn't one of the few, so she thanked Florence and replaced the receiver. Bold Victory, whatever it was, was located in Jacksonville, Florida. Perhaps someone else had heard of the company. Dimple sat down to one of her Victory Muffins and a cup of ginger mint tea. The morning was half-spent and she had visits to make.

CHAPTER TWENTY-FIVE

Opening her umbrella to ward off the blazing August sun, Miss Dimple started out for a visit with the Jarretts. The umbrella, once a vibrant shade of violet, was now streaked and faded, she noticed. When this war was over, Dimple decided, a new umbrella would be one of the first things she'd purchase.

Attempting to stay on the shadier side of the street, Dimple walked a little faster. She was eager to give Clay's family an update on the latest developments with Mary Joy, and also to boost their hopes after her recent conversation (if you could call it that) with Jasper Totherow.

She found Chloe Jarrett and her daughter, Loretta, tightening the lids on glistening jars of green beans that lined the kitchen table and countertops.

"This should be the last of the batch," Chloe said, welcoming her. "This makes seventeen more quarts to add to the thirty-something I put up earlier. I usually detest canning," she confided, "but at least it's kept me busy—not too busy to worry, but it helps a little." With a damp dishrag, she carefully wiped off the bright green rows of jars. "Please take some of these home with you, Miss Dimple. We've plenty to spare and they're a lot better than the canned ones from the store."

Miss Dimple accepted gratefully and hoped she would be invited to sit somewhere other than in the steaming kitchen.

Loretta, thank goodness, was of the same mind. "For heaven's sake, Mama, it's hot as Hades in here!" She untied her apron and tossed it over the back of a chair. "Let's sit out on the porch, where it's cooler."

Chloe rinsed out the dishrag and draped it over the sink. "Of course! What was I thinking? And how about a glass of iced tea? I could use one myself."

"That would be most welcome," Miss Dimple admitted. After the long, hot walk from town, the cold drink was appealing. The three took their glasses to the shady end of the front porch, where a slight breeze ruffled the leaves on the pecan tree at the corner of the house. Already the tight green hulls had formed around the shells inside which nuts would soon mature. Amos, the old Collie, slept nearby under the overhanging branches of a drooping spirea bush.

"I'm afraid we don't have any encouraging news from our Clay," Chloe began, setting her glass aside. "I've told Bobby Tinsley over and over that he was out picking peaches when Prentice was killed. Came in a little after noontime to get cleaned up so he could make deliveries for Harris Cooper. I don't know how they think he could be in two places at once!"

"Well, I believe I might have a bit of good news, or at least it's worth looking into." After drinking most of her tea, Dimple continued to hold the frosty glass, relishing its coolness. "I spoke with Jasper Totherow yesterday and he said something I found intriguing."

Loretta frowned. "But, Miss Dimple, you can't believe a thing that crazy old man says!"

Her mother, eager for any word of encouragement, quieted her daughter with a wave of her hand and leaned forward. "What was that, Miss Dimple?"

"He said he saw someone light that fire at Leola Parker's the day she was found dead." Miss Dimple told her how, according to Jasper, Leola had tripped and hit her head.

"Did he know who it was?" Chloe asked.

"He didn't get a good look because whoever did it was wearing a Klan hood that hid his face, but Jasper said he was driving a black car."

"A lot of cars are black," Loretta said.

"True, but someone in a black car attempted to follow us when several of us went to see Leola's daughter, Mary Joy, down near Griffin. We managed to evade whoever it was, or so we thought, but now Mary Joy tells me a man has approached her about buying her mother's property." She explained how Leola had been badgered by someone with the same goal in mind.

Chloe gripped the arms of her chair. "Do you think this same person might have been responsible for setting that fire?"

"Perhaps not the same person, but one of his associates," Dimple replied.

"I wonder why he wants that particular piece of land," Loretta said.

"I wish I could answer that, but perhaps it will eventually come to light." Miss Dimple drank the rest of her tea and set the glass aside. "But it does seem there's a definite connection to Leola's death, and possibly Prentice Blair's."

"I don't suppose Mary Joy recognized the man who approached her," Chloe said. "Did he leave a name?"

"No, but he did leave a card with the name of a

291

company, or I assume it's a company. It's called Bold Victory, and Florence tells me that according to the phone number, it's located in Jacksonville, Florida."

"And there was no other name on the card?" Loretta asked.

Miss Dimple shook her head. "Just the name, Bold Victory, a phone number, and the initials in large black print. Mary Joy says it looks like the *B* is superimposed on top of the *V*."

Loretta, who had been slowly rocking, suddenly stopped. "I think I've seen that card before," she said. "It sounds familiar somehow."

"Has someone showed interest in the property here?" Dimple asked.

"Heavens no!" Chloe gasped, although sometimes she wished they would. "I'm sure I would've heard about it if they had."

Then where? Miss Dimple rose to leave. "If you remember where you saw it, you will let me know, won't you?" she said to Loretta.

"Of course, but I can't think of anybody here who has dealings with a company in Florida. Who in the world could it be?" Loretta stood, too. "Mama, I have to go now, but I'll call you tomorrow. Miss Dimple, why don't you let me give you a ride? Those quart jars are too heavy to carry."

And Dimple Kilpatrick thanked her and accepted.

Elberta Stackhouse nibbled at her scrambled eggs and cheese. Prentice had always enjoyed that supper, heaping spoonfuls of peach jam on toast or biscuits, but now Bertie cooked it only because it was easy and cheap. She didn't even miss the bacon or sausage she used to serve before the war made such things precious. She glanced at the empty place beside her where Prentice usually sat and from where she'd filled her aunt in on what was going on in her young life.

And now that life had ended. Bertie's stomach lurched and she pushed her plate aside. Would life ever hold meaning for her again? Life without Prentice? Remembering the not-so-late depression, she scraped the eggs into the trash can but set the toast aside for later. She had been raised to believe it was a sin to waste food, but what could you do with cold scrambled eggs?

And then Bertie stood in her kitchen doorway and tried not to think, but it didn't do any good. It was after six o'clock, but the sun was still bright and a cardinal sang in the old pear tree by the window; a dog barked not too far away; a plane rumbled overhead, and once again she felt the dark, heavy surge of grief welling inside her. *How long? How long?* Bertie took a deep breath and let herself go limp. It was time.

In Prentice's room, her blue-flowered bedspread

was pulled carelessly over the pillows, the way she had left it before leaving for her job at the Peach Shed. The book she had been reading, Daphne du Maurier's *Rebecca*, lay open, facedown, on the bedside table. Sitting on the side of the bed, Bertie picked it up and looked at the date in the back. It was way past a month overdue from the Elderberry Library, but kind Virginia had not sent a reminder. Prentice's clothes still hung in the closet. Her hairbrush, threaded with long, fine, sunshiny strands, waited on the glass-topped vanity along with a jar of Pond's cream with the top screwed on crooked; and several squares of bathroom tissue, blotted with the pink lipstick she'd loved covered the bottom of a wastebasket.

Bertie gathered the tissues and the hairbrush and clutched them to her. She ran her fingers through the brush and rubbed the tissues against her cheek in an attempt to absorb the last essence of the fine and beautiful woman she had raised and who had been as much a part of her as if she had carried her in her womb. And then she cried. She cried for the woman Prentice might have been, the children she might have had, the bleak certainty of a life without her. She cried until her body ached from the exertion of it and she was left empty and dry.

In another two weeks, school would begin, and more from habit than from anything else, Bertie had already begun planning for her classes. She had always enjoyed being around young people, and loved the challenge of inspiring them, but the thrill that usually came with the start of a new school year just wasn't there, and she missed it.

This wasn't right. It wasn't fair—not only to her students but to herself. Bertie went in the bathroom that connected Prentice's room with hers and dashed cold water on her hot, puffy face. She stripped Prentice's bed and bundled the sheets to take to the laundry, then carefully folded her clothing to donate to the Bundles for Britain drive sponsored by the Parent Teacher Association. Her niece's hairbrush and personal items were tucked lovingly away in a small wooden box.

Dusk had arrived by the time she finished packing everything away, and the room was soulless and bare as if it had been vacuumed of energy, of joy. Bertie poured herself a glass of tea and sat out on the porch. Across the road, neighbor children laughed and shrieked as they raced through a sprinkler on the lawn. Bertie smiled as she watched them. *Life goes on, with or without you, Elberta Stackhouse. How are you going to spend it?*

And she took her empty glass inside and picked up the telephone.

Thank goodness Knox himself answered. If it had been Chloe, she would have had no choice but to tell her the truth. Chloe deserved that, but it would have made both of them uncomfortable, to say the least.

Knox's first thought was that she had found something or remembered something that might help in Clay's defense, or, God forbid, something that would convict him, but she spoke with a calmness that defied that.

"I need to speak with you, Knox," Elberta told him. "Would it be convenient for you to drop by for a few minutes? It shouldn't take long."

He frowned. "Well, of course, Bertie. I'll do anything I can. I think you know that."

Knox didn't tell Chloe where he was going, only that he had an errand and wouldn't be long. He found Elberta waiting on her porch when he arrived there a few minutes later.

"How are you?" he asked.

"About as well as half a person can be, but I'm thinking of changing that," she said, offering him a seat in one of the wicker porch chairs. Elberta took the other one, facing him.

Knox Jarrett looked at her for a long time and knew that she knew his suffering couldn't begin to equal hers, although it came pretty damn close. "Bertie," he began, "I'm so sorry—"

She shook her head. "Knox, I know Clay wouldn't have hurt Prentice. It had to have been somebody else who put her ring in his truck. One of these days, maybe they'll find out who did this, but I wanted you—and Chloe, too—to know I don't believe Clay had anything to do with it."

He didn't even try to hide the tears that came—tears of relief, tears of regret, tears of compassion. "Bertie, I'm sorry," he repeated. "Sorry for everything."

Sorry for everything. The words were heavy. They weighed a million pounds, and Elberta Stackhouse felt as if she had been lugging them around for over a quarter of a century. She stood and took his hand. "Thank you," she said.

On the other side of town, Dimple Kilpatrick sat down to a supper of pimento cheese sandwiches and canned tomato soup. Phoebe's cook, Odessa, had gone to a funeral that day. As one of the flower-bearers, she knew she would be too late to cook, but she had left a tray of homemade pineapple sherbet for dessert. After helping with the dishes, Dimple and Annie took their sherbet to the porch, where lightning bugs blinked in the twilight, and next door Willie Elrod and some of his friends played One-Two-Three Red Light Stop! attempting to soak up as much fun as possible in their dwindling summer.

The other women stayed inside to listen to a program on the radio, so the two had the porch to themselves, and Miss Dimple took the opportunity to tell Annie about her visits with the Jarretts and Jasper Totherow. Annie had learned earlier of Mary Joy's offer from the stranger and of Miss Dimple's attempt to place a long-distance call to the company in Florida.

"Clay's sister Loretta seems to think the name of the company and the initials on the card sounded familiar," Miss Dimple confided. "She was almost sure she'd seen them somewhere before."

"I can't imagine where," Annie said. She closed her eyes and let the creaking of the swing lull her. Maybe tonight she would be able to sleep. Every day now for longer than she wanted to count, she would tell herself, *This might be the day I hear from Frazier!* But it wasn't. Day after day, it wasn't. She knew Charlie had received several letters from Will all at once, because Jesse Dean Greeson had told Odessa about it when she'd stopped to buy a bag of rice at Harris Cooper's store, and, of course Odessa, being happy for Charlie, had told everyone else.

What kind of horrible person am I, Annie thought, to be jealous of my best friend's good fortune? *Of course* she wanted Will to be safe, just as she wanted the same for her brother, Joel, and for Fain, for Delia's Ned, and for Phoebe's young Harrison, but she wanted it for her own Frazier, too! This awful waiting was wearing her down and wringing her out.

Tomorrow, Annie thought, I will get up early and join Miss Dimple on her morning walk, watch the sun rise from the hills above town, and look ahead to a day when the war will be over.

But by the time Annie awoke the next morning, Miss Dimple had already circled the town and was enjoying a poached egg on toast with a dab of strawberry preserves on the side, so Annie set off alone, determined to begin her day on the right course.

Odessa was out sweeping the front walk when the boy on the black bicycle turned into their street and stopped right in front of the house.

Odessa pretended she didn't see him. If she didn't see him, maybe he would go away, but when she looked up, he was still there.

"We don't want no dealings with you," she told him as he bumped his bicycle over the curb. "You just go along now."

"I'm afraid I can't do that," the boy told her. "I have a telegram for Miss Annie Gardner. Somebody will have to sign."

Odessa's eyes widened. Did he think she couldn't sign her name? Why, Miss Dimple Kilpatrick had taught her how to read and write when she'd first come to work for Miss Phoebe. "Lemme have that pencil!" she said, and took the telegram from his hand. Then she turned and hurried inside, leaving the broom in the middle of the walkway along with her hopes for a bright new day.

Lily Moss had finished her late breakfast of

cornflakes and milk topped with fresh sliced peaches. "Who was that, Odessa?" she asked, and then she saw Odessa's face and the yellow envelope in her hand.

"Oh, dear God! Phoebe, come quick! Odessa Kirby, don't you dare pass out on me!" Quickly, she snatched an armchair from the dining room—barely in time for Odessa to plop down on it—and began to fan her with the Elderberry telephone book, which happened to be the closest thing at hand.

"Let me see that!" Phoebe rushed in from the kitchen, followed by Velma Anderson, who, with her graying hair tied up in a bandanna, was on her way to the high school to get her classroom ready for the beginning of the school year.

"Oh no! This is for Annie. . . . It's what she's been worrying about." Phoebe examined the telegram as if she could read it with X-ray vision. "Oh, that poor girl!"

Miss Dimple, who had gone upstairs to freshen herself, wasn't aware of what was going on below until she started back down and saw the tableau. At the same time, Annie, having walked for what she assumed was an appropriate amount of time, sauntered into Phoebe's walkway, picked up the broom, and encountered the lot of them staring at her in alarm.

"What's going on?" she asked. And then she saw the telegram and knew it was for her.

300

Miss Dimple put the telegram in her hand and, leading her into the parlor, seated her in the soft plush chair by the window.

Annie put her face in her hands. "I can't read it," she said. "Somebody, *please!* Won't you read it for me?"

Silence reigned. No one, it seemed, wanted to be the announcer of worse-than-bad news. Finally, Miss Dimple stepped up. "I'll read it," she said.

CHAPTER TWENTY-SIX

D imple Kilpatrick stood by the window, her hand on Annie's shoulder, and willed herself to speak calmly. The other women hovered nearby in terrified silence as Miss Dimple adjusted her bifocals and read:

**SMALL PROBLEM BUT AM OK stop
LETTER ON WAY stop
LOVE, FRAZIER**

"Oh, glory hallelujah!" Odessa, who had been clutching the arms of her chair, sprang to her feet and threw her hands in the air.

"Amen to that!" Annie said, laughing, as Miss Dimple gave her the telegram. Her hand trembled as she read it again. *He was safe. Her Frazier was safe!*

"I wonder what he meant by a small problem," Phoebe said.

"I don't know, but he's *alive!* Thank goodness, he's alive!" Annie jumped up and hugged them all. "I have to telephone Frazier's parents. . . . Maybe they've heard something more."

"I was getting ready to call you," Frazier's mother told her when Florence was able to make the connection. They had received the same telegram, she said, but nothing more.

"I can live with that," Annie admitted. "At least for a while—and he *did* say it was a *small* problem, didn't he?"

Charlie! She must tell Charlie! Telegram in hand, Annie cut through the backyard and ran across Katherine Street to find Charlie in the kitchen making tuna croquettes for the noon meal. Was it almost time for dinner? Except for the arrival of the telegram, she had little recollection of the rest of the morning.

At the news, Charlie forgot her hands were covered in raw egg and cracker crumbs and threw her arms around Annie, flinging gobs of breading about. "I'm so happy for you! I can't tell you how relieved I am. . . ." And she sank onto a kitchen chair and cried into her apron.

"Why, Charlie . . ." Annie knelt beside her. "What's wrong? This is *good* news. Why are you crying? Will's all right, isn't he? Odessa told us about your getting all those letters."

"It's what was in the letters," Charlie began. "I didn't want to tell you, worry you even more, but Will had to ditch his plane. He's in a hospital in England."

"Why didn't you tell me? What happened? Is he going to be all right?"

"I didn't know myself until all those letters came at once. It had been a while since I'd heard from him, so I was getting more concerned than usual."

Charlie rose and washed her hands at the sink. "It happened near the end of July, during a raid over France. The Germans shot out his engine and it caught on fire. Will said he managed to jettison the engine and was trying to make his way back to England when the plane began to plummet over the English Channel."

Annie stiffened, finding it hard to breathe. This easily could have happened to her brother, Joel, as well. "Dear God! How terrifying, Charlie! What happened then?"

Charlie wiped away her tears with a dish towel and smiled. "He pulled the rip cord on his parachute."

"And then what?"

Charlie shrugged. "Will doesn't remember. He woke up in a hospital a day or so later. He has a broken collarbone and is pretty banged up, but he's going to be all right." She sighed. "Frankly, I hope they'll keep him there until this awful war's over."

That evening, Phoebe brought out a bottle of champagne a former boarder had given her and invited Charlie to join them in a toast to all their brave men. Even Odessa, a strict teetotaler, downed her portion without protest.

Miss Dimple was in the front yard the next morning, clipping a few roses for the table, when Clay's sister, Loretta, pulled into the driveway and hurried toward her. Dimple's first thought on seeing her was that something had happened concerning Clay, and she became so careless with what she was doing that she received a bad jab from a rose thorn.

Laying the flowers aside, she quickly wound a clean handkerchief around the bleeding finger and went to meet her. "What is it, Loretta?"

"You asked me to let you know if I remembered where I'd seen the card you were telling us about—the one that said 'Bold Victory' with the combined initials. Well, this morning when I first woke up, it came to me. It was Mrs. Kirkland—you know, the one with all those names."

Loretta followed Miss Dimple to the porch, where they sat in the shade. "I was helping Daddy in the Peach Shed a few weeks ago and she had written down what she wanted on the back of a card like that. I remember thinking it was an interesting name, and I believe I commented on it, but she said she'd just picked up the card from her son when he was at home a few days before."

"Chenault." Miss Dimple nodded.

"Do you think *Chenault* had anything to do with what happened to Leola and Prentice?"

Miss Dimple hesitated before speaking. "I think it would be worth our while to find out," she said. "I wouldn't mention this to anyone else yet, Loretta. Let me think about it a bit and I'll see what I can come up with."

Who would best be able to find out about the mysterious company in Florida? She couldn't think of one person in Elderberry who might be able to help her. Miss Dimple took the roses into the kitchen to arrange in Phoebe's lovely blue crystal bowl. It would have to be someone who had the means and incentive to look into this on Clay Jarrett's behalf. . . . Miss Dimple jammed a rose stem into the bowl and pricked another finger. *Why, his attorney, of course!* Chloe had told her the lawyer's name. Someone from Atlanta, she said, and he was supposed to be one of the best. Tisdale, Chloe had said. Curtis Tisdale.

Dimple put the roses in water and went to the telephone to call the Jarretts.

On meeting the attorney at the Jarretts', Miss Dimple was surprised to learn that she had gone to college with his aunt Lavinia at Georgia State College for Women in Milledgeville and had, in fact, roomed across the hall from her in the large drafty house heated by fireplaces.

"I've heard stories about how you girls used to secretly make fudge on the hearth," he reminded her once introductions were made. He had immediately driven from Atlanta when Knox Jarrett telephoned him about the possible connection between Leola's death, and, ultimately, Prentice's, and the unknown company in Florida.

After learning of Jasper's statement, Curtis had spent some time attempting to interview him, but had come away unconvinced of the man's testimony. "I believe he did see someone set that fire," he told them, "but I have serious doubts as to whether it would hold up in court. Jasper, I'm afraid, doesn't come across as a very reliable witness."

"But you can't argue with the fact that someone—or some corporation—is extremely interested in buying the land Leola's daughter now owns," Knox said. "All we know is that it's located in Jacksonville and that Chenault Kirkland may or may not have something to do with it."

"And that's what I'm trying to find out," Curtis assured him. "I've already made some inquiries and hope to learn more soon."

It had been late afternoon when he arrived and

the Jarretts and Miss Dimple gathered on the porch of the farmhouse, where Loretta and her mother served fruit punch and gingersnaps for the ladies, while Knox invited Curtis Tisdale back to the kitchen for something a little stronger.

Miss Dimple sipped her punch while watching shadows lengthen across the lawn. In a short time, September would be upon them, and most of the summer, it seemed, had been overcast by heartbreak and murder. Curtis Tisdale, she thought, appeared competent as well as confident, and for the first time since that awful day she and her friends were summoned from the orchard, she felt they might begin to see the light.

Being of clear conscience, Dimple usually fell asleep soon after her head hit the pillow, but that night sleep wouldn't come no matter how many verses of Scripture she remembered or fruits and vegetables she named in alphabetical order. Finally, in exasperation, she went downstairs to brew a cup of ginger mint tea, and discovered Annie in the kitchen before her.

"You, too?" Annie sat at the table, sipping a cup of steaming milk, and Miss Dimple told her of the meeting with Clay's attorney while waiting for her water to come to a boil.

"I certainly hope we'll hear something soon," she said, "and that it will make a major difference in Clay's defense."

Annie agreed. She hoped, too, that she would

finally receive that long-awaited letter from Frazier.

But the next day passed uneventfully. It wasn't until the day after that Chloe Jarrett telephoned Dimple to tell her Clay's attorney had found a definite connection between Chenault Kirkland and the mysterious undertaking called Bold Victory. Chenault, Curtis had discovered, owned stock in an obscure offshoot of a huge chemical plant with ambitions to branch out in Georgia.

"That seems all on the up-and-up," Chloe explained further, "although Griffin Kirkland denies any knowledge of the company. Leola's land backs up to the river, you know, and I understand that's important in the production process and would be a valuable asset to this particular industry."

From what Chloe had learned from Curtis Tisdale, they planned to manufacture synthetic fabrics such as nylon and viscose rayon, and that some of these materials would be used in the making of parachutes and coverings for light-weight planes, in addition to affordable clothing.

"Surely they could find other places with access to a river," Miss Dimple said. "It seems both Leola and her daughter made it clear they weren't interested in selling their land."

"It looks like there's more to it than that," Chloe told her. "It seems that particular piece of land would be perfectly suited for what they need. Mr.

Tisdale explained that access to raw materials, energy, and transportation would be determining factors in selecting a site, as well as the water supply and the mild climate here." She hesitated. "What's of interest to the police is how they apparently chose to go about getting their hands on the property."

Miss Dimple had to admit to herself that she had never cared for Griffin Kirkland; nevertheless, she couldn't see him dressing in Klan attire to frighten Leola Parker. For one thing, it would ruin his reputation if anyone found out.

"Griffin claims to be in the dark," Chloe continued, "but they do have that testimony from Jasper—for whatever it's worth. However, there's no way to prove who was behind that hood."

"What about Chenault?" Dimple asked. "I would assume he'd deny it, as well."

Chloe Jarrett paused. "They haven't been able to question Chenault yet."

"He's stationed over at Fort McPherson, isn't he? Shouldn't be too hard to find him."

"That's exactly what I thought," Chloe said. "Frankly, I don't understand it, but maybe we'll hear something soon."

Dimple certainly hoped so. She was usually a patient person, but her patience, it seemed, had been tried to the limits lately.

When they still had no word from Chenault Kirkland the next day, things took a different turn. His father said he had no idea where he was, and, naturally, his mother claimed she didn't, either. When his commanding officer verified *he* had no knowledge of his whereabouts, Chenault Kirkland was officially declared absent without leave, and in less than twenty-four hours, he was arrested at his girlfriend's house in Savannah.

"What I don't understand," Charlie said, "is why Chenault would run away like that when there's a good chance he might never be connected to what happened at Leola's." She had stopped by Phoebe's after giving her small nephew a ride in his stroller, and now she sat on the back steps while Tommy attempted to throw fallen apples into a bucket in the backyard.

Miss Dimple sat beside her as Annie raked up apples from underneath the tree nearby. "I believe there may be more to it than that," she said, clapping as one of Tommy's apples went into the bucket with a bang. "It must have something to do with what Hattie said. Remember, Hattie claimed she *knew* something—even led people to think she might have found something important?"

Annie paused in her work. "Do you think that's why she was killed?"

"I think she bragged to the wrong person, someone who wanted to silence her before she was taken seriously," Dimple said.

Charlie shook her head. "I don't know. If she

really found anything incriminating, then where is it?"

"And *what* is it?" Annie asked. "If Chenault ran away because he was afraid something Hattie found would connect him to a murder, it must've been important. It doesn't seem likely, though, that they can prove he was the one who set that fire."

She wasn't counting, however, on Mimosa Armstrong. Mimosa did the weekly washing for the Kirklands, picking it up on Monday and delivering it in a large wicker basket early Friday morning. Mimosa didn't own a washing machine and had never heard of a dryer. She boiled the clothing in a big black wash pot in her yard, stirring it with a long wooden paddle, and, once it was rinsed in several waters, hung it on the line to dry. The articles, including sheets, were then ironed with a flatiron heated on the stove in Mimosa's kitchen before being returned, usually on foot, to her customers. Only once in a while, if the weather was bad, would Hardin Haynesworth Kirkland drive over in her car to collect the clean laundry.

Earlier in the summer—and Mimosa remembered exactly which day it was because it was the same day her papa scared them so with those bad chest pains and Dr. Morrison had to take him to the hospital over in Milledgeville—she had taken

311

the Kirklands their clean laundry. Mrs. Kirkland always made her wait while she counted everything, and this time she was short one sheet and a pillowcase. Mimosa knew exactly where they'd been because she'd seen Chenault take them out of the dirty clothes pile when she went to pick up the laundry, and naturally, she'd asked him if he didn't want her to wash those, too. He'd told her not to worry about it because he was planning to use them in some kind of entertainment at the fort.

In spite of Mimosa's claims, she was blamed for stealing the bed linen and was paid less than half of what she was owed. Later, when she heard rumors about somebody in a sheet setting that fire at Leola Parker's, it was only a matter of checking her calendar to set the wheels of justice in motion. But first, she needed a little help from Doc Morrison.

Still simmering from hurt and anger over being treated unjustly, Mimosa went to the doctor in tears. Who would believe a colored woman over people as rich and powerful as the Kirklands?

Ben Morrison understood her problem, but he also understood human nature, and he had treated most of his patients in Elderberry long enough to be a pretty good judge of character. And that was when he got in touch with his friend Dimple Kilpatrick.

With Mimosa and the good doctor to back her

up, it took only a short time for Miss Dimple to convince Sheriff Holland something was rotten with Chenault Kirkland in addition to his being AWOL. She had shared her suspicions earlier with him that someone had deliberately started the fire in order to frighten Leola from her property.

"Still, I'm afraid it's going to be difficult to prove the sheet Chenault took was the one used to frighten Leola," the sheriff told her.

"He probably used some of that sheet to wind around the cross he made," Doc Morrison said. "And I suppose he must've soaked it in kerosene or something to make it burn."

Dimple turned to Mimosa. "I'm sure you do laundry for people other than the Kirklands, don't you?"

Mimosa nodded. "Why, yes, ma'am. I wash for lots of folks."

"And how do you keep the clothes separate? Most sheets look pretty much the same, don't they? How do you know which sheets belong to whom?"

"Oh, they's marks on them, Miss Dimple," she explained. "Some folks sew on some kind of tape, but most just put initials or a name on theirs with a marker that don't wash off."

"Do you remember how the Kirklands marked theirs?"

Mimosa thought for a minute. "It was just the

last name, Kirkland, on the hem at the bottom, always in the same place. Miss Hardin, she's real particular about that."

Miss Dimple turned to Zeb Holland. "Sheriff, do you still have what's left of that burned cross?"

"Of course." Sheriff Holland smiled. "Well, it's a long shot, but it's worth a look-see." He paused, thinking. "And he had to put that thing together somewhere. Where you reckon he'd go to do that?"

"The garage, I suppose," Miss Dimple replied.

Zeb Holland nodded. "But you know we're talking about something that happened a couple of months ago. I'd think he would've cleared away any evidence by now."

"I believe most people would," Miss Dimple began, "but probably not Chenault Kirkland. I'm afraid that young man believed he was above suspicion, and I doubt if it would even have occurred to him at the time that his actions would be in question."

"Part of that cross was burned and what's left of it was exposed to mud and water, so I'm afraid the odds are against finding a name on there, but I'll sure see what turns up. As for the other, it could take me a little while to get a search warrant, but I'll see if I can get ahold of the judge," the sheriff told them. "If we're lucky, I might be able to send somebody over there this afternoon. Meanwhile, keep this to yourself. We don't want any word of this getting out."

"You will let us know what you find, won't you, Sheriff?" Miss Dimple asked. "This has been going on much too long, and I'm . . . well, I'm sure we're all grateful for your help."

But the sheriff held up a hand. "Don't be too quick to thank me, Miss Dimple. Even if we find something, it's probably just going to be circumstantial evidence."

Dimple Kilpatrick only nodded. At this point, circumstantial evidence was better than no evidence at all.

CHAPTER TWENTY-SEVEN

Well, I suppose you've heard," Lou Willingham said to her sister Jo. "The sheriff found the Kirklands' name on a piece of sheet wrapped around what was left of that burned cross. It was faded and dirty, but he said you could make it out plain as day. And more torn strips turned up out in the Kirklands' garage. Sure looks like *somebody's* been up to something dastardly."

Dastardly? Jo laughed. "Sounds to me like you've been watching too many of those old melodramas at the picture show."

If they weren't speaking over the telephone, Lou would have been tempted to shake her sister. "You know good and well what I mean, Josephine Carr! Seems to me it's obvious Chenault Kirkland had a hand in what happened at Leola's, and he must've had a good reason for running, or he wouldn't have gone AWOL. Why, I wouldn't be surprised if he didn't have something to do with killing poor old Hattie McGee, as well."

"I heard Charlie say Hattie found something that might incriminate somebody," Jo said. "I'll bet that somebody was Chenault. Charlie was talking over the phone and didn't know I was listening. Have you noticed how she's gotten downright tight-lipped about telling me a blessed thing? And frankly, I've had about enough of it. I don't understand why she's become so secretive—and Annie and Dimple Kilpatrick are the same way."

Lou pulled out the chair by the telephone in her hallway and made herself comfortable. This looked to be an interesting conversation. "I wonder what she found," she said. "I'll bet she's hidden it somewhere."

"Well, whatever it was must not have turned up, or I think we would've heard about it," Jo said. "Chloe Jarrett told Bessie Jenkins at church last Sunday that the old trailer Hattie lived in had been turned inside out, things just thrown everywhere. If somebody was searching for something, they must not have found it."

"I imagine that place was a mess to begin with," Lou said. "Poor Hattie! I doubt if she was much of a housekeeper." Lou picked up a pencil and made meaningless doodles on the pad by the telephone. "But if it's not in the trailer, then where is it?" Her doodles tuned into circles, and the circles turned into curlicues, and then the curlicues began to look like primitive flowers. *Roses.* "Jo, think of all those roses she planted! Maybe she buried whatever she found in there."

"If you want to go and dig around in all those bushes in ninety-degree temperatures, go right ahead," her sister told her. "Besides, whoever's been looking for something out there might come back and find us."

"Oh, good heavens, Josephine! Chenault Kirkland is locked away, and bound to stay that way for a good long time. And think, if she *did* bury something there, the soil would be disturbed, wouldn't it? At least it's worth our time to look. Think of Clay Jarrett wasting away in that awful jail! Why, I took him some of my apple cobbler the other day and the poor thing just set it aside. Seems to have lost his appetite."

"That's because everybody in town has been feeding him," Jo said. "I'm sure he managed to choke it down later." Her sister was a fabulous cook, and Jo couldn't imagine a young man Clay's age turning down anything she had to offer.

317

"And I doubt if the Jarretts would think kindly about our poking around on their property," Jo added.

"Naturally, I was planning to ask their permission," Lou explained. Of course she hadn't thought of doing that, but it was a good idea. "I would think they'd welcome anyone who wants to try to clear their son's name."

"By all means, but I doubt if you'll find anything. You know how Hattie carried on," Chloe told Lou when she telephoned a few minutes later. "When would you like to come?"

"The sooner, the better," Lou said. "It should be cooler in the early morning."

"Knox and I will be at a funeral in Social Circle tomorrow. Knox's aunt Rose Ellen—would've been eighty-nine her next birthday—and of course there'll be a big dinner to follow, but we should be back by three.

"We're closing the Shed for the day, but if you need anything to dig with, Hattie kept a couple of tools underneath the trailer," she added. "I sure hope something turns up!"

Louise Willingham did, too. Her sister was not happy being roused from bed at such an early hour and expected to dig into dry red earth as hard as marble.

"I thought you said the soil would look different if it had been disturbed, Lou. It all looks the same to me. I worked all day yesterday at the ordnance plant and I didn't plan to spend my entire morning digging in the hot sun!" Jo leaned on her hoe and blotted perspiration from her brow with a red bandanna.

"I worked yesterday, too, Jo, and we've been here less than an hour," Lou reminded her. "I brought a Thermos of ice water if you want some. It's over there under that oak tree. Why don't you take a break and get something to drink?"

Jo willingly laid aside her hoe and did as she was advised. Refreshed by the water, she found a mossy spot and sat down under the tree to take note of her surroundings. It was at least ten degrees cooler here and she was in no rush to start digging again. Two robins played tag in the old oak's branches and a soft breeze rustled leaves in the sassafras tree beside her. Their mother had been a firm believer in the pinkish tea made by brewing the roots of that plant, as it was supposed to purge you of all kinds of impurities and tasted a little like root beer. It had been a long time since she had chewed a twig of sassafras, and Jo reached over to break off a piece. That was when she saw the trail.

At first, she wasn't sure it was a trail because it was so overgrown with weeds it was difficult to make out the pathway. It was probably made by some kind of animal, she thought; there were plenty of them around: rabbits, raccoons, possums. Still, it would be interesting to see where it went. Jo stood and wandered closer.

Briars clutched at her skirt as she waded through yellowing grass that brushed her ankles as she passed. Trees grew closer together here and dry twigs snapped under her feet as she stepped cautiously, her eyes on the trail.

She almost didn't see it because the trail—or what there was of a trail—ended in a small woodland clearing carpeted with leaves so deep, her shoes sank into them with each step. Looking closer, she noticed a mound of vines heavy with muscadines climbing high into a black gum tree in the swell of the hill. In another few weeks, the plump green grapes would ripen into a dark, pungent purple.

For a few seconds, she had that peculiar feeling, like somebody had walked over her grave. Ignoring it, Jo crept nearer. It looked like some kind of cave. Did an animal burrow here? But what kind of animal would lean branches over a low overhanging limb to make a crude framework for the thick thatch of grass and underbrush? Jo leaned closer. It appeared to be a tent of sorts—a tent just large enough for one person.

"Lou!" Jo shouted, shuffling back through the scratchy grass as quickly as she could. "Louise! Come here, and hurry! I think I've found something."

Her sister, red-faced and perspiring, let her spade drop where she stood and followed, fanning herself with a large straw hat as she ran. "What is it? Where?"

The two of them stopped short at the bramble-covered burrow in the woods and Jo dropped to her knees to examine it closer. "Hattie must've made this, Lou. Somebody had to drag that limb in front of the entrance to hide it." And with one hand, she shoved aside the limb.

"What's in there? Can you see?" Louise squatted beside her but had no desire to crawl into the mysterious tunnel of grass. No telling what was in there. Spiders? Snakes? Lou Willingham shivered. It was one thing to dig in a rose bed, but this wasn't at all what she'd had in mind.

"Let's wait on the Jarretts, Jo. They should be back before too long. Let Knox find out what's in there."

But Jo had come this far and she was not to be deterred. "Aren't you even curious? I don't want to wait that long." And she crawled on her hands and knees until she disappeared inside.

This time, it wasn't difficult to find where the soil had been disturbed, although someone had attempted to disguise it with a scattering of dried grass. "There's something buried under here," Jo announced, shoving the earth away with her hands.

"What? *What?*" Her sister crouched closer.

"Wait a minute . . . it's a . . ." Jo brushed off the dried red earth. "It's nothing but an old cocoa tin!" She shook it and something rattled inside.

"You mean *real* tin? Then it must be old—or at least from before the war. I think they're made out of pasteboard now. What's in it?" Lou urged, leaning closer.

Jo backed carefully out of the narrow confines of the makeshift tent and wiped the dirt from her skirt as she stood. "I need something to pry off the lid," she said, shaking the tin again. "Sounds like there might be a couple of things in here."

"Hattie had all kinds of junk underneath that trailer," Lou said. "I'm sure we'll find something there."

Using a small hand spade with a broken handle, Jo pried off the rusty top and emptied the contents onto the hard-baked earth behind the now-abandoned trailer.

"This is what I was afraid of," Jo groaned as she looked at the trinkets scattered on the ground. "All that work for nothing!"

Lou picked up the single opal earring and a tarnished ring with a chipped red stone that obviously had come from the dime store. "These were Hattie's treasures, so they must've been important to her. It's sad, isn't it? What's that in the bottle?"

Jo made a face as she removed the top. "Ugh— Blue Waltz perfume!" She set aside a lapel pin with several rhinestones missing; a small plastic whistle that looked as if it had come from a Cracker Jack box; a gold tab from a key chain; a man's pocket watch with a broken crystal; four dollar bills folded together, and thirty-six cents in change.

Lou put the broken key chain in the palm of her hand to examine it more closely. "This is the only thing that looks like it might be worth anything. I think it's gold—and look, there's something engraved here."

It looked as if the delicate links of the chain had been separated from something—probably a ring of keys—but the thin rectangular tag remained attached. Lou held it up to the sunlight, and although it was almost noon and the sun was high in the sky, she felt a frightening chill.

"Can you read it? What does it say?" Jo leaned closer, wishing she'd brought her reading glasses.

"Jo, it's *Chenault's!*" Lou narrowed her eyes to read the inscription: *G. Chenault Kirkland.* She closed her fingers over the metal. "Good grief, Jo—this must be why Hattie was killed. She knew too much—"

"And talked too much," Jo added, reaching for the gold trinket and turning it over in her hands. "Look, it's engraved on the back, too: *Love, Linda—6/12/44.* That must be his girlfriend in Savannah. I guess she gave it to him on his birthday or for some special occasion. . . ." She dropped the key chain into her sister's hand. "Only a few weeks before Prentice was killed."

Lou examined it more closely. "It looks like the link has been pulled apart here from the rest of the key chain. Hattie must have found it somewhere."

"And I think I know where," Jo said. "Chenault probably dropped it behind the Peach Shed during his struggle with Prentice. Delia said a train passed through about that time, so I doubt if anybody across the road at Grady's would have heard her."

Jo felt familiar tears welling at the thought, but this time they were tears of anger at the person who had brought it about. "We need to take this to the police, Lou. Maybe now they'll believe Clay had nothing to do with this."

"But you know Chenault will deny everything. He could've lost that thing anywhere, and now Hattie's not here to tell where she found it." They had started back to the car, which Lou had parked in front of the Shed, when Jo, who was in the lead, stopped suddenly and held out her hand to her sister. "Did you hear something?" she whispered.

Lou shook her head. Jo was fond of teasing. "What am I supposed to hear? Some of Hattie's Nazis? Or Yankees, maybe?"

Annoyed, Jo shushed her once more. "I'm not kidding. Sounds like somebody's in the woods back there and they're trying to keep quiet. I've had the strangest feeling the whole time we've been here—like we were being watched."

"All the more reason to leave," Lou urged her. "Come on, let's get going!" And she gave her sister a slight shove.

Clutching the engraved tab, Lou trotted after Jo, thinking of how refreshing it would be to stop at Grady's for an ice-cold Coke before presenting their newly found evidence to the authorities. She began to walk faster.

She didn't know where the limb came from, but suddenly it was right there in front of her, where it hadn't been before, and Lou pitched headfirst over it and fell sprawling on the weed-choked path. The gold key chain sailed out of her hand and landed in a mound of twigs and pine needles. Stunned, it took Lou a few seconds to realize her tumble had been no accident, for, in the act of getting to her feet, she was shoved to the ground again as someone behind her snatched the broken key chain and took off running, the rustle of footsteps fading in the distance.

"Jo!" Lou called, stumbling to her feet. But her sister had taken her advice and gone on ahead. "Jo! Come back!" She didn't have time to chase after the two of them, Lou decided. Jo would eventually notice she wasn't behind her, and if she hurried, she might be able to track down the person who had tripped her.

The wooded area they had just left covered several acres between the Peach Shed and the Jarretts' home, with orchards surrounding it, and the thief could be anywhere by now.

Not one to give up easily, Lou took a deep breath and gave chase. Although she couldn't see her face, from her quick glimpse of the fleeing figure, she could tell it was a woman, slender and slight of build, and, unfortunately for Lou, swift of feet. She was tempted to yell at her to come back, but why waste her breath? Of course she wasn't going to come back. Louise picked up a burst of speed and ran after her, and soon heard Jo and someone else close behind her.

Lou felt a sharp pain in her side and every breath stabbed like a knife. She would never be able to catch up with this woman, she thought, but if she slowed, she would certainly lose her. The woman dodged around a mulberry tree, the ground underneath spattered with wine-colored berries, and hesitated at a leaf-carpeted gully on the other side. Lou took advantage of the respite to get a second wind just as her sister and Grady Clinkscales caught up with her. She learned later that Grady had become concerned and had come over to investigate when he noticed her car had been parked there for so long.

The thief turned to look back right before she jumped, and for the first time, they could see her face. *Hardin Haynesworth Kirkland!*

Louise Willingham knew there was no way she could clear that ditch without breaking her neck, and she wasn't sure about her sister or Grady, either. The three of them watched as Hardin, just before jumping, caught her foot on a root and tumbled headfirst into the shallow ravine.

*C*HAPTER *T*WENTY-EIGHT

W hat do you think of your mama and aunt Lou being heroines of the day? Or should I say of the year?" Phoebe asked Charlie a few weeks later when she and her family were invited over for ice cream from the last of the peaches. School had begun the week before, and even though it was still too hot to wear the colorful fall clothing advertised at Rich's Department Store in Atlanta, Miss Dimple thought she detected a slight crispness in the air on her early-morning walks.

Jo gave her squirming grandson a kiss before setting him down to play in the yard. "Lou isn't going to be satisfied until she gets us both killed," she said, but she smiled when she said it, and her sister rolled her eyes and shrugged.

"I thought we'd be perfectly safe with Chenault Kirkland locked away. How was I to know *his mother* was the one who killed poor Hattie

McGee? And if I remember correctly, *I* was the only one who came away with battle scars. I still have bruises on both knees."

"If you hadn't been in such a hurry to play detective, we would have learned Chenault was with his company on maneuvers during the time Hattie was killed," Jo reminded her.

"But he did kill Prentice," Delia said, and she spoke with such vehemence, her toddler puckered up and began to cry until she picked him up and soothed him.

"He knew I usually went across to Grady's for cold drinks and waited until I was inside," Delia continued, speaking softly. "He must have parked behind the Shed and asked for help loading the peaches into his car. That was probably where she broke his key chain." Delia hugged little Pooh and kissed the top of his head. "If I know Prentice, she would've put up a fight. . . . If only I had heard her!"

"Honey, I doubt if you could've heard anything with the train passing by, and she probably didn't have a chance after that," her mother said, and then looked as if she regretted having said it. Everyone knew Miss Dimple had heard a scream at about that time, but it was only *one cry,* and they had learned from the coroner's report that Prentice had been strangled from behind.

"I don't think Chenault went there intending to kill her," Dimple said. "He probably planned to use his charm to reason with Prentice, try to expain his actions, but she believed he had been responsible for killing the one person, aside from her aunt, she loved best in the world—"

"And was having none of it," Charlie added.

"Prentice must have recognized his car when he set that fire at Leola's," Delia told them. "I knew something was bothering her. At first, I thought it had to do with her breaking up with Clay, but I believe she was trying to decide what to do about Chenault. His car was one of those expensive Ford Tudor deluxe sedans. It was a four-door model with sealed beam headlights with chrome trim. Prentice told me he gave her a ride in it one time when she was walking home from town, and she even pointed it out to me once when she saw him in it. It had chrome strips on the sides and another down the center of the hood, and as far as I know, was the only one like that in town. She must have already made up her mind to confront him, and threatened to go to the police."

"Then why would she take a chance on helping him load those peaches, and *behind the Shed* at that?" Phoebe asked. And no one answered because no one wanted to say it aloud. Even before he enlisted in the military, Chenault had access to weapons. Like many in the area, the family kept firearms in their home, and it was possible he had taken along a pistol. *Her actions hadn't been voluntary.*

Annie slapped at a mosquito buzzing about her arm. "I'm sure Chenault came back to look for that key chain as soon as he realized he'd dropped it," she said, "but by then Hattie had probably found it."

"She didn't miss much," Miss Dimple said. "And I'm not sure that was *all* she saw."

Phoebe was passing around a plate of sugar wafers, giving Pooh one for each chubby fist, but she almost spilled the lot at Dimple's announcement. "Oh, Dimple! You really don't think Hattie saw what happened, do you?"

"She said she did, remember?" Delia reminded them. "When we were leaving the church after Prentice's funeral, Hattie cornered me in the hallway—nearly scared me to death."

Charlie nodded. "That's right! Of course she had everything all mixed up with Yankees and Nazis, and no telling what else, but she did say she saw who took Prentice, and she'd found something gold. That must've been the key chain. I didn't pay much attention to her, but I remember you tried to convince her, Miss Dimple, to report anything she saw."

Phoebe shook her head. "Well, I reckon she did report it, but it was to the wrong person. Do you think Hardin followed Hattie with the intention to kill her?"

"She swears she didn't," Delia said. "Clay told me she said she just wanted to try to talk Hattie into telling her where she'd hidden that gold tab that came off the key chain, but Hattie wouldn't do it, and Hardin was afraid Hattie would eventually tell what she'd seen."

"And it only took a push," Phoebe added.

"But why the rose petals?" Annie asked. "I heard she scattered rose petals over the body, and if she didn't bring them with her, she would've had to *come back* and leave them. Oh, poor Hattie!"

"I guess she was trying to mimic the Rose Petal Killer," Charlie explained. "We didn't learn until later the first killer only used white ones."

"To tell you the truth, I'm surprised Chenault confessed," Miss Dimple admitted. "Except for the laundry marking, most of the evidence against him might be considered circumstantial. If his mother hadn't killed Hattie to try to cover up what he did . . ."

"And then trip you in an attempt to get back the evidence," Jo added. "Well it didn't leave much doubt, did it?"

"And don't forget—she was the one who planted Prentice's class ring in Clay's truck," Delia added. "They finally got her to admit it."

She wiped cookie crumbs from her son's face. "What a horrible person she is! I'm really not surprised. Sometimes it was all I could do to be polite when she came to the Shed."

"Do think she knew all along what Chenault had done?" Annie asked. "To Leola and Prentice, I mean."

Jo made a face and snorted. "Oh, I'm sure she knew about Leola. It was probably her idea to try to frighten her away, and I imagine Chenault must've told her what he did to Prentice, or she wouldn't have tried to get that key chain from Hattie."

Delia set her empty ice-cream bowl aside and shuddered, as if she could dispel a pesky thought. "It's crazy, isn't it, that she should've been the first person to show up after I learned Prentice was missing?"

Phoebe gasped. "Oh, Delia! Do you think she *knew* what had just happened?"

But Delia shook her head. "No, I really don't. After I finally made it clear that we were dealing with an emergency, she seemed to be concerned." She sighed. "Well . . . either that or she's a darn good actress!"

"Huh!" Charlie muttered. "I'll bet it didn't take long for her to put two and two together. Clay told me that Griffin Kirkland had planned for Chenault to go to law school and join his firm after the war," she added, "but his mother had been secretly saving for years so he could become independent of his father."

Phoebe began to scrape the ice-cream churn, ladling the rest of it into a container. "I never did understand why Hardin Haynesworth what's-her-name paraded around town pushing a wheelbarrow dressed like Hattie. Can somebody please explain that to me?"

"I don't believe she wanted anyone to realize Hattie was missing," Miss Dimple said. "I suppose she thought the longer the body lay there, the harder it would be to determine the time of death, and everyone would think she was killed by the Rose Petal Killer. Also, it would give her more time to look for the tab from the key chain Chenault lost."

At that moment, little Tommy took a tumble from the wooden kiddie car his grandmother had given him for his first birthday, and Delia had to steel herself not to run to his aid. She smiled as the child picked himself up from the grass and climbed back onto his toy. He was growing so fast! She could hardly wait for his father to see him. Wouldn't Ned be proud?

"Clay told me he enlisted in the navy," she said finally. "He's been wanting to do that for a while, and I think it will be good for him to get away. There are too many reminders here of Prentice." She shook her head. "She was part of my life for as long as I can remember. I've lost a good friend."

Jo Carr gave Delia's hand a squeeze. "I'm happy that Bertie has finally agreed to marry Adam. I understand they'll have a quiet ceremony during the Christmas holidays, and she's accepted a teaching position in January as head of the English Department in Clifford."

Miss Dimple smiled. "Good. I can't imagine Elberta *not* doing the thing she does so well." And everyone exchanged knowing smiles because they were thinking the same thing about her.

Annie held out her bowl for more ice cream. "This is *so good,* Miss Phoebe. I can't seem to get enough."

Charlie laughed. "Funny how your appetite has improved. I wonder—could it have anything to do with that letter that came the other day?"

"Yes, I've noticed you seem to have perked up a bit," Phoebe added, refilling Annie's bowl.

Annie smiled and patted the pocket where she kept the letter from Frazier, folded and unfolded, and read and reread. " 'O wonderful, wonderful, and most wonderful, wonderful! And yet again wonderful . . .' "

Miss Dimple recognized the passage from Shakespeare's *As You Like It*. "I believe we get the message," she said, laughing. Of course everyone already knew what was in the letter Frazier had sent from Coustanus, a little town in Normandy. Several in his unit had been killed by Allied bombs during the breakout at Normandy in Operation Cobra in late July, and Frazier and another young officer became separated from the rest. Soon after that, the other officer was badly injured during fighting to take over a bridge from German troops.

Surrounded by the enemy and suffering himself with an infection from a wound on his leg, Frazier managed to get his injured captain to a bombed-out shell of a farmhouse, where the two survived on stale cheese and sprouting potatoes until American forces captured the bridges and neighboring towns, eventually driving the German army across France. The wounded officer was still recovering, but Frazier had since been reunited with his unit.

There was not one person in Phoebe Chadwick's backyard that sunny September afternoon who didn't join Annie in rejoicing over the news in her long-awaited letter, for all of them were united in the cause of victory, and every one of them had a loved one on some foreign shore.

And Miss Dimple Kilpatrick had more than anyone.

Center Point Large Print
600 Brooks Road / PO Box 1
Thorndike ME 04986-0001 USA

(207) 568-3717

US & Canada:
1 800 929-9108
www.centerpointlargeprint.com